Rescued heart

Georgia Beers

Rescued heart

© 2016 BY GEORGIA BEERS

THIS TRADE PAPERBACK ORIGINAL IS PUBLISHED BY BRISK PRESS, BRIELLE NEW JERSEY, 08730

EDITED BY LYNDA SANDOVAL
COPY EDITED BY HEATHER FLOURNOY
COVER DESIGN BY STEFF OBKIRCHNER
FIRST PRINTING: JANUARY 2016

ISBN-13: 978-099667742-4

ACKNOWLEDGEMENTS

I've never written a series before, so this was a new undertaking for me. It's also been different in ways I never expected, and I'm really proud of the way it's coming together. I hope you enjoy it as well. There are several people to thank, people without whom my writing career would be nonexistent...or at least much less gratifying.

Steff Obkirchner has been designing my covers for years now, and I'm continually amazed by her artistic eye and her ability to bring to life what I've put inside the book. She hits a home run every single time, as far as I'm concerned. (The fact that she's one of my best friends in the whole wide world doesn't hurt either.)

The other two thirds of the Triumvirate are essential to my sanity (and sometimes, my insanity). Nikki Little often makes me laugh when I want to cry, and I don't always realize how much I need that. Melissa Brayden says helpful things like, "Why are you watching Netflix instead of writing?" or "What about *this* photo for the cover?" They are different sides of my daily conscience and I am so, so grateful to have them on my side.

My editor, Lynda Sandoval, kicked my author ass with this book, and I owe her a debt of gratitude. In my fifteen years as a published writer, I've never been through a harder edit, and I have never been happier to come out the other side holding a novel that makes me swell with pride. She's taught me so much already, about writing in general and about writing romance in particular. I can't wait for the next project.

Heather Flournoy put her eagle eyes to work and managed to catch things that Lynda and I both missed in several passes. My editing team is the best I could have asked for, and I plan on keeping them.

The folks at Brisk Press...what can I say that I haven't already in my previous books? They continue to be awesome, and that's all I could ever ask for in a publisher.

My wife, Bonnie, who has put up not only with me, but with this crazy, unpredictable career of mine—and has done so with impressive grace, never-ending love, and an unfailing sense of humor. I'm ashamed to say that I often forget to be thankful. She's become a pro at throwing everything against the wall to see what sticks as far as plot points go. She doesn't write, but she's my idea factory, and sitting at a bar with her while we sip good wine and iron out the next novel is by far one of my favorite things to do in all the world. I hope we never stop.

Last but never, ever least, I thank you, my readers. Your never-ending support keeps me going on those days when I'm sure I am a total fraud and have no business pretending to be a writer. Thank you for the e-mails, the Facebook messages, the gifts, the handshakes, and the requests for book signings. Please keep them coming. It all means so much more than you could ever know.

DEDICATION

To anybody who has ever rescued an animal in one way or another. Your time, your love, your home, your money...it all counts. This book is for you.

And to all the animals of the world...if only we humans could give love as unconditionally...

CHAPTER ONE

"CRAP."

Ashley Stiles was running late. Again. It was the story of her life, really. The bakery had been a madhouse with the rapidly approaching Easter holiday, and she'd ended up stuck there for way longer than she'd expected. Thank God she'd learned to pack a bag when she left in the morning so she didn't have to show up at Junebug Farms in her bakery whites, covered with cookie batter and cake frosting. It was colorful, sure, but it was also really distracting to try and walk dogs that wanted only to lick your clothes.

Winter was finally fading away, and that made Ashley happy. She'd been in Upstate New York her entire life. Born and raised. She could handle winter. But the past couple had been brutally cold and longer than she remembered them being when she was a playful kid building snow forts and sledding. Here it was, almost the end of March, and there were still large banks of filthy brown snow left in corners of parking lots, at the mouths of driveways, piled on some sidewalks. Winter was fading, but it wasn't going quietly, and now that she was almost thirty, she wished it would just go rather than hang on and continue to add footnotes to the season. As if to punctuate the point, a chilly gust of wind forced Ashley to hunker down into herself as she hurried across the wet and muddy parking lot to the main building of Junebug Farms.

"Hi, Mr. Tracey," she called to the tall, thin man in coveralls standing on a stepladder near the door and doing something indiscernible to the large overhead sign with a wrench and a screwdriver.

"Hi, Ashley. And it's Bill," he told her with a grin and a shake of his head, as he'd told her exactly the same thing the half dozen times he'd seen her since she began volunteering to walk the dogs.

"I know," she said with a grin, giving her stock answer. Bill Tracey wasn't old, but he was old enough to be her father, and Ashley was raised with manners. Calling him anything other than Mr. Tracey felt disrespectful to her. Still, she was working on it.

She stomped her feet on the industrial black rubber mat inside the door, despite the utter lack of snow on her shoes, and took a look around.

Junebug Farms was almost always bustling in some way, shape, or form, and today was no exception. The main lobby was large, airy, and open with high ceilings and a dark concrete floor painted to look like marble—and almost succeeding. To Ashley's immediate right was Paws and Whiskers, the small gift shop that sold everything from basics like collars and bowls, to extravagant splurges like flannel dog coats and Tempur-Pedic pet beds. She waved to Maggie Simon, the shop's manager, who waved back even as she conversed with a customer. The woman was a master of multitasking, and Ashley had vowed to take lessons from her one day.

Junebug Farms had a very particular smell, a combination of animal, hay, excrement, and disinfectant, and it was surprisingly not unpleasant. Ashley had grown used to it, grown to expect it as she entered, actually looked forward to it, and she smiled now as she inhaled and glanced to her left at the open seating area. In addition to the smell, there was the sound.

2

A never-ending cacophony of barking, howling, meowing, and the hum of human conversation was a permanent part of the atmosphere. A white noise, really. Junebug Farms was not the place to go if you had a headache—that was for sure.

A handful of people milled around, looking at the photos and letters that lined the walls in frames of various sizes and shapes. They told the story of Junebug Farms, how it came to be, who worked here, what it did for the community and its animal population. Walking past the wall of windows where dozens of homeless cats waited for somebody to adopt them, Ashley waved to various people she passed, people on their way here or there, people behind the enormous front desk, some she knew, some she didn't. Not a lot of people actually worked here as paid employees; most were volunteers. Of those who were actual employees, a very small percentage was full-time. Junebug Farms operated almost solely on donations and grants, and there was never a time when money wasn't tight. Ashley learned more about the ins and outs of how the place ran each time she came to spend a couple of hours. Though she wanted to stop and coo at all the cats, a glance at her cell phone reminded her that she was already nearly thirty minutes late, and Lisa was not going to like that one little bit.

Shaking her head, Ashley picked up the pace and let herself in to the employee break room. Lockers covered one entire wall, and she found an empty one, shed her coat, stowed her bag, and pocketed the locker key. Hurrying down the hallway, she smiled at everybody she passed, hearing her mother's voice somewhere in the back of her head as she almost always did: *It doesn't take any effort to smile and be nice to people.*

Mom was right.

Lisa Drakemore hadn't had that same lesson, obviously. She was sitting at her desk and barely spared Ashley a glance when she entered the dog area of the building. She simply held up a red canvas leash, said, "You're late," and handed Ashley a clipboard.

"I know. I'm sorry. Easter rush. We had cookie orders coming out of our ears today." Ashley tried hard not to notice that Lisa smelled wonderful, like vanilla and...sandalwood, maybe? She couldn't put her finger on it, but it was comfortable and inviting. Which made no sense because Lisa couldn't look less impressed if she'd put every ounce of energy into it. Ashley bit her bottom lip, took the leash and clipboard, and muttered, "I'm sorry."

"Mm hmm."

Irritated with herself, Ashley headed for the door that opened onto what sometimes felt like the saddest hallway in the world, as far as she was concerned. She tried not to look at it that way, but every once in a while the wretchedness of it would punch her right in the throat.

The dog wing was a good hundred yards or more long. Each side had cage after cage after cage, and each cage contained an unwanted, lost, abused, or just plain unlucky dog. As she did each time she stepped through that door, Ashley took a moment, inhaled slowly, exhaled even more slowly, and willed herself into a calm, loving place. Junebug Farms was a no-kill shelter, and that was the only way Ashley was able to do what she did. None of these dogs would be put down. Not one. But some would never leave.

Off to the left was another set of doors that led to the medical suite where dogs and cats were neutered or spayed, given vaccinations or general well-being exams, and tended to if they came in with cuts, bruises, or worse.

"There you are." Tammy Renner seemingly appeared out of nowhere, as she always did somehow. "I was beginning to think you weren't coming." Her blue eyes slid up to Ashley's head. "Somebody throw a cake at you today?"

Ashley squinted, then reached up to realize she was still wearing her Carter's Bakery hat. Her ash-blond ponytail was pulled through the back and a large chunk of blue buttercream frosting fell to the floor when she touched the front.

"Damn. I forgot to change my hat."

"I'm sure the dogs won't mind," Tammy said good-naturedly.

"I'm surprised Lisa didn't say something."

"Me, too. She's in a mood today."

"Great." Ashley scanned her clipboard to see what dogs needed walking, which were new, which might need extra attention.

"No worries. The dogs are happy." Tammy held up a matching clipboard, her list different from Ashley's, though Tammy's had three visible red check marks.

"Oh, good. Let's see who we've got today."

This was the best and worst part for Ashley. Most dogs were so sensitive, so in-tune with the world around them. Some of them were just elated to see her, to have some time out of their cage to get some exercise and soak up the attention of a human. Each cage was attached to an outdoor run so the dogs could get outside any time they wanted, but nothing beat the loving attention of a person. Some of them jumped, howled, did spins, so excited were they for Ashley's company.

She loved when that happened.

Others were obviously depressed. Those were the ones Ashley spent extra time with, gave extra love to, sat down on the floor of the cage next to them and just talked to them, pet them, loved them.

Jax was one of those depressed dogs, and he was on Ashley's list today. He was very large, which was a big part of why he hadn't been adopted yet. He was also ten years old, another part of the reason. A Lab/shepherd mix of some kind, he'd been dropped off by the grandson of his owner, who had passed away six months ago. Nobody in the family had been able to take him, so the grandson dropped him and left without so much as a backward glance. Ashley was one hundred percent sure Jax understood that his master was dead and he'd been abandoned, and it broke her heart to look into his sad and lonely brown eyes. He would get all the extra love she could shower on him today.

When they put their lists together, Tammy and Ashley surmised that three new dogs had arrived that morning: a terrier mix that had been found wandering behind a 7-Eleven and two pit bulls that had been seized from their owners, most likely under suspicion of dog fighting. Ashley didn't let herself think about that at all; the entire subject sickened her.

Instead, they went to work. Rather, Ashley went to work and Tammy continued to work and they walked dogs together for the next two hours, chatting with each other about life, love, and family.

"What's new in the land of baked goods?" Tammy asked.

"Not a lot." They stopped along the path as the dogs sniffed various trees and leftover snow mounds. "We were busy today, though. And my manager is still an idiot. I'm so glad she's leaving." She took a deep breath of late winter air. "What are the garden plans for this year? Did you decide to compost again?"

Ashley always thought of Tammy as a hippie born twenty years too late. Somewhere in her early fifties, she had long chestnut brown hair shot through with strands of silver and almost always braided down her back. Her taste in clothes tended toward worn jeans and T-shirts with a denim shirt thrown over. She never wore makeup, was fond of hammered silver jewelry and cowboy boots, and had been married to her husband since she was seventeen. She was a vegetarian and had an impressive green thumb and an amazing garden each year, from what she'd told Ashley, and though Ashley didn't consider herself spiritual or earthy or anything like that, there was a quiet, peaceful energy that Tammy gave off. Being around her was relaxing. Ashley thought that was why the dogs gravitated toward her. Working with her was enjoyable, and Ashley was always happy to see her face.

"My husband bought a new compost barrel, so we'll see how it goes. And your manager *is* an idiot. You could do her job in a heartbeat. Have you talked to the owner about who's going to replace her? Have you applied for the job?"

"Not yet," Ashley said with a shake of her head.

Though the wind kicked up every now and then, the weather generally cooperated and allowed them to get through their lists, walking a total of sixteen dogs in 120 minutes. They were in agreement that each dog deserved at least fifteen minutes of fresh air. On the weekends, Ashley liked to walk longer, but it was a weeknight and on most weeknights, she wanted to get home, eat some dinner, and decompress a bit. Bakery hours began very early and by six or seven o'clock, she was usually beat.

Back inside, they hung their clipboards on the wall next to Lisa's desk.

"She must be on her dinner break," Tammy commented at the empty desk chair. "I think it's one of her nights."

Ashley nodded, knowing Lisa's schedule varied each week, and honestly happy not to run into her.

"I'm going to head out," Tammy said, her hand on the swinging door of the break room. "You coming?"

"I thought I'd go sit with Jax for a bit," Ashley said.

Tammy gave a knowing smile. "He'd like that, I bet. Okay. See you tomorrow?"

"I'll be here." They waved their goodbyes and Tammy disappeared into the break room. Ashley turned back to the hall of cages and walked halfway down until she came to the one she sought.

Jax was curled up on the blanket in the far corner and didn't lift his head when he saw Ashley, though his tail thumped the floor twice. Ashley unlocked the cage and let herself in.

"Hey, big guy," she said softly, taking a spot on the floor next to the enormous dog and burrowing her fingers into the fur around his neck. He lifted his head then, seemed to look right into her eyes, and not for the first time, Ashley got a quick flash of something almost human. She smiled warmly at him and he laid his head on her thigh as she began to talk.

"So, let's see. What can I tell you about today? Oh! The girl at work I told you about last week? Katie? Remember her? She dropped an entire tray of macaroons on the floor this morning. An entire tray, Jax. Do you know how many macaroons are on one tray? Like, three dozen. I wanted to kill her. But you'd have been proud of me. I kept my cool. I didn't yell. I helped her pick them up and then got her started making another batch." She rubbed at her cheek. "I may have cracked my jawbone clenching my teeth so hard to keep from blowing a gasket at her, though." She continued to stroke Jax's fur, soft and thick, and she grinned when he gave a little groan of contentment and shifted his body so he was closer to her.

This had become their routine over her past several visits, and it was as relaxing for her as it seemed to be for him. Sometimes, she walked him. Other times, he'd already been walked and there were other dogs that needed the outdoor time. But she always set aside the end of her shift to sit and talk with Jax. It had become necessity. "Oh! I know what I forgot to tell you. Remember that silver Lexus I told you about last week, the one that cut me off on the way here? I swear to you, the *exact same guy* did it again today. Can you believe that? I should get his license plate next time. And do what with it, I have no idea, but I should totally get it. You think?"

Jax was watching her with rapt attention, his brown eyes fixed on her face as she spoke.

"You know what, Jax? It's not so bad here, right? I mean, it's warm. You get fed. You're not homeless. I get that being adopted would be best, but...it wouldn't be terrible if you just ended up staying here. You know?" She bent to place a kiss on the top of his big, square head.

"It's getting late."

Ashley flinched at the voice, then raised startled eyes up to the door of the cage to see Lisa Drakemore's tall form leaning against it, arms folded across her chest. The outfit she wore was simple, almost utilitarian, but she somehow made khaki pants and a green polo shirt look sophisticated and even a little sexy, if Ashley was going to be totally honest. Her short, light brown hair was highlighted with a bit of gold, swooped to the side and tucked snugly behind her ear where small silver hoop earrings sparkled in the harsh overhead lighting. High cheekbones held a hint of pink, and the woman had the face of a model, something discussed by more than one employee here. Her green eyes—which Ashley had always found utterly dreamy despite the intimidation she felt around Lisa—crinkled a bit at the corners, and Ashley was shocked to realize Lisa was almost smiling at her. Lisa Drakemore was not a woman who smiled often, at least not in Ashley's experience. That didn't make her mean or angry or scary. Ashley just thought of her as…serious. Lisa was a very serious person, and serious people did not smile much.

"Yeah." Ashley tossed her an uncertain half-grin. "He's a good listener."

Lisa continued to level that green-eyed gaze at her, face unreadable.

"Okay. I'm heading out in a minute."

With a nod, Lisa turned and left.

Ashley sat blinking at the empty space where she'd stood, then inhaled slowly to catch the last bit of Lisa's intoxicating scent as it wafted away down the hall. Lowering her voice to the tiniest of whispers, Ashley leaned down to Jax and said, "That was actually three whole words. I think that's the most she's talked to me since I've been coming here." In response, Jax lifted his head and licked the front of Ashley's hat. Her eyebrows climbed up in surprise as she reached up, felt the hat on her head—still coated with large, dried chunks of frosting—and closed her eyes in mortified irritation, remembering once again that she hadn't changed her hat before coming in the building. "Oh, that's just great. God, I am *such* a dork."

CHAPTER TWO

"SHE ALWAYS SMELLS LIKE cupcakes. Ever notice that?" Bill Tracey asked, waving goodbye to Ashley as she left through the door of the dog wing.

"Hmm?" Lisa asked, looking up from her desk, but not having really heard the question. That was normal when it came to Bill, a guy who talked endlessly. It was simple self-preservation to tune him out, lest your ears fall off from overuse. If she had to estimate, Lisa would guess she only actually heard about half of what the man said. Ever.

"Ashley," Bill clarified, gesturing to the now-closed door. "She smells like cupcakes."

Lisa followed his arm. "Huh." She had noticed, actually, and Bill was completely right. Ashley Stiles, of the cute little blonde ponytail and frosting on her head, smelled liked baked goods, sweet and warm and tempting. *All the more reason to keep my distance.* Not that that would be anything new; Lisa kept her distance from most people at work. From most people in life, really. More self-preservation. At least, that's what she told herself.

She tuned back in to Bill in mid-sentence, saying something about a hinge on the door to cage seven. "... tomorrow, okay?"

She blinked at him, tried to focus without looking like that's what she was doing, and nodded her assent. "Sure, Bill. That's fine."

He bid her goodnight, and she realized, if he was leaving, it must be past nine. A glance at her watch confirmed her suspicions, but not before it occurred to her that Ashley had stayed later than usual as well. Must have been talking poor Jax's ear off. The thought made one corner of her mouth quirk up as she neatened her desk and then made one last trek down the dog wing to check on everybody. The barking had died down at this hour, though it never completely stopped. Junebug Farms was not a place that was ever quiet, not for a minute, but Lisa had learned to filter it, or at least push it to the background of her brain, in the five years she'd been working there. Assured everything and every animal was in its place for the night, she hit the light switch to "overnight," and the wing dimmed considerably. Donning her jacket and then shouldering her bag, she said quietly the same words she said to them every evening. "Good night, dogs. Sleep tight. You're safe. Everything's going to be okay."

The wind had gone from cold to icy since Lisa had been out for lunch earlier that day, and she huddled inside her coat as she speed-walked to her car, which sat alone in the empty lot looking like a single life raft floating in the middle of the ocean. Once ensconced in the driver's seat, she cursed herself yet again for not splurging on the remote car starter when she'd leased the Toyota two years ago. This was her second winter of climbing into a freezing cold car in the dark and she was just about over it.

The drive home was easy. Traffic was light and she pulled into her assigned space at her townhouse complex less than twenty minutes after she left Junebug. She hauled her stuff out of the car and waved to Mrs. Benchley, who was giving her poodle its final walk for the night. She slipped her key into the lock, turned it, and entered her small, cozy townhome, a sigh of comfortable relief pushing from her lungs as she shut the door behind her and four meowing cats of varying sizes and colors, and one very slow dog, came running (or meandering on the dog's part) from all areas of the house.

"Hello, my brood," she said, bending to scoop up Groucho, a white cat with three legs and a black spot of fur just below his nose. She flopped him over her shoulder like a stole and he happily rode around the house that way as she put her things away and got their dishes out.

At thirty-two years old, Lisa wasn't old enough to be the Crazy Cat Lady, but she was well on her way, and she knew it. It only worried her sometimes. But not tonight. Tonight, she was happy to just be home and alone with her babies.

Groucho was the newest addition to the family, having been in the Drakemore household a mere three months. His foot had been caught in an illegal trap in the woods not far from Junebug Farms, and a hunter with a heart had rescued him and brought him in. One amputation later, Lisa took him home. Clyde was the oldest of her quartet, a huge gray tabby with only one eye. He was discovered wandering a field. The farmer who found him wanted to keep him, but worried his disability would make him an easy target for his other barn cats. It was a good call, as it became apparent early on that Clyde was not an outdoor cat, nor a hunter. He preferred to sit on a comfortable chair in the sun all day and have his food delivered to him, thank you very much. Hubbard was a gray tiger cat and had been a stray, brought in to Junebug so pregnant, the staff was surprised she didn't simply burst. She had a litter of five healthy kittens, all of whom were adopted, but became so depressed and despondent without her babies that she stopped eating. Lisa had taken to hand-feeding her and did so for weeks until the cat came back to herself. By then, Lisa was attached to Hubbard and Hubbard to her. She moved into the townhouse the next day. Tiny was just that: tiny. Black and white and itty bitty. He looked like a kitten despite his three-year age, his growth having been stunted by a mother who was malnourished and abused during her pregnancy. Only Tiny and one brother had survived the birth. He was another one Lisa had hand-fed, this time with a bottle. She couldn't give him up. Keeler was a Lab mix of some sort, a stray that had been brought into Junebug Farms by Animal Control, who'd found him on Keeler Street, and he'd been a mess. Abused, malnourished, and skittish, with haunted brown eyes and a frightened distrust of just about everybody. He was shaky and pathetic and did his best to make himself as small and unnoticeable as he could—which was difficult, as he was not a small animal. Lisa had worked hard over the years to school her emotions, to lock her feelings up tight when things bothered her, but something about Keeler got to her. From the moment he was brought in, she was the only one he trusted and they'd become inseparable. It was a foregone conclusion pretty early on that she'd be taking him home.

She filled dishes with a small amount of wet food, added a little dry, and set them all down in various corners of the room for the cats. Hubbard and Groucho were not fond of other cats anywhere near their food, so they ate in the far corners. Tiny and Clyde ate side-by-side, happily munching and purring. Keeler got his own corner and took his time eating the raw diet Lisa painstakingly prepared for him. As he chewed, he looked up at her with adoring eyes. She smiled and he wagged his tail, then bent for another bite. It was their routine.

As dinnertime progressed, Lisa grabbed a wineglass from the cupboard, opened the fridge, and filled the glass with white wine from the boxed Reisling on the top shelf. She allowed herself one modest glass each evening after work, sort of a reward for not killing anybody during the day. Today hadn't been bad, but on days when abuse cases were brought in or somebody dropped off an animal because they were too damn lazy to care for it properly, Lisa allowed herself a second glass. Keeping her opinions to herself was not always easy, but it was necessary for the success and reputation of Junebug Farms.

She sipped her wine and watched her animals finish up their meals, enjoying the blessed silence, which didn't last long, because her cell phone beeped, signaling an incoming text. Hoping it wasn't a problem at work, she dug her cell out of her bag and cautiously glanced at the screen.

Been too long since we talked…

With a grin, Lisa dialed. It was picked up after two rings.

"Is this my favorite niece?" came the beloved voice

"Only if this is my favorite aunt." Lisa felt her entire being relax. The voice of her Aunt Joyce was like a balm to sore muscles, a massage to an aching back. Everything just felt… bearable when she talked to Aunt Joyce.

"How are you, sweetie? Was it a work night?"

"It was. Last one this week, though." Lisa took her wine, kicked off her shoes, and flopped onto the couch. Crossing her feet at the ankle, she propped them on the coffee table and was immediately besieged by cats wanting to be close to her. Keeler laid himself under her legs.

"How many assholes since the last time I talked to you?"

Lisa choked back a laugh. Despite her age—68—Joyce Meredith had a mouth on her that would make a lumberjack blush, and she'd been known to let loose a string of profanities that brought an entire room to a screeching, silent halt. She was unapologetic about it, and Lisa loved her for that. She wished she had half the balls her aunt did.

"Only one this week. Two pit bulls were brought in from the same house."

"Dog fighting?" Aunt Joyce knew many of the ins and outs of Lisa's job, including from where certain dogs came.

"Of course," Lisa said, her voice colored with anger. "The poor things have no idea what to do with gentle treatment. Jamie's going to work with them, see what she can do." Jamie O'Connor was the resident dog trainer and behaviorist at Junebug Farms and sometimes, the girl had her work cut out for her.

"How many is that now?"

"Pit bulls? Ten as of today." Lisa found a good spot on the back of Groucho's head and his motor kicked up several notches. "I think people are starting to understand that they're really great dogs who get a bad rap, but people still tend to be afraid of them. We've placed about six in the past two months, though."

"That's great."

"It is. Placing ten more would be better."

"There must be a fundraiser coming up soon, right?"

"Aunt Joyce, you just donated last month."

"Hush. You don't get to tell me what to do with my money." Her tone was playful enough to take any sting out and firm enough to let Lisa know there was no room for argument.

"Yes," Lisa said. "Later next month. I need to round up my volunteers next week for that."

"Some worthy ones this time?"

Lisa chuckled, reminded of two fundraisers ago when she was stuck with a large number of volunteers who rarely showed up to the shelter. It was common practice with high schoolers. They liked to choose the shelter as their required community service for school, but few of them realized it was actual work to be there. Her mind flashed to this newest batch. Tammy and Ashley and Mark and Christian. They were all responsible volunteers that Lisa was certain would do more than their share of work during the endless hours of fundraising. "I've got a few."

"Well, that's good. You should mention it to your mother. I bet she'd like to help."

Lisa barked a laugh, causing Groucho to flinch and jump away. He was immediately replaced by Hubbard, and Lisa continued scratching as if nothing had changed. "Subtle, very subtle."

Joyce had the good sense to laugh along. "I thought it was. No?"

"Not so much."

"Well. How many of her calls have you dodged this week?"

Lisa felt her face heat up, unsure if it was from anger or the shame of being called out. "Only a couple." *Or six. Maybe seven...* "I did answer one, but I was at work, so I couldn't talk."

"Convenient. You know what you could do? Be the bigger person."

"I was the bigger person. For my entire childhood, I had no choice but to be the bigger person thanks to her." Her voice was hard, despite her attempts to keep it nonchalant. It happened whenever the subject came up, which was why Aunt Joyce didn't take offense.

"Don't you get tired of carrying it around?"

17

"Carrying what around?"

"That big, heavy grudge."

Lisa pressed her lips together and said nothing as she let out a frustrated breath.

"Never mind," Aunt Joyce said, obviously understanding she'd pushed enough. "I just want you to think about it. She's been back in town for almost a year now, Lisa, and she'd just like to spend more time with her daughter." When Lisa stayed silent, her aunt repeated, "Just think about it. Okay?"

"Okay." Lisa sounded very much like a teenager with that answer, and she knew it.

"I love you, Favorite Niece of Mine. You know that."

She was never able to stay mad at her aunt, a fact she found incredibly frustrating sometimes. "I do. I love you, too."

"All right. Well, have some wine before bed. It'll help you sleep."

"I am way ahead of you. Though mine's not in a tumbler like yours."

"Too bad for you."

They hung up laughing, Lisa staring at the phone for a long beat afterward. Thank God she had her aunt. There were times when it really did seem like Aunt Joyce was the only person in the world who got her, who completely understood what she was thinking and feeling and why. She may have had little input from her actual mother from her late teens on, but Aunt Joyce had never let her down.

Lisa sat there for another half hour, sipping her wine, loving her animals, and allowing her brain to decompress. Her job wasn't stressful beyond belief, but it could get hectic. Combined with having to monitor her volunteers and the never-ending noise of the place, it was a lot, and Lisa's favorite thing to do when she got home was sit in the blessed quiet and just…breathe. Just be. The cats surrounded her like the Greek gods around Mount Olympus, and she spent the next several minutes scratching, petting, cuddling, and cooing to each of them. Animals amazed her. With their unassuming trust and their unconditional love, she would much rather be around them than people. That's why the job at Junebug Farms was so perfect for her. True, she often wanted to throttle people who dropped off pets for ridiculously lazy/stupid/asshole-ish reasons, but she had become a pro at controlling her facial expressions so she looked completely neutral. Opinionless.

Which she was not.

All she had to do was remember what Keeler looked like when he was brought in. Or look at Groucho's stump of a leg or Clyde's closed-up eye socket or think of Tiny's beaten and abused mother to get her ire up. But she'd also learned not to do that. Instead, she looked at her cats with love. They were her babies. They loved her no matter what her hair looked like, whether or not she came home late, with no regard to the anger she had toward her own mother. They were sure and solid and Lisa held onto them like a buoy when she felt herself drifting into sad or worrisome territory in her head.

"Okay, gang. This girl has had a long day. Let's head up."

As if they completely understood her, all four cats jumped off the couch and followed her into the kitchen. She rinsed her glass, set it in the dish drainer, and scooped a handful of small cat treats out of the cookie jar on the counter and two dog treats from the smaller jar next to it. Then she headed upstairs to her bedroom, four cats trailing behind her like a string of children following the Pied Piper, Keeler slowly bringing up the rear.

This was Lisa Drakemore's life and she was fine with that.

CHAPTER THREE

THOUGH APRIL HAD COME in on the heels of a very angry, windy, and unseasonably cold March, it leveled off and ended up being a rather pleasant month. By the third week, it was gorgeous out, which was perfect for the Pawsitively Spring Junebug Farms Fundraiser.

It was always better when they could set part of the event up outside on the grounds. Better for many reasons, the two main being that A. it allowed the buildings to be less crowded. Fewer people milling around meant less stress on the animals. And B. it allowed the public to roam the grounds, get a good look at where its donations went, see what Junebug did for so many neglected, abused, and abandoned animals in the community. There was usually a bump in donations if people got up close and personal.

Lisa was thrilled that the fundraisers were only four times a year, but even that could be a lot. They took a ton of organizing and careful planning and institution. She was not the head of fundraising (thank *God* for that), but she still ran around like a nut for most of each event.

The vibration from her phone in her back pocket tugged at her attention, and she pulled it out. A text from her mother. With a roll of her eyes, she tucked the phone away without even reading.

It was a lovely Sunday afternoon, too lovely to deal with that woman. The sun was a warm, bright ball in an electric blue sky. The temperatures hovered around sixty degrees, and the smell of spring combined with wet dirt, hay, and animals made for a scented atmosphere that Lisa adored. She was rarely happier than when she was outside on the Farms, in the sun, with people wandering and opening their wallets. She could see the three horses and two donkeys in the corral a hundred yards away. She could hear the goats bleating for more food from the families that surrounded their pen. And of course, the never-ending barking coming from both inside the building (the doors were propped open) and from the dog runs out back.

"This is amazing!"

Lisa turned to regard Ashley Stiles standing next to her, and the first thing Lisa noticed was that Ashley was hatless. Lisa didn't think she'd ever seen the woman without a hat on, and her cascade of wavy blonde hair was a pleasant surprise. The sun glinted off it, highlighting different shades of gold. She was casually dressed in jeans and a soft-looking waffle-weave Henley in light blue, a white fleece vest serving as a jacket. A rectangular nametag was stuck to her chest, labeling her *Ashley – Volunteer*.

"Is this your first fundraiser?" Lisa asked her.

"It is. I had only just started volunteering when the New Year one happened, and I couldn't make it."

"Well," Lisa said, making a sweeping gesture with her arm. "Here it is. Welcome."

They stood side by side in silence, just watching. The vendor tents were sprinkled across the still-brown grounds like mini marshmallows floating in hot cocoa, their occupants all hawking their wares. Dog and cat food suppliers, a pet photographer, training classes, pet supply manufacturers. Donors and customers brought their own dogs with them and/or they were here to adopt, and people and animals milled about everywhere. It was impressive, the turnout, and Ashley said so.

"We've done a good job promoting the fundraisers so that they've become a pretty well-known part of the community. We've got a great P.R. crew. Wait until we do the televised one." Lisa glanced at her. "It's crazy."

"I've watched it on TV before."

"Being there is a whole different ballgame. It's sort of wild how it all comes together."

"When is it?"

Lisa squinted up at the sky as she thought. "It changes all the time. Last year, it was in the fall. Sometimes, it's in the spring. I'm not sure, I'd have to look it up."

"I'd like to be a bigger part of that, I think," Ashley said and then yawned. Mortified, she covered her mouth. "Oh my God, I'm so sorry."

Lisa's chuckle seemed to put her at ease.

"I've been here since six and I didn't sleep very well last night."

Lisa knew exactly when she'd gotten there because Lisa had been there first. She was in charge of the volunteers and their assignments for the fundraiser. But Ashley was obviously embarrassed, if the color of her cheeks was any indication, so Lisa just smiled.

"What can I do next?" Ashley asked, and her enthusiasm despite being tired was admirable.

Gazing across the grass to her left, Lisa asked, "How do you feel about checking the food supply for the goats?"

"Are you kidding? I *love* the goats." And Ashley was off.

Lisa watched her go, watched the gentle swing of her hips and the way the light breeze pushed all that hair off her shoulders. She watched her for a long moment before catching herself. Deciding she needed to check on the other volunteers, she gave her head a literal shake and moved off in the direction of the barns.

⊷

How was it possible for one woman to smell so good all the time? Especially a woman who worked in a building filled with animals and animal feces and animal stink? Ashley couldn't understand it. Nothing smelled better than standing next to Lisa Drakemore. It was a conclusion she'd come to in the last ten minutes. She smelled like… Ashley closed her eyes and inhaled, trying to take in any scent particles that might possibly remain in her nostrils. Vanilla? Lavender? Honey? Okay, so she smelled warm. Warm and comforting. And Ashley worked in a bakery, so that said a lot. Furrowing her brow as she thought, she found it disconcerting that she had no idea what Carly smelled like…

"Excuse me." Ashley's daydream was interrupted by a young mother, who gestured to the gumball machine-type contraption that held the goat food. "How does this work?"

Ashley smiled at the women and at the toddler next to her. "You want to feed the goats?" she asked the little girl, who nodded so enthusiastically her brown pigtails bobbed. "Okay, come here." Ashley squatted down to be at eye level with the girl, then looked up at the mother. "Do you have a quarter?" The woman handed it over and Ashley took a Dixie cup from the holder. "Okay. You hold this." She put the cup in the little girl's hand and then situated it under the machine's opening. "Right here. Don't move it. Okay? You got it?" The girl nodded some more and Ashley deposited the quarter, then turned the knob. Dry kibble fell into the cup and the girl giggled

24

delightedly. "That's all there is to it. Now if you go over there," she said as she pointed toward the side of the pen. "My friend Tammy will show you how to feed them the right way. Okay?"

The mother smiled and thanked Ashley, then the two were on their way. Ashley pushed herself through the crowd to head back toward the building, and a sense of pride washed over her and she took in her surroundings. The vendor tents, the dogs running agility near the barn, the swarms of people and leashed pets. It was all kind of amazing, and though she was simply a volunteer, Ashley felt warm and happy to be a part of it all.

Her attention was focused on a couple with two Westies on leashes, and she wasn't watching where she was walking... which became clear when she ran smack dab into a rock solid chest.

Strong hands closed around her upper arms and kept her from falling. "Whoa! Careful there," said a deep male voice.

"Oh, my God, I'm so sorry," Ashley said, trying to right herself. She looked up into cool blue eyes smiling at her.

"It's no problem at all. I'm glad I caught you." His grin was wide and friendly enough, but Ashley felt a weird tingle run up her spine as she tried to place his familiar face. "It's not every day I run into a beautiful woman."

Ashley felt herself blush. "Thanks." She moved to go around him, but his grip tightened just slightly.

"I don't believe we've met," he said.

"Oh. No, we haven't." Ashley purposely took a step back, which forced him to either let go of her arms or follow her. He did the former and she held out her hand. "Ashley Stiles. I volunteer here."

His large hand engulfed hers and held on. "Clark Breckenridge."

The name instantly sent bells clanging in Ashley's head, as the Breckenridge family donated huge amounts of money to Junebug Farms each year as well as other local charities. She immediately changed her entire demeanor, not wanting to do anything to annoy him. "Oh, Mr. Breckenridge. It's so nice to meet you. I've heard a lot about you."

He lowered his voice and leaned toward her conspiratorially. "Don't believe what they say. I'm really a nice guy."

She chuckled as she was expected to and took another subtle step away, a little weirded out by his closeness, putting more space between them. "We're having such a great turnout, aren't we? Are you enjoying yourself?"

"I am now," he told her, a gleam in his eye.

Ashley broke into a nervous sweat and was trying to figure out how to extricate herself from Breckenridge's cloying company when an unfamiliar voice reached her ears.

"Clark. There you are. I've been looking everywhere for you. Are you charming the socks off our volunteers again?" The woman had a gorgeous smile, a small dimple appearing on her left cheek. She was tall and looked out of place in her business attire. Her navy blue pantsuit was pristine and the white blouse with blue pinstripes was crisp and bright. She had chestnut brown hair in a French braid, and behind the black-rimmed glasses were startlingly blue eyes. "I have a few board members who really want to meet you." To Ashley she said, "You don't mind if I borrow him, do you?" Without waiting for a response, she tucked her hand into Clark's elbow and gently led him away, tossing a wink over her shoulder at Ashley.

"Who the hell was that and what the hell just happened?" Ashley said aloud softly.

"That was Catherine Gardner and I'd say she just rescued you from the lecherous Clark Breckenridge." Jason Reed tossed his head, a habit Ashley had noticed he'd developed to keep his sandy, too-long hair out of his eyes. He was young—Ashley put him at around eighteen—and had been volunteering at Junebug since a project he did for a class his sophomore year. He was sweet, a little geeky, and a senior in high school. Ashley liked him very much.

"Who is Catherine Gardner?"

"She's the accountant here. She keeps the books, tallies the donations. She's the money chick." He pushed his wire-rimmed glasses up his nose with a finger.

"I've never met her."

"She's got a big office in the back and she's there most of the time. That's probably why you don't see her." Jason met Ashley's gaze and shifted from one foot to another as he added, almost as an afterthought, "She's my aunt."

Ashley raised her eyebrows in surprise.

"She's my mom's sister." Jason was a good six inches taller than Ashley and he gazed off over her head now. "She tries to keep an eye on Breckenridge. He just…he's kind of pushy and he thinks the size of his checkbook should get him whatever he wants." His eyes met hers again as he gave a little shrug. "He's usually right." Before Ashley had time to be insulted by the insinuation, Jason said, "Looks like Jamie needs me. Later." And he was off. Ashley followed his line of sight to see Jamie O'Connor, one of the dog trainers, waving her arm from the agility course. Jason's volunteer time often coincided with Jamie's hours and he was terrific with the dogs. Ashley had watched more than one training class.

The rest of the day flew by and by six o'clock, most of the attendees had gone home. The vendors were closing up shop, packing their wares and their literature. Bill would take down their tents tomorrow. The goats in the pen were all lying down, likely exhausted from all the attention and the constant eating. Even the dogs in the dog wing seemed more subdued than usual. The air had chilled a bit, and Ashley had traded her vest for her gray Junebug Farms hoodie an hour ago. Now, she headed inside the building to see if anything else had to be done before she left. She was exhausted and if she didn't eat something soon, she was pretty sure she'd keel over.

A handful of people milled around inside, but not many. The doors to Paws and Whiskers were closed, but Maggie Simon was visible through the glass calculating her sales. Bill Tracey was mopping the floor in front of the windowed cat display. Ashley waved to him as she went by. A glance through the window of the closed door to what Ashley knew was the conference room told her that Catherine Gardner and Clark Breckenridge were in there. She hurried past and pushed through the doors to the dog wing.

Lisa sat at her desk, head down, fingers poking at letters on a keyboard, and Ashley slowed her pace so as not to disturb her. She was a few feet away when Lisa looked up.

"Hi," Ashley said, giving a little wave. "Didn't mean to bother you."

"No problem."

"Do you need me to do anything else before I go?"

With a shake of her head, Lisa said, "Nope. I think we're good." She paused, then surprised Ashley by asking a question. "Want to hear something cool?"

Ashley grinned, surprised by the friendly tone in Lisa's usually professional, detached voice. "Always."

"Eight dogs were adopted today. And fifteen cats."

Ashley's eyes widened in surprise. "Seriously?"

"Seriously."

"That's *awesome.*"

"It really is."

Lisa looked different to Ashley somehow, and she tried hard to put her finger on it. Something about her was…more relaxed? Maybe that was it. And the fact that the corners of her mouth were actually turned up slightly gave her face an entirely different look. A nice one. But when no other words came, it was clear to Ashley that the conversation was over, and she moved on past Lisa's desk to the employee break room and her locker.

Well, there was a smile and what could be considered a conversation, albeit a tiny one. Twice today. Progress! Ashley grinned as she retrieved her belongings and headed back out, tossing a wave to Lisa. Who didn't look up from her desk.

Inside her car in the Junebug Farms parking lot, Ashley checked her cell. Three texts from three different friends reminded her they were all meeting out at Sling at seven for Mo's birthday, and a fourth from her best friend, Jenna, that said simply, "You had BETTER be here." Ashley was beat and really just wanted to go home, but she also wanted to see her friends and not incur the wrath of Jenna. Before she could second-guess her decision, she texted that she'd be there and to order her a cheeseburger before she fainted from hunger. Then she put away her phone, shifted her car into gear, and hit the stereo, Rihanna singing to her as she drove.

Sling was a gay-owned bar and restaurant that had done surprisingly well for itself, given the unimpressive track record of previous gay-owned establishments in the area. The décor was urban contemporary, with a restaurant and bar downstairs, and a second bar and a dance floor one flight up. The food was decent, the drink prices reasonable, and the atmosphere welcoming. As tired as she was, Ashley was happy to be there, even on a Sunday night. Apparently, her friends were just as happy to see her, as a cheer went up the second she walked through the door.

A large, rectangular table was set up against a wall and nearly a dozen of Ashley's friends and acquaintances were seated around it. Balloons in a rainbow of colors bobbed in the breeze of passersby, their red ribbons tethered to the head chair where the birthday girl sat. Ashley headed in that direction.

"Happy birthday, Mo-Mo," she said as she hugged her friend. "Thirty's a big year, you know. No more screwing around. Or so I hear." She grinned at Mo's "ppffffttt" and gave her an additional squeeze.

"Carly saved you a seat," Mo said to her, then waggled her eyebrows. Ashley playfully slapped the bill of the Birthday Girl hat she wore.

"You made it," Jenna said by way of greeting as Ashley took the chair in between her and Carly where a cheeseburger waited for her. Jenna bumped Ashley with her shoulder and grinned. "Good to see you, Ash-hole."

"Hey, cutie," Carly said as Ashley turned to her. She stretched her arm possessively across the back of Ashley's chair, used that hand to rub her shoulder gently. The table was a bit rowdy, so she had to lean close to Ashley's ear to be heard. "How did today go?"

"Really well," Ashley said, meeting the brown-eyed gaze. "There were a ton of people and almost two dozen animals were adopted."

"Really? That's fantastic." Carly leaned in and kissed Ashley quickly on the mouth. "Good for you."

As was her usual reaction, Ashley was momentarily startled by the move and forced a smile onto her face. She had been seeing Carly for a few weeks now, and the overall consensus was that they were great together. Carly was cute, kind, and fun...and she made it abundantly clear that she was beyond attracted to Ashley. That was something Ashley hadn't felt in a long time, and she liked it. *So shoot me.* She knew all she had to do was tell Carly she wanted to be exclusive and it would happen. They would be girlfriends. There was no reason not to be. No reason at all.

Pulling herself out of her head, she took a bite of her burger and turned her attention to the table, to her friends—some of whom she'd known since college, some of whom she'd only met in the past year or so—and three women she'd barely laid eyes on before. Jenna was the only one she knew from her elementary school days; they'd been best friends since the sixth grade. Introductions went around and Ashley smiled and waved and shook the hands of those she could reach.

"Are you two together?" one of the newbies asked, using a finger to circle around Ashley and Carly.

"Oh, well..." Ashley said.

"Pretty much, yeah," Carly said at the same time. They glanced at each other and laughed, though Ashley's laugh was nervous and Carly's seemed uncertain.

"We're very new," Ashley said to the newbie (Chrissy? Christy?). "Still working it out."

"Ah. Got it."

She could feel Carly stiffen a bit next to her, but thankfully, she didn't contradict what Ashley had said. A glance in Jenna's direction and was met by inquisitively raised eyebrows, but like Carly, Jenna said nothing. Ashley knew she'd be dealing with this later, and she was not looking forward to it.

Other than that bump, the evening was fun. Sling wasn't terribly busy on a Sunday night, so it felt like they had the place to themselves. Ashley wolfed down her cheeseburger and fries so fast she surprised even herself. When she looked up to meet Jenna's grin, she shrugged. "I was starving."

"Obviously," Jenna said. Then, "I have to pee. Come with me."

Ashley rolled her eyes, but wiped her mouth with a napkin, asked Carly to order her a second beer, and followed Jenna.

The ladies' room smelled strongly of some sort of orange air freshener that wouldn't be unpleasant in a larger room or a smaller dose. The walls were painted a muted orange, and three stalls were separated by gray metal dividers. Jenna went into one. Ashley figured she might as well go while she was there and took the one next to her.

"Things with Carly seem to be going well. Yeah?" Jenna asked through the steel that separated them.

"Yeah."

After a beat, Jenna said, "Jesus, Ash, stop overwhelming me with all the flowery language. I can only take so much." Ashley laughed. When they were both at the sinks washing their hands, Jenna met her gaze in the mirror. "Seriously, though. You're good?"

Ashley pulled her eyes away and moved to the paper towel dispenser. "Yup. I'm good."

Jenna wasn't convinced—Ashley could tell by her expression—but she didn't push. Instead, she said simply, "I just want you to be happy. You've been on your own for a while now. You deserve to have somebody who thinks you're amazing. Like I do." With a wink, Jenna kissed Ashley's temple and left the room.

Ashley looked at her own reflection for a long moment before she followed her friend back to the table and eased into her chair, under Carly's arm once again.

By eleven o'clock, conversation died down a bit and the group started to disperse, most claiming work the next day. Ashley hadn't known how long she'd be at the fundraiser, so she'd smartly taken tomorrow off. Even so, she'd been regularly yawning for the better part of an hour.

"Ready to go?" Carly asked as two others stood and gathered their things.

"I am. I was up at five this morning."

They stood together and Carly held Ashley's hoodie so she could slide her arms in. Goodnights went around the table and the group slowly milled out the door. Carly's hand slid down Ashley's arm and grasped her hand. Her grip was warm and firm as they walked to the parking lot.

"So…I'll call you tomorrow? After work?" Carly asked as they reached Ashley's car.

"Sure." Ashley hadn't told Carly she'd taken the day off, and she still didn't tell her. She didn't want to examine why.

"Good." Carly smiled, her teeth shining white in the dim light of the lot. She really was quite attractive, her dark hair a wavy cloud around her head, her brown eyes soft and kind. She moved in closer to Ashley, gently pinning her between the car and her body, and she bent down to Ashley's mouth for kiss.

Their lips pressed together, and Ashley closed her eyes, willed herself to relax and just chill. Carly's mouth worked slowly against hers, her tongue eventually seeking entrance, which Ashley allowed. It was a nice kiss. It was fine.

It was fine.

Somewhere in the back of her mind, a voice questioned whether fine was acceptable. It was. Wasn't it? This wasn't a romance novel or a romantic film. This was real life and real life didn't always come with fireworks and attraction that was near combustible. Right? Real life was calm and comfortable. Easy and stable.

Like kissing Carly. It was nice.

Ashley extricated herself from Carly's arms. She wanted to get in her car and drive home as quickly as she possibly could, but she also wanted to spare Carly's feelings and not just rush off. So she forced herself to move slowly, to smile, to be kind. "I really have to go. I'm so tired."

"Okay," Carly said, her grin wide, her eyes unassuming. "Talk to you tomorrow."

"Sounds good."

Carly leaned in for one more kiss, then backed away slowly and lifted one hand in a sweet little wave. Ashley waved back, got in her car, closed and locked the door. She keyed the ignition, then looked at herself in the rearview mirror, squinted.

It was fine.

Everything was just fine.

What more could she ask for than that?

CHAPTER FOUR

MANAGER MEETINGS HAPPENED every Monday morning at eight, and today was no exception. Lisa took her usual seat on the side of the long, cherry conference table, Starbucks cup in hand, notebook opened in front of her. A couple other people had tablets or laptops for note taking, but Lisa liked to go old school, liked the feel of pen on paper. She was exhausted from yesterday's activities, but the coffee was helping.

The meetings were generally attended by eight people, if everybody was present, and this morning, everybody was. Lisa looked around the room at her peers. Some were her friends. Some were simply acquaintances, colleagues. Some were friends with each other, some were not. Her gaze landed across the table and on Catherine Gardner, looking impeccably better dressed than anybody else in the room—as always—in a gray pantsuit, her black-rimmed glasses perched on her nose as she looked over a paper Lisa could only assume was full of numbers.

Three seats down sat Anna St. John, their public relations person who hated to be called cute, but that's exactly what she was. Her blond hair was pulled back in a ponytail, one hank of it hanging down next to her left eye. She wore jeans and navy T-shirt with a gray zip-up Junebug Farms hoodie as a jacket, her outfit the antithesis of Catherine's formal business attire. The dark circles that had underlined her soft brown eyes as of late seemed less prominent this morning, which was good, and she squinted slightly as she looked at something on her phone.

As she did so, one corner of her pink-glossed mouth quirked up in a half-smile. Lisa was glad any time she saw Anna smile lately, as she'd had her heart broken not so long ago. By Catherine.

David Peters sauntered in then. Lisa was constantly amazed at how much he got done, as she always thought he seemed to move slower than everybody else, which she was starting to realize was an optical illusion, maybe because of his bulk. He was the head of fundraising at Junebug Farms, and that alone should have had him running around like a lunatic yesterday, but his speed never varied from his usual saunter. Bald head the color of milk chocolate, it gleamed in the overhead light. His broad shoulders and solid biceps strained against his oxford shirt and Lisa felt a strange sympathy for the fabric that was trying so hard to contain his musculature. Lisa would bet money he'd just come from the gym. He took a seat, plastic tumbler in hand and filled with something unappetizingly green.

Donna Christianson, the event coordinator for Junebug Farms and Maggie Simon from the gift shop rounded out the meeting, the two of them with their heads together chatting about something Lisa couldn't hear. They didn't have to wait long for the head of things to show up.

Jessica Barstow didn't go as far as Catherine did when it came to dressing for work, but she still managed to look several cuts above everybody else in the room. Always. Navy dress slacks and slight heels made her look slick and professional. The powder blue silk blouse with the sleeves already rolled up at 8am gave her the air of a stern businesswoman who was completely in charge of her company. Her auburn hair was pulled into a loose ponytail this morning, the escaping strands softening her entire look. Well, the escaping strands and the big smile on her face. Pam Redmond, Jessica's assistant and right hand, trailed in immediately behind her. Pam took the chair nearest Jessica, extracted a notebook from her bag, and looked up expectantly, pen poised.

"Good morning." As murmured greetings went around the room, Jessica continued. "I am happy to report that yesterday was a huge success, assuming I'm reading the reports correctly." She set down a faux leather portfolio and a mug of coffee, then took a seat at the head of the table. "I want to thank you all for your hard work."

They did the usual Monday meeting agenda. Jessica gave them a summary of the previous week and touched on headline issues that each manager would talk about in more depth as they went around the table. She finished up, then turned things over to David, then Maggie, and so on. Each person gave a report about yesterday, complete with lots of smiling and joking. Catherine's report was the most anticipated, as she was all about the money. She gave them the total that had come in from donations during the fundraiser and the number earned enthusiastic whoops and cheers.

"The Breckenridge Foundation came through, as always, with a huge chunk. Oh, and Lisa," Catherine looked over the rim of her glasses. "Seems Clark's chosen his newest conquest and she's one of yours. Amber? Andrea? Something with an A. That cute, perky blonde that's always smiling."

"Ashley," Lisa said, on a sigh.

"Ashley. That's it."

"Thank God it's not one of mine this time," Maggie said quietly from her end of the table. She threw a sympathetic look Lisa's way.

"Can't you keep a leash on him?" Lisa tried unsuccessfully to keep the irritation out of her voice. "Every fundraiser he has to do this?"

Catherine shrugged. "They're all adults. Not my problem."

Lisa shook her head in disgust, and tried to ignore the fact that Clark anywhere near Ashley made Lisa decidedly uncomfortable. She wasn't about to analyze that. Catherine's response was not unexpected, which was annoying, as usual. She tiptoed around the Breckenridges because of the money they donated, and part of Lisa understood that. But they'd had more than one woman at Junebug who'd fallen for Clark's questionable "charms," and they always ended up hurt, angry, or both. Plus they *never* ended up staying.

Jessica stepped in and nipped the potential, all-too-familiar argument in the bud. "Let's just keep an eye on things, okay?"

They finished going around the table. Reporting on the adoptions from yesterday went a long way toward making Lisa feel better—or at least let go of her irritation for the time being.

"That's fantastic," Donna said. "That's a lot of cats to get scooped up in one day."

Lisa nodded happily. "It was a good day."

The meeting wrapped up, and everybody stood to head off in their own directions. Jessica left the room first, walking half a speed faster than the average person. Pam followed on her heels and Lisa grinned to herself, as she always thought of Pam as Jessica's soccer mom tail. Everywhere Jessica went, there was Pam, right behind her. Always.

"I'm not unsympathetic, you know."

Catherine's voice surprised her, as did the fact that she was suddenly right next to her. Lisa met her gaze. "I know that. But this isn't news. He does this all the time. How many volunteers have we lost thanks to him?"

Catherine didn't argue. "I know. You're right. But…"

She didn't have to go on. Lisa got the message. "His checkbook is worth more than a dozen volunteers. Says you."

"It's not just me, Lisa. It's fact. I am doing my best to keep him in check. In fact, I rescued your girl from him yesterday. That's how I knew he had the hots for her. He told me. The 'little blond cupcake,' he called her."

"Charming," Lisa said, revolted. "And she's not my girl."

"Oh. Well. You know what I mean." Catherine gave her a wink and left the room, Lisa watching her go.

"Sometimes, I can't stand that bitch," she muttered, gathering her things. At the sound of a muffled chuckle, she looked up to meet Anna's brown eyes across the table.

"Get in line," Anna said.

Mondays were notoriously quiet and this one was no exception. Lisa spent the day doing intake paperwork, as well as filling out forms and making phone calls and arrangements for the people who had adopted dogs and cats at the Pawsitively Spring event. Only a few people came in to wander the dog wing, one of them a petite, dark-haired woman in jeans and a Carhartt jacket who set Lisa's gaydar to pinging like a car alarm. The woman strolled up and down the corridor three or four times, each time stopping in front of the same cage door: number sixteen.

Lisa pulled the file, saw that the dog in cage sixteen was fairly new. He was some sort of terrier mix, about twenty-five pounds with a black, wiry coat and soulful brown eyes. He'd been brought in last week as a stray, and Lisa was kind of surprised he hadn't been adopted yesterday. Dogs his size and breed usually went quickly.

The woman paced once more, stopped in front of the cage, and squatted down. Lisa could hear her gentle murmurs, and the security cameras allowed her to watch on one of the four monitors behind her desk what was transpiring. The dog had his nose to the cage door and the woman was stroking him with whatever fingers she could fit through the mesh fencing. The dog's tail wagged slowly, uncertainly, as he sniffed the woman. He didn't back away. Rather, the wagging of his tail sped up a bit. Lisa grinned. This was a good sign.

After ten or fifteen minutes of quiet conversation with the dog, the woman took her leave. As she reached Lisa's desk on her way out, she winked at her and said simply, "I'll be back."

"We'll be here," Lisa said with a smile. Excellent. The terrier mix was most likely going to get a home.

Adoptions were the best part of Lisa's job by far. People were filled with such joy when they were about to take a pet home. And frankly, so were the pets. Especially the dogs. Lisa had read a study once that claimed dogs instinctively knew that being in a shelter was bad and when somebody adopted them —essentially saving them from the shelter—they knew that, too, and experienced the canine equivalent of undying gratitude. Shelter dogs were often said to be more loyal and loving than dogs who had never been in the same situation.

It was close to six by the time Lisa was wrapping things up. Tammy Renner, who had been a volunteer at Junebug Farms for close to ten years, had offered to take over for the evening shift, since there were three more appointments scheduled for adoption pickups. While she was not the kind of person who was comfortable handing over the reins to the department she ran like a drill sergeant, Lisa didn't mind turning things over to Tammy. She was one of the few volunteers Lisa trusted to handle things and handle them correctly. Plus, Lisa was exhausted from yesterday.

"These people are coming at seven. They're adopting the black Lab mix." Lisa ran a fingertip down the schedule on her computer monitor so Tammy could follow. "These people are taking Old Gertrude."

"Old Gertrude got a forever home?" Tammy asked, obviously delighted to see their nearly ten-year-old feline resident find someplace to live. "That's terrific."

"It's a nice, newlywed couple. I liked them."

Tammy smiled and gave a nod.

"And this woman is taking the bulldog mix."

"Got it." Tammy was still smiling.

"You know, I don't say it nearly enough, but thank you for all you do here."

There was a quick flash of surprise on Tammy's face, but she covered it quickly and patted Lisa's arm. "You're welcome. And I love it here, so it's not work to me."

"Well." Lisa pushed an arm into the sleeve of her jacket. "Thank you anyway."

"Have a great night," Tammy called as Lisa exited the dog wing and pulled out her cell to check for texts as she strode across the lobby.

"Lisa. There you are."

Lisa looked up from her cell and into the cool blue eyes of none other than Clark Breckenridge. She stopped walking and cleared her throat, reminding herself not to let on how truly repulsive she found the man. It was largely due to his family that Junebug Farms was able to run as easily as it did. "Mr.

Breckenridge. Hello. Are you looking for Catherine?" She craned her neck in the direction of the accounting office, praying she'd see her and be able to hand him off. No luck.

"Please. Call me Clark." Breckenridge smiled, but it didn't reach his eyes. Lisa had noticed long ago that it almost never reached his eyes. "And no, in fact, I was looking for you."

"Me?"

"Yes. I was wondering if that cute little cupcake of a volunteer of yours was working tonight."

Lisa ground her teeth and mentally counted to five before she made a show of scrunching up her face in thought and saying, "Hmm. I don't know who you're talking about."

He held his hand flat next to his shoulder. "About so high? Blonde? Always smiling? Great ass?"

Lisa squinted at him and shook her head. "Sorry. Doesn't ring a bell."

His look of irritated frustration was totally worth it. "Ashley," he finally said. "I'm pretty sure her name's Ashley."

"Oh! Ashley." Lisa nodded as if she *finally* understood whom he meant. "No, I'm sorry. She's not working tonight."

"Aw, bummer. Do you know when she's on next?"

Wednesday at five o'clock, she thought as she made another big show of wracking her brain. "Hmm. Let me think." She went so far as to tap her chin with a fingertip. "No, I'm sorry. I don't know for sure." Before he realized it, she stepped around him, wanting to make an exit before he asked her to look up the volunteer schedule, which she had no way to deny him. "Good to see you, Mr. Breckenridge. Take care." She walked as fast as she could to the door without actually running away from him and made it through without incident. *Not that he won't just go ask Tammy*, she thought to herself, knowing that's exactly what he'd do. And he'd get his answer. Lisa wasn't sure why she felt so protective of Ashley. She hardly knew the woman. It was true that the idea of any woman with a creep like Breckenridge kind of grossed her out. But the idea of him with Ashley made Lisa's skin crawl.

She didn't let herself analyze why.

━◆━

Lisa found the last piece to finish the border of the puzzle. Finally. She snapped it into place with a victorious, "Yay!" She glanced again at the box top, depicting the entire picture the puzzle would presumably show once she was finished. It was a field of purple flowers, each one looking very much like the next, and for an instant, she wondered how in the world she thought she'd be able to put it together without tossing herself off the roof in frustration. The border had obviously been the easy part. But she took a deep breath and remembered how many equally difficult puzzles she'd mastered in the past year: twenty-three.

"I got this," she said to Groucho, who was draped around her shoulders in his usual impression of a feather boa. "No worries. I totally got this." She was scanning all the pieces she'd laid out on the card table, trying to plan a strategy, when her cell rang. She looked at the screen for a long moment while she did a quick calculation to figure out how many of these calls she'd ignored.

Too many, really.

With a sigh, she pressed the answer button. "Hi, Mom."

"Hi, sweetheart. Is this a bad time?"

"No." *Yes. Isn't it usually?*

"Oh, good. Um…" her mother hesitated, sounding a little nervous. Which was par for the course during these conversations. "I haven't spoken to you in a while, so I thought I'd call and say hi. See how the fundraiser went."

Lisa poked this inside of her cheek with her tongue. She knew where this was coming from. Though the fundraiser was well-publicized, she suspected Aunt Joyce had a hand in creating a conversation starter for Lisa's mother. She suppressed a sigh.

"It went well," Lisa said, matter-of-factly. "We had a good turnout. Adopted out lots of animals."

"Great. That's fantastic. You're so good at what you do. It makes me proud."

"Thanks."

"How are those animals of yours?"

"They're fine." Purposely not elaborating, Lisa rolled her eyes at herself and her own passive-aggressive tactics. Apparently, the fruit doesn't fall far from the tree.

"Good." A beat of silence. "Have you talked to your brothers lately?"

She hadn't in over a week, and it irritated her that her mother pointed it out. The same mother who had gone for weeks and weeks at a time without talking to the children she'd left behind. "I've been really busy." She tried not to dwell on the fact that her brothers rarely called her. She was the one who seemed always to do the reaching out.

To her mother's credit, her tone held no judgment. "Well, Eric got a promotion," she said proudly. Eric was five years younger than Lisa and worked for American Express as a financial planner. At twenty-seven, he was one of the youngest in his office, but the guy was a whiz with numbers. Always had been. Something Lisa was not. And had never been. She envied him.

"Good for him," she said, picking up a puzzle piece and turning it different ways.

"He's doing so well there. And apparently, Ben has picked up six new contracts for this summer. *Six*. And he's kept all his old ones."

"He's going to be working his tail off," Lisa said, grinning with pride even through her annoyance. Ben was two years younger than Eric and despite the fact that they couldn't possibly be more different, they were as close as twins. Eric was clean-shaven and wore a suit and tie every day. Ben was lucky to shave four times a month and preferred worn jeans, flannel shirts, and work boots. The two of them were tighter than almost any other pair Lisa had ever seen. And as much as she loved her little brothers with all her heart, she had often felt left out, not included in their circle, probably because she'd been thought of as more mother than sister. "Starting that landscaping business of his worried me, but he's really done well."

"He has. I'm so proud of him."

"Me, too."

Turned out, the boys were a fairly safe subject, and they actually chatted about them for several more minutes before the conversation lagged, as it always did with Lisa and her mother.

"We should have lunch soon," her mother said. "Or dinner. Either works for me."

"Sounds good," Lisa replied, using the same stock answer she gave every time her mother suggested a get together of any sort. "Let me check my schedule and I'll toss you some dates."

"Okay, sweetheart." Was that a note of dejection in her mother's voice? A stab of guilt poked Lisa in the ribs, but she slapped it away. "You let me know. I'd love to see you. It's been too long."

Lisa couldn't recall how long it had been. Dodging phone calls or e-mails when she wanted to was easy. Sidestepping her in person was much more difficult, and since her mother had come back to town a little over a year ago, Lisa'd become a virtual master at avoiding her. *I'll hear about it from Aunt Joyce*, she thought as she hung up the phone and stared at it in her hand.

It's not like she'd never tried to deal with these feelings inside. There was a stack of books upstairs in her bedroom. *The Children of Divorce. Adult Children of Divorce. Forgiveness is a Choice. Mother Daughter Wisdom.* There was a time when she'd read endlessly on the subject, snapped up any book she could find that had to do with children of divorced parents, kids who had a strained relationship with one parent or another—anything that she thought might relate to her situation. But for whatever reason, she just had trouble letting go of the past and moving forward with a clean slate. She'd never been able to give her mother that: a clean slate. Her best friend Grace told her she had "mommy issues." Aunt Joyce was always telling her how unhealthy it was to hang on to "that big, heavy grudge," how it stressed her heart and her psyche and her soul, not to mention her outlook on every other aspect of her life.

They were both right. Lisa knew that; she wasn't an idiot. But no matter how hard she tried, she couldn't seem to pry her fingers open long enough to let go of the whole thing. She held on with both hands, as if letting it slip from her grasp would mean she'd lose a major piece of herself. Which was silly. She knew that, too. And the truth was, she *wanted* to let go. Being quietly, endlessly angry was nothing short of exhausting. But whenever her mother called and used that sweet, friendly voice, never striking back even when Lisa was downright mean to her (which didn't happen often, but did happen), it just made Lisa hold on tighter.

A puzzle piece flying off the table caught her attention and pulled her from her ruminations. Tiny was on the card table, apparently wanting to help.

"Oh, no you don't," Lisa said, swooping him up and depositing him on the floor. He was the only one of the four felines who climbed up on things. The kitchen counter. Her dresser in the bedroom. The curtain rod in the living room. Keeler's back. "Am I going to have to use the squirt gun on you, buddy?" He looked at her with his big eyes as if he knew just exactly what she'd said, then ran away into the hallway, Lisa smiling after him.

The phone call—and the unpleasant thoughts it brought with it—gone for the moment, she scratched Groucho's head and picked up another piece of the puzzle. It was obviously a piece of the sky, the blue surprisingly warm. Turning it in her fingers, Lisa gazed at it, the color settling into her, reminding her suddenly of the sparkling blue of Ashley Stiles's eyes.

Wait. What?

With a head tilt to the side, she furrowed her brows.

Where the hell had that come from?

CHAPTER FIVE

"I'M LATE. I KNOW. I KNOW." Ashley hung her jacket on the hook inside the door of her mother's house and scooted up the three steps into the kitchen. Her mother pulled a chicken from the oven, and when she stood up, Ashley kissed her on the cheek. "I'm sorry."

"Honey, the day you show up on time is the day I start to wonder if the world is about to end." Monica Ribisi set the pan with the roasted chicken down on the counter and slid off her oven mitts.

"I brought wine," Ashley said, by way of apology, holding up a bottle of Pinot Grigio.

"Then all is forgiven."

Ashley uncorked the bottle and opened a white cupboard door, only to see a stack of navy blue plates where the wineglasses should be. "Mom. Did you rearrange the cupboards? *Again?*" She opened three more doors before finding the correct one. "What are you trying to do to me?" She poured two glasses and handed one to Monica.

"I felt like a change," Monica said with a shrug as they clinked glasses.

Ashley shook her head with an affectionate grin, and they sipped.

"Are you two hogging all the wine for yourselves?" asked Ashley's big sister, Kelly, as she entered the kitchen.

"Wine? What wine? I have no idea what you're talking about." Ashley held her wineglass behind her back.

"Ha ha. Very funny. I want some." Her brown hair, which she had recently cut short, looked stylish and hip, and she had eyes the exact same shade of blue as Ashley's. She poured herself a glass and sipped.

"How's life?" Ashley asked as she carried a bowl of salad into the dining room.

"It's not bad." Kelly followed her with butter and the salt and pepper shakers. "Not bad at all."

"Right on time, Ash." Vincent Ribisi gave Ashley's shoulder a gentle squeeze and winked at her as he went into the kitchen to help with the rest of dinner.

"Never gets old, all the late jokes," Ashley said to her stepdad, shaking her head.

Monica came in with the potatoes and Vince followed with the chicken on a platter. "You've been late since the day you were born, sweetie," she said to her daughter. "It's just who you are."

The five of them sat down to dinner. Doing so on a Tuesday night was unusual, but it happened to be a day everybody was available, and Ashley's mother liked to round them up whenever she had the chance. Everybody had their own lives, their own crazy schedules, and getting everybody on the same page could be crazy difficult. So today, they ate cheerfully and caught each other up on their lives, just as they always did during family dinners, happy to be together.

"You still doing volunteer work at the shelter, Ash?" Kelly's husband, Stephen, asked.

Ashley nodded. "A couple times a week, if I have the time. They're really great about being flexible with my schedule."

"They had a big fundraiser last week, right? One of my colleagues works with them." Stephen was in advertising.

"Really? You guys have us for a client?"

"Yeah…I think Kristin…" He gazed at the ceiling as if looking for the answer up there. "Well. Not important. But yeah, we do work for them."

"Cool." Ashley swallowed a bite of chicken. "I really like it there. Nice people. They're good to the animals. I enjoy it."

"Does it get hard?" Vincent asked. "Like…sad, I mean?" He was a very large, very Italian man of sixty who'd been Ashley's and Kelly's stepfather for the better part of ten years. Physically, he looked like he could crush a bowling ball in one hand. In reality, he was a huge sap of a man with an enormous heart and a soft spot for animals. Ashley loved him for that.

"A little," she replied. "The older dogs have much less of a chance of being adopted. That can be hard. I mean, it's a no-kill shelter, so they won't be put down. But still. I wish I had a huge farm with tons of land. I'd just take them all home with me." Her thoughts shifted to Jax, his big, soft eyes sad with loneliness.

"Yeah, I'd have a tough time with that," Vince said and took a sip of wine. "You're a stronger person than I am."

Ashley puffed up a bit with that, and her mother smiled at her. After a beat, Monica asked, "Have either of you talked to your father lately?"

Kelly looked at Ashley and they each shrugged. "I talked to him a couple days ago," Kelly said.

"I think he left me a message the other day, but I haven't called him back yet." Ashley made a mental note to do just that.

"Well, I spoke to him yesterday." Monica took a sip of wine and said nothing more.

"Okay, you obviously have something you want to share," Kelly said with a grin.

Divorced for nearly fifteen years, Monica and her ex-husband Rick had surprised everybody by becoming very close friends. They spoke on the phone several times a week, and Rick was always invited to parties or gatherings hosted by the Ribisis. Most people found the whole situation oddly disconcerting, but Ashley just thought she was lucky. The idea of her parents disliking each other—or worse, hating each other—wasn't something she could ever even imagine. They just made better friends than spouses. It was as simple as that.

Monica leaned forward slightly and lowered her voice as she said, "I think he's seeing somebody."

"You mean he has a new flavor of the month," Kelly corrected.

"Stop that," her mother scolded.

"Mom. Come on. He dates somebody for a month or two, then finds a reason to stop seeing her and moves on to the next. It's what he's done for how long? Since he started dating? You know this as well as we do." Kelly looked to Ashley for confirmation.

Ashley shrugged. "She's right."

"Well, I think this one might be different. He sounds… smitten."

"Smitten?" Ashley looked to her sister, who grinned back at her. "What is this, 1943?"

"Stop that," Monica said again. "You know what I mean. Call him and see for yourselves."

"Gonna have to now," Ashley said.

"Hey, how's the cookie business, Ash?" Vincent asked as Kelly stood and excused herself to the bathroom.

"Things have died down since Easter, so we've all had a chance to breathe. That's been nice." Ashley's job tended to be very cyclical, revolving around holidays and major life events. "Next up will be weddings and graduations. Then the Fourth of July."

"You've got baked goods for everything," Stephen commented.

"True story."

Kelly returned a few minutes later and took her seat. "Are you still seeing that girl?" she asked around a forkful of food, avoiding eye contact with her sister.

Ashley blinked at her, shot her the silent sister-to-sister *Really?* look before saying, "Sorry?"

"What girl?" Monica and Vince said at the same time.

Looking smug, Kelly went on. "Ashley's been seeing some girl. Carol? Karen?"

"Carly," Ashley said, irritated. "And I'm not really *seeing* her. We're just…sort of dating."

Her mother furrowed her brow. "Isn't that the same thing?"

"It is exactly the same thing," Kelly confirmed.

Lifting her shoulders in a shrug, Ashley said, "It's not at all the same thing. It's not the least bit serious."

"For you," Kelly said.

Ashley whipped her head around to gape at her sister.

"What?" Kelly asked. "I ran into Jenna the other day."

"Yeah, well. Jenna doesn't know everything."

But Kelly didn't give up. "She knows you pretty well. And really, Ash, you're going to have to get serious about somebody eventually or you're going to end up a lonely old woman. You'll be the house the kids all avoid on Halloween because you scare them."

The wink Kelly shot in Ashley's direction did little to take away the sting of the words, but before Ashley could give a smart-ass reply, her brain tossed her a quick picture of Lisa Drakemore, smiling one of her very rare smiles. *What the hell?* Ashley thought with surprise, then did her best to tamp that image down and ignore her sister's comments. She shoveled a forkful of potatoes into her mouth to keep herself quiet.

Luckily, the subject died down and conversation turned to other topics, but the Carly dilemma stuck in her chest, like heartburn. They ate and talked and laughed for nearly another hour before Ashley stood and began to clear the table, reminding everybody that she had to be to work at five a.m. "And then I'm going to go walk some dogs after that," she told her mother.

In the kitchen, Monica put a hand on her daughter's back. "I want you to know how proud I am of you."

Ashley blinked in surprise. "Where did that come from?"

Her mother shrugged as she handed Ashley a plate to rinse before lining it up with the others in the dishwasher. "I'm not sure. I just think I need to tell you more often. Your job, the time you put in at the shelter, your visits here…you're a good girl, Ashley. I'm proud of you and I want you to know that."

The welling up of her eyes caused Ashley to blush slightly as she put her arms around her mother and squeezed. "Thanks, Mom. I love you."

"Love you, too."

The entire ride home, Ashley could feel the grin stretched across her face.

Life was good.

>─◇─<

Ashley spent her entire Wednesday putting out one fire after another, which was a relief only in that she didn't dwell on guilty thoughts about Carly. Two different deliveries were incorrect and one was missing altogether. A cake order had a misspelling. One of the bakers called in sick and another decided to simply not show up for work (this was the third time he'd done this and he was going to get fired, Ashley just knew it). A disgruntled customer caused a scene. And one of the industrial mixers decided to just stop working. Ashley was stressed out, frustrated, and tired, but for some reason, the direction of her apartment wasn't the way she pointed her car when she slid behind the wheel. Instead, without even thinking about it, she headed straight for Junebug Farms. And when she pulled into the parking lot, she felt a sense of relief settle over her.

Interesting.

Remembering to change her hat this time, she pulled off her batter-covered white one and donned a hot pink hat with a white Nike swoosh on the front. She tugged her ponytail through the back and checked herself in the rearview mirror, determined she would never again show up covered in frosting. Her white coat and floured shoes were left at the bakery, and she'd changed into comfortable jeans and tennis shoes before she'd left. She surprised herself by wishing she had a little makeup on (she rarely wore it to work), and gave her lips a quick coat of gloss with the tube she kept in the center console of the car. Then she headed in.

It didn't make sense that the noisy chaos of Junebug Farms would feel relaxed and calming compared to working in a bakery, but such was the case for Ashley and she smiled as she was bombarded with the familiar sounds and smells. Disinfectant, the buzz of conversation, endless barking. It hit her the second she opened the door, surrounded her like a fog, and she felt oddly at home. She waved to Maggie Simon on her way by the gift shop and then again at the two volunteers behind the front desk area of the lobby. Bill Tracey was precariously perched on a ladder doing something to an overhead light, so Ashley refrained from distracting him and stayed quiet as she walked by.

The volume of the barking increased exponentially as she pushed through the double doors leading to the dog wing, and Ashley was happily surprised to see ten separate people meandering up and down the row of cages, stopping here and there to coo to a dog or read the chart attached to its cage door. There was a family of three, two couples, and three individuals, and Ashley simply stood next to Lisa's desk and watched.

"Wow," she breathed after a few moments.

"I know, right?" Lisa replied from her seat. Lowering her voice to just above a whisper, she asked, "See that woman near cage sixteen? The short one with the dark hair?"

Ashley nodded.

"She was here on Monday, too. Looking at the same dog. I think he might get lucky."

Ashley grinned. "That's awesome."

"And the parents with the boy? They want to see Jax. Again. Tammy's walking him, but should be in soon."

As if on cue, the back door opened and Tammy entered with Jax on a leash. It was as if Jax recognized that the family was there to see him, and his large tail began to wag, like a fur-covered baseball bat swinging back and forth. The boy was maybe ten, and Ashley watched in awe as he dropped to his knees so he could look the dog in the eye. Ashley turned to say something to Lisa, but the expression on her face stopped the words in Ashley's throat.

Lisa was smiling.

Widely.

Her green eyes seemed radiant, sparkling with a joy that Ashley hadn't seen before. She looked undeniably beautiful. And when she lifted a hand, brushed it through her hair, and gently tucked a chunk behind her ear with her fingertips, her eyes never leaving the family and Jax, Ashley felt a sizzling jolt run through her. It shocked her so much, she took a small step back. Away.

Lisa glanced up at her, and a sudden look of concern creased her face. "You okay?"

Ashley raised her eyebrows in question, buying herself some recovery time by asking, "I'm sorry, what?" even as she felt heat flush her cheeks and her body break out in a sweat.

"I asked if you were okay. You have a weird look on your face."

Nodding, Ashley replied, "Oh. Yeah. I'm fine. I'm good. I'm great. You?"

Lisa squinted at her, but didn't press. "I'm good."

"Oh, good. That's good. Um…" She pointed in the general direction of the restrooms. "I just…I'll be right back." And suddenly, she couldn't get away from Lisa fast enough. Thankful to be the only person in the ladies' room, she threw a handful of cold water on her face—which felt like it was broiling—and looked at her reflection in the mirror. "What the hell was that?" she hissed. "Pull yourself together, for God's sake. This is not the time or place to decide you have a crush. Geez." The door opened, and Ashley was grateful to have an excuse to stop talking to herself. Tammy grinned at her in the mirror.

"I think those people are going to adopt Jax." She went into a stall and shut the door, but kept talking. "They were here on

Sunday. He seems to really connect with the boy. Did you see them?"

"I didn't. But that's great," Ashley replied, and she meant it.

Her voice echoing from inside the stall, Tammy said, "It's a little bittersweet, though, I have to admit. I'll miss him."

Ashley stopped with her wet hand halfway to the towel dispenser as she took in Tammy's words. "Oh. Yeah, I hadn't thought of that." And she hadn't. A flash of melancholy hit as she realized Jax could be leaving and she'd never see him again.

The toilet flushed and Tammy bent over the sink to wash her hands. "It can be a tough part of the job. I mean, it's not the same as it would be at a shelter that's not no-kill, but it's still difficult. You get attached." She reached around Ashley for a towel. "You try not to, but sometimes it can't be helped." With a small smile, she left Ashley standing in the ladies' room alone.

The next couple of hours went by quickly as Ashley walked several dogs and made an appearance at the goat pen just for a change of pace. Back inside, she watched as the dark-haired woman filled out paperwork to adopt the terrier mix. *Lisa called that one*, she thought with a smile. Then she helped mop out a couple of empty cages. It was nearing six by the time she realized how hungry she was and decided that once she finished mopping, it was time to pack up and go home. Tammy was putting the last of her walkers back in his cage when Lisa spoke from her desk as she set down the phone.

"It's official, ladies," she said, and the rare smile on her face was gorgeous, Ashley couldn't help but notice. "Jax has been adopted. They're coming back tomorrow morning to pick him up."

"Fantastic!" Tammy said, clapping her hands together. "I was pretty sure we'd have him here for the duration."

"So was I." Lisa walked down the aisle to stand next to Tammy at Jax's door. The Lab/shepherd mix stood proudly, enormous head up, tail wagging, as if he knew he'd just accomplished something major. "That boy is going to love you to pieces," Lisa said to him.

Ashley watched all of this from two doors down, and it was true that she was beyond happy for Jax. She was ecstatic. This was huge for him. Dogs his age and size? They were rarely adopted. Most spent their remaining days here at the shelter, and though they were well-cared for and loved, it wasn't the same as having a forever home and their very own family to love and protect. This was great news. It was a very, very happy day for Jax.

Ashley quietly leaned her mop against the wall and headed to the employee break room, which was thankfully empty. She tried to keep herself quiet, to get her emotions under control, but a small sob escaped from her throat before she could clap a hand over her mouth. Her eyes filled with tears just as a warm hand lay on her shoulder.

"Hey," Lisa said softly. "You okay?" Gentle pressure from her fingers slowly turned Ashley to face her. One look at the shimmering wetness in her eyes was all it took.

"I'll miss him," Ashley whispered.

"I know," Lisa said. "So will I. It's okay. Come here."

Before Ashley could say anything more or launch any sort of protest, she found herself enfolded in Lisa's arms, and the warmth of that embrace melted any barriers Ashley had put up to keep her emotions penned in. Once the tears spilled over, there was no stopping them and she cried quietly against Lisa's shoulder. She could feel Lisa's hand on her head, the other on her back, stroking gently. She could hear the tender murmurs close to her ear, telling Ashley she understood, promising that it would be okay, that Jax would be very happy, that Ashley being sad to see him go just proved what a big heart she had. She was pretty sure she felt Lisa press a gentle kiss against her hat, but she chose not to think about it too hard. It was all a bit surreal to Ashley, being held by this woman she'd always labeled as a bit cold, a bit removed. And oh, my God, did she smell good. That same mixture...honey, vanilla, and something slightly different this time. Jasmine? Ashley didn't know for sure, but what she did know was that she could stand right there, wrapped up in Lisa's warm, soft embrace, until the end of time and be perfectly, amazingly content.

It was that thought that finally made her extricate herself. Slowly. So she could remember what it felt like, as the likelihood of it happening again was slim. It had to be slim. Ashley wouldn't survive it a second time, which she realized when she had trouble pulling her eyes away from Lisa's mouth.

With a loud clearing of her throat, Ashley took a step back and gave a weak smile. "Sorry about that." She wiped at her face, glad after all that she had no mascara on. Glancing around the room, she located a box of tissues and snagged a couple, wiped her face, blew her nose. Lisa watched her the whole time, a mix of sympathy and amusement on her face.

"No need to apologize. I completely get it." There was that smile again.

Why don't you smile more often? God, you're gorgeous when you smile. Lisa reached out and squeezed Ashley's shoulder, but didn't step any closer. "I don't want volunteers who feel nothing for the animals. You know?"

Ashley nodded and blew out a breath. "Yeah, I do. I'm happy for Jax. I really am. I'm just…a little embarrassed now." She shrugged.

"It'll be our little secret." Lisa made a show of twisting an imaginary key in front of her lips and tossing it over her shoulder. "No worries." She held Ashley's gaze a beat longer, then winked at her and left the room.

Ashely waited until the door closed, then dropped forward, bracing her hands on her knees, and a groan escaped her lips. "Oh, my God," she said aloud, albeit quietly. "What the hell was that?" It didn't take long for her sadness to morph into total mortification. She covered her face with both hands as she straightened back up and shook her head back and forth slowly. "I cannot believe I did that. I am such an idiot." She finally dropped her hands and blew out another, bigger breath. Near the bank of lockers was a small mirror, and she used it to clean herself up. She blew her nose one last time, downed a paper cup of water from the cooler, and shook her hands out at her sides, willing herself to pull it together. She smoothed her hands down her shirt, straightened her hat. Deep breath in, slow breath out, and she was ready. She needed to say goodbye to Jax as he'd be gone the next time she was here. It wouldn't be easy, but she knew if she didn't, she'd regret it. Plus, he deserved to know how much she cared about him and how happy she was for him.

As she pushed the door open, she tried not to notice that she could still smell Lisa on her clothes.

☙

Lisa wasn't sure what to make of those five minutes in the employee break room, and she was still rolling it around in her head an hour later as she packed up her things to head home.

It was completely out of character for her and she knew it. The emotions of other people were not things she enjoyed getting wrapped up in. In fact, she stayed as far away from them as she could manage. She'd done more than her share of taking care of people in her young life. She had no desire to do it again. But something about Ashley, about Ashley's sadness— it called to her, tugged at her, and she'd had no choice (which kind of ticked her off). She'd understood exactly why Ashley had excused herself and regular Lisa would have shrugged in indifference. This new, weird Lisa hadn't even thought twice before following. And holding her while she cried? How the hell had that happened? Lisa couldn't remember the last time she'd been the pillar of support for somebody. Definitely not her forté. And also, not anything she wanted to do. Why would she? People did nothing but take from you, why hand over a shining opportunity? But it had felt...right. Ashley was only an inch or two shorter than Lisa and her head fit naturally against Lisa's shoulder like that's where she belonged. Lisa could still feel the warmth of Ashley's body, the solid softness of it, Ashley's hand at the small of her back. And the smell of cupcakes. Always cupcakes. Lisa squinted in confusion at the memory.

What a weird freaking afternoon.

She shook herself back to the present.

Both Tammy and Ashley were scheduled for another half hour. Lisa put on her jacket, shouldered her bag, then found Tammy to let her know she was leaving. She didn't purposely avoid Ashley, but not seeing her again tonight was probably best for both of them. For Ashley so she wouldn't be embarrassed all over again. For Lisa so she had some time to purge her brain of the day's nuttiness.

The avoidance wasn't total, however.

On her way to her car, Lisa could see Ashley some distance away walking one of the pit bulls. But who was that walking next to her? A quick glance at the parking lot and Lisa's gaze landed on the black Mercedes coupe, confirming her suspicions. Goddamn Clark Breckenridge.

"Ugh, I hate that guy," Lisa whispered into the evening air. She kept walking toward her car, but had trouble pulling her eyes away from the couple. Clark was walking rather close to Ashley, who laughed at something he said. Lisa could hear it from where she stood, fumbling with her keys, trying to find the right button to unlock the door so she could get inside and not listen to that blowhard playboy make Ashley laugh again. Even though it was a really, really nice sound.

"Goodnight, Lisa," she heard Ashley call to her. She looked up to see Ashley waving at her. She gave a half-hearted wave back before throwing herself into her car and pulling the door shut, suddenly overwhelmed by the need to escape.

So she did.

The next day handed Lisa a pounding headache the moment she opened her eyes. She'd slept fitfully, unable to find a comfortable body temperature, and when she had slept, her mind had been plagued with strange, exhausting dreams that should couldn't remember. All she knew now was that she felt like she'd slept for a grand total of fifteen minutes and she was running dangerously low on Motrin. One of the cats had left her a lovely present of a pile of vomited hairball, though nobody was ratting anybody else out. And worst of all, she was out of coffee. She briefly thought maybe she'd just go back to bed to avoid the disaster this day was obviously going to be, but at the last minute, decided against it. She took the last handful of Motrin, cleaned up the puke, and headed to work. A stop at Dunkin' Donuts on the way in cured the coffee problem, and she was pleasantly surprised to see Tammy Renner there before she was. The woman might as well be a full-time employee; that's how much time she spent at Junebug Farms. Too bad every volunteer didn't have such dedication and unlimited amounts of free time…not to mention the love for the animals.

"Morning, boss," Tammy said with a warm smile. She wore jeans and a flannel shirt over a white T-shirt. Lisa made it a point not to be friends with her employees as she felt it undermined her authority, but Tammy was easily one of the kindest people she'd ever met, and she felt her mood warming up almost immediately when she saw her grinning face.

"Hi, Tammy. How are you?"

"Can't complain." Tammy's stock answer. "I mopped out the empty cages—boy, I love seeing those."

"Me, too."

"And I gave Jax a bath."

"Oh, right," Lisa said, remembering that the old boy was heading to his new forever home this morning. "Fantastic."

"I swear he knows what's going on. Prancing around like he's Mr. Big Shot."

"Funny how that happens, isn't it?" Lisa asked. "I think he *does* know. Dogs are so much smarter than we ever give them credit for." She watched as Tammy nodded, a different thought entirely poking at her brain. As Tammy started to walk away, Lisa asked, "Hey, how late was Ashley here last night? Do you know?"

Tammy furrowed her brow and pursed her lips. "Hmm. I'd say maybe an hour after you left?"

"Was Clark Breckenridge here the whole time?" Lisa tried to ask it innocently, but wasn't sure if she'd succeeded.

Tammy rolled her eyes with a scoff. "He was. Followed her around like a puppy. Lucky for him, she's polite. I'd have told him to take a hike." As if remembering exactly who Breckenridge was and what he did for Junebug, she added, "Gently, of course."

"You said Ashley was polite." Lisa again tried to feign only vague interest. "You don't think she's interested in him? That maybe they'd make a good couple?"

"Ha!" Tammy laughed. "Um…no."

"Really? Why not?"

A beat went by as Tammy studied her before saying, "Oh, honey, I don't think Mr. Breckenridge is…" She seemed to search for the right words, scanning the ceiling before finishing simply with, "Ashley's type." With a wink, she headed down the aisle to the golden retriever mix in the last cage.

Lisa could do nothing but stare after her for a full thirty seconds.

What the hell did that mean?

CHAPTER SIX

KATIE STANGER WAS INCOMPETENT.

Okay, maybe that was harsh. Maybe "not terribly competent" was better. Ashley didn't like to judge. In fact, she preferred to keep her head down, her mouth shut, and just do her job. But Katie was a menace to the bakery without meaning to be. And that was the hardest part for Ashley: she liked Katie. Katie was bubbly and enthusiastic and cute as a button and *nice*. And she always tried *so hard*. But she was a klutz, constantly tripping, spilling, or dropping. She didn't follow directions well because she was so excited to get started that she didn't fully listen, and she was making Ashley's day a living hell that consisted of picking up slack and correcting mistakes that were not her own. Her patience had worn as thin as the phyllo dough the pastry chef used to make the baklava and she couldn't wait until the end of the day.

Which was another five hours away.

"I might not make it," she said to her friend Stella as they worked together frosting the half-moon cookies. "I might dive headfirst into the vat of cake batter and just end it all."

Stella gave a snort of agreement. "I get it." Lowering her voice as she looked around, she said, "I hid in the walk-in freezer for almost twenty minutes to avoid her constant questions. I still can't feel three of the fingers on my left hand." She held up the hand in question and tried to wiggle her fingers. They stayed immobile.

From one steel work table over came a quiet chuckle. Ashley turned toward Martha, who was decorating a cake. "Are you talking about you-know-who?" she asked quietly, jerking her chin in the direction Katie last bounced. At their nods, she shook her head. "She dropped an entire container of frosting this morning."

"I know. I had to help clean it up." Even though everything they were saying was true, Ashley felt bad about their conversation. "Well, maybe she just needs some time to get the hang of things." With a grimace, she added, "Some more time, I mean."

Before anybody could say anything more, the subject of their dismay practically skipped into the frosting area, her joyful exuberance almost tangible. "Hi, Ash," she said with a grin, her brown hair creating little wings as it tried to escape from under her hat. Even when she reached her destination next to Ashley, she couldn't seem to keep still, shifting her weight from one foot to the other, doing a slight bounce, her eyes filled with the excited delight of somebody much younger. Like, toddler younger. "Can I do something to help?"

The question sent Ashley into a silent, internal panic because she didn't want to give *anything* to Katie to do, lest she spill it, drop it, or ruin it in some form or fashion, which was always a distinct possibility with her.

"Um…" She looked around, noticed that both Stella and Martha looked pointedly away, avoiding eye contact. Damn them. Her eyes landed on some stainless steel bowls and utensils she'd used earlier. "How about taking those dishes to be washed?"

"You got it." Katie bounced to the pile Ashley had indicated and swooped them up in a precarious armload that would not have surprised anybody had it crashed noisily to the floor. Shockingly, it did not, and Katie sprang along and out of sight.

Ashley grunted and shook her head, hating the dread she felt around Katie, hating that such a nice, kind human being made her cringe so badly. Katie had been at the bakery for more than five years, so she definitely did something right or the owners wouldn't have kept her on. She was actually an excellent baker, and a couple of the new cookie styles had been hers. Those were probably the reasons she hadn't been let go.

"Hey," Stella said, pulling her out of her ruminations. "Did you see they've posted a department manager position?"

"In addition to the manager position Becky's leaving?"

"Yup. It's in your e-mail. From what I read, they're going to hire a couple different department heads over the next year or so. You should apply for this one."

"You should apply," Ashley countered. "You've been here way longer than I have. You'd have it locked up."

Stella shook her graying head. "No, thanks. I've been here for a long time, but I like this role. Besides, I'm only a few years from retiring. Why on earth would I want more responsibility?"

Ashley laughed, completely understanding. "Well, I don't know that I want more either." Giving Stella a sheepish grin, she added quietly, "Well. That's not entirely true. I actually would like more. It's the 'getting it' part that makes me nervous. The application and the interviewing and the selling myself stuff. I hate all of it. Stresses me out."

Stella cocked her head, gave Ashley a stern, parent-like look. "Honey, you're young. You need to think about your future. Moving up would be a good thing for you. Are you just going to frost cookies and cakes your entire life?"

Making a noncommittal sound, Ashley raised a shoulder in a half-shrug. "I don't know."

"What's not to know?" Stella asked. "You've been here since you were in high school. They trust you. You're good at your job. Put on your Big Girl Panties and apply."

"I might."

"Yeah, I've met you and that means you're placating me and you will not apply."

Ashley grinned. "But maybe I'll surprise you."

Stella snorted. "That'd be nice, but I'm not holding my bre—"

A loud crash interrupted them. Ashley looked at Stella. "And there it is."

"Honest to God, that girl would drop her own head if it wasn't attached to her shoulders."

With another groan, Ashley put down her tools and headed in the direction the ruckus had come from. Around the corner and in the kitchen, Katie was picking up utensils from the floor. When she saw Ashley approach, she gave a sheepish grin. "At least they were already dirty. They had to be washed anyway."

Her smile was contagious. Ashley couldn't help but smile back as she squatted down and helped grab up the fallen tools. "Here you go." She handed a ladle and a giant spatula over.

"You've been here for a long time," said Katie, apropos of nothing.

Ashley nodded. "You've got some time logged in, too."

"Only five years and three months. Not like you."

"Hey, five years is nothing to sneeze at."

Katie gave a half-shrug. "I guess."

She couldn't help it, Ashley reached out and gave Katie's shoulder a squeeze of encouragement. "Don't sell yourself short. Okay? That doesn't do anybody any good."

There was that infectious smile again. "I won't," Katie said with a nod. "Thanks, Ashley."

"Any time." Ashley headed back to her own workstation, feeling better about her earlier thoughts. Katie was a good kid. Ashley chuckled internally. Kid. Katie was only three years younger than she was. Calling her a kid was silly.

An hour later, Ashley and Stella had finished the cookies and Ashley had a chance to sit at her small desk in a tiny corner of the back area and rest her feet. Looking down at her battered —in more ways than one—sneakers, she absently realized it was probably time for a new pair. She stretched her legs straight out and pointed her toes like a dancer, willing the muscles to relax. Then she turned to her computer to check her e-mail.

Stella was right. There it was, an e-mail from the owners asking for applicants to fill not only Becky's soon-to-be empty position, but two department managers as well, and more to come in the future. The application was attached. Carter's Bakery was large and employed upwards of fifty people, so Ashley was sure there'd be plenty of candidates. Lots of people had been there longer than she had.

Also, she'd been there longer than lots of people.

Chewing on the inside of her cheek, she reread the e-mail. Her cursor was hovering over the little paper clip icon when her cell phone vibrated, moving it slightly on the desktop next to the keyboard. Carly's name showed in the screen.

Ashley breathed in and let the air out slowly. She picked up the phone, her thumb hovering over the green button when an enormous crash startled her so badly she literally popped out of her seat for a second. Hand pressed to her chest, she spun around and met Stella's laughing eyes across the room.

"Well, it *has* been over an hour since she dropped anything," she said with a shrug.

Ashley couldn't help but smile as she stood to go help. "This is true."

CHAPTER /EVEN

MEMORIAL DAY WEEKEND COULD not have presented better weather to the people who attended the annual volunteer thank you picnic Junebug Farms threw every year. They used to wait until later in the summer, but discovered that it was more difficult to gather everybody together the better the weather became. Moving it to Memorial Day weekend did force them to compete with camping trips and long weekends out of town, but over the years, the management team for the shelter had found the end of May to be the best time.

This was the fourth year they'd had it on this date and the third time it had been held at Lisa's aunt's waterfront beach house. Lisa had initially hated the idea and still did. Every year, she and her aunt had the exact same discussion. Every year, Lisa lost.

"What if they break stuff? It'll be a bunch of strangers in your house, Aunt Joyce. And by late evening, many of them will be drunk."

"Are they adults?" Aunt Joyce had asked.

"Yes, for the most part. We do have a couple high school kids."

"Who will not be drinking, I assume?"

"No. Jessica's really good about watching that."

"Then there's nothing to worry about."

Lisa made a sound indicating she was trying to think of another reason why this was a bad idea.

"Lisa. Listen to me." Aunt Joyce's voice took on the slightly stern quality that she didn't use often, only when she felt she wasn't being

heard. *"My beach house is beautiful. I love it. But it does not get nearly the use it should. I am overjoyed by the idea of people having fun there. Don't worry. I'll pop by and make sure everything is running smoothly. Just tell Jessica it's a go. And stop stressing."*

Of course, she couldn't tell Aunt Joyce the real reason this gathering bothered her. Aunt Joyce wouldn't understand that Lisa's worlds were colliding and how much that weirded her out. She didn't like to mix her work life and her private life, and Aunt Joyce was as much a part of her private life—as was this house—as anything. Having her work colleagues poking around the place where Lisa grew up felt...invasive somehow. But she sucked it up and put it on a shelf in her brain and let her aunt do what made her happy.

Now, Lisa stood on the beach, watching the water from Lake Ontario lap gently up over the shore. The sun shone brightly down, bouncing off the water as if it were a sheet of glass, forcing Lisa to pull her sunglasses off her head and over her eyes. The sky was a clear canvas of electric blue and the bright white sail of a boat in the distance made Lisa's view almost as perfect as a painting. Her phone buzzed and she pulled it out. A text from her mother.

Hope the picnic goes great today! 😊

Lisa blew out a breath and tucked the phone back into her pocket.

"This is going to be fantastic." The voice from behind her startled her slightly. She turned to raise her gaze and meet the Ray-Ban-covered eyes of David Peters.

"You think so?" she asked him. He was decked out in crisp khaki pants and a tight black T-shirt that hugged his muscular torso like it was painted on him. The sun glinted off his bald head and his teeth seemed bright white against his dark skin.

"Are you kidding? It's always great. Look at this place." He waved a massive arm in a very Vanna White-like gesture. "It's beautiful. We've got food. Drink. A gorgeous lake. A fire pit for later. The makings for s'mores. What's not to like?" At what must have been a grimace on Lisa's face, David laughed and laid a warm, heavy hand on her shoulder. With a squeeze, he said, "Lisa. Honey. You really need to lighten up. Take a page out of your aunt's playbook. She's already got some wine."

His deep chuckle resonated in the pit of Lisa's stomach even as he was walking away. She blew out a breath. Maybe he was right. If Aunt Joyce wasn't worried—and she rarely was—maybe Lisa shouldn't be either. She headed toward the house, toward the makeshift bar, thinking maybe her aunt had the right idea.

Three hours later, the barbecue was in full swing. Hot dogs and hamburgers sizzled on the grill where Maggie Simon's husband, Bill, was dressed in a Kiss the Cook apron, tongs in hand, flipping away. Various volunteers—some that Lisa knew and some from other areas of the shelter that she didn't—were bunched up in small, departmental cliques, talking, laughing, eating and drinking. The volunteers for the barn animals were together. Three girls that gave time to Paws & Whiskers were chatting with Maggie. Jamie O'Connor was sitting near the fire pit with four of the people who helped her with her behavioral training and agility classes. And on the back deck of the beach house sat Tammy and Ashley, who had driven together, along with six other volunteers.

Lisa stood off to one side of the yard holding a bottle of beer, watching her volunteers laugh and converse with one another. A hand on her arm startled her enough to make her jump, and Aunt Joyce covered a laugh with a sip from her Tervis tumbler of iced white zinfandel.

"Why don't you go sit with your people?" she asked, her eyes slightly glassy from the wine.

"I was thinking about it," Lisa lied. She would rather stand where she was and observe from afar. *I like this view,* she thought as she watched Ashley bust into a fit of laughter at something a volunteer named Will said. Her cheeks were rosy —whether from the day's sun or the alcohol, Lisa wasn't sure, but she liked the color—and she looked adorable, which she tried not to think about. She'd done her share of mingling, of thanking various volunteers in various departments for all their hard work. She took a swig of her beer, then turned to her aunt, trying to ignore the erotic pull Ashley seemed to have on her, even as she stood this far away. "Having fun?"

"I am," Aunt Joyce said, the watery smile apparent in her voice. "You know I love these gatherings." She hooked her hand around Lisa's elbow. "Come on. Introduce me to your volunteers." And with a gentle tug, they were walking toward the deck.

"Hey there," Ashley said, and grinned as her blue eyes settled on Lisa's with a rather bold directness as Lisa pushed her sunglasses back up onto her head. The eye contact caused a surprising—and sensual—tightening low in her body, and Lisa cleared her throat, forced herself to pull her gaze away. Which was not easy.

"Folks, this is my aunt, Joyce Meredith. This is her beach house you're partying in," she said with a half-grin.

Her volunteers didn't disappoint her, jumping up to shake hands or hug Aunt Joyce, sucking her into their circle like a cell absorbing nutrients. Lisa watched, smiling, loving how playful and friendly Aunt Joyce was with the staff. A glance up had her locking eyes with Ashley again, and this time, the gaze held for one, long, delicious beat until Ashley smiled at her in a way that could be described as nothing other than totally sexy before slowly and casually looking away. *Jesus Christ.* Lisa wet her lips and took a sip from her beer, suddenly parched. *What the hell is happening here?*

Ashley looked great today. Sexy. A little hot, even. Okay, a lot hot. Lisa had noticed. Not intentionally, but she couldn't seem to help where her eyes went—and that fact irritated her a little bit each time they pulled her gaze in Ashley's direction. Which was often. White shorts with flapped pockets on the back, a black tank top, and a white hooded jacket with the sleeves pushed up her forearms. Black sandals and a long silver chain with a fish dangling around her neck finished off the outfit, and Lisa tried not to stare at the waves of blonde hair cascading around Ashley's shoulders. It was still somewhat unusual to see her with her hair down rather than in a ponytail and covered with a hat. Lisa liked it down. She liked it down a lot, and she found herself daydreaming about what all that glorious hair would feel like in her hands. *God...*

That thought jarred her hard enough to get her to return to reality and, draining her beer, she turned away from the group and went in search of something or someone less distracting to focus on. Anything. Anything at all.

Unfortunately, she ran directly into the solid chest of Clark Breckenridge.

"Hello, Mr. Breckenridge," she said, amazed by how *not* aggravated she sounded, since what she really wanted to say was, "What the hell are you doing here?" Even in casual clothes, he was ridiculously handsome, his dark hair just wavy enough to make a woman (not Lisa) want to run her hands through it. Broad shoulders stretched the blue golf shirt as tight as possible without making it look too small, and his torso tapered down to a trim waist, chinos cinched with a brown leather belt that probably cost more than Lisa's entire outfit.

"Lisa," he replied with a gallant tip of his head. "I told you. It's Clark." But his eyes were focused over Lisa's shoulder and she knew without looking who he was focusing on. "Nice to see you," he said, and with a gentle brush of his hand to her arm, he sidestepped her and beelined for the deck. And Ashley. Lisa didn't want to look, but couldn't seem to stop herself as she pulled her sunglasses back down to cover her eyes and turned to take a glance.

Was that dread on Ashley's face when she saw him?

It could be, but Lisa wasn't sure. If it was, Ashley had done a masterful job of covering it quickly. If it wasn't…Lisa could have been mistaken. It was possible. They hadn't ever spoken about him. Maybe Ashley was fine around him. Maybe she liked his attention; lots of girls did. Maybe she was happy to see him, despite what Tammy had said about him not being Ashley's type. Though Tammy did tend to be a really good judge of character…

"God, stop it," Lisa muttered in disgust. Not wishing to subject herself to any further analysis about why she was suddenly so concerned with how Ashley chose to occupy her time, she forced her head back around, detoured past the coolers to grab herself another beer, and headed toward the fire pit. Jamie's crew always tended to be a fun bunch. Maybe they could distract her from this…distraction.

"Lisa. Come sit with us," Jamie O'Connor said with a grin as she saw Lisa's approach. Catherine's nephew, Jason, jumped up from the collapsible chair he was occupying and offered it to Lisa as he pushed his glasses up his nose with a finger.

"Thanks, Jason," Lisa said, taking the seat.

"For those of you who haven't met her, this is Lisa Drakemore. She's in charge of adoption and intake at Junebug." Jamie gave her head a toss to shake her dark hair out of her eyes. Murmurs went around the circle, which was made up of six other people besides Jamie and Lisa.

"Intake?" a young woman asked. "You must want to kill people on the daily." She sported a chestnut brown ponytail and startlingly blue eyes.

Lisa cocked her head. "What do you mean?"

The woman shrugged. "Just…some of the animals that are brought in are abused or neglected, right?"

"Oh." Lisa nodded and scratched her chin. "Some are. That's true."

"How do you not go off on those idiots?" the guy sitting next to Jason asked. He looked to be maybe thirty and his head was intentionally bald, judging from the slight wheat-colored stubble prickling his scalp.

"She drinks," Jamie said with a grin, earning laughter around the circle. Lisa lifted her bottle and took a sip.

"It takes practice," she told them honestly. "Some days are easier than others. I just try to remind myself that whatever that animal has been through, it's over and we're going to give it a better home than what it had."

Nods and more murmurs went around the circle. "Well, I don't think I could do what you do," the same woman said. "Here's to you, because somebody's got to do it and most of us aren't strong enough." She lifted her red Solo cup and the rest of the group followed suit.

Lisa felt herself blush. "Thanks," she said, her voice quiet. It was weird, all this praise. It felt…unnecessary. Unwarranted. To Lisa, this was her job. She did her job. She liked to think she did it well, but she rarely stopped to think about how difficult it might be for some people to see and know the things she saw and knew. There were far too many instances in which mankind should be ashamed of itself.

As if reading her mind, Jamie leaned close to her, her dark eyes intense, and whispered, "They're right. Just accept it and smile."

Lisa did as asked.

The balmy afternoon slid into a satisfyingly cool evening while the partygoers were paying little attention, and Lisa was surprised to look out at the lake and see lights twinkling along the shore. The temperature was perfect for a fire, and more people had gathered around it as time had passed. Lisa had been sitting around the fire with Jamie and her crew, listening to them, laughing with them, for longer than she'd realized and her perfectly pleasant buzz was almost worn off—though not quite.

Excusing herself, she stood to make a trek to the ladies' room. Plus, she wanted to see if Aunt Joyce was still around… or, more importantly, not passed out somewhere. The woman liked her wine a little too much, and as she'd said to Lisa the one time she ventured to bring up the subject, "I am an old woman and if I want to drink too much wine, I will drink too much wine, damn it. It's nobody's goddamn business." Lisa had turned a deep shade of crimson, mortified that her aunt had scolded her like a child—something she'd never done when Lisa actually *was* a child. Learning her lesson, she hadn't mentioned it since. Instead, she simply did her best to keep an eye on her aunt and make sure she was safe.

Surprisingly few people were inside the beach house, and Lisa found the bathroom blissfully empty. She locked herself in, sat down, dropped her head into her hands, and blew out a large breath. These gatherings took their toll on her. She enjoyed them, yes, and she'd had a great time chatting and joking with Jamie's crew around the fire. But she also found group situations generally exhausting, and she wanted nothing more than to get back home to her animals, her puzzle, and some quiet. She felt drained.

After folding the hand towels neatly (they'd been in a damp heap on the vanity) and hanging them up, Lisa exited the bathroom and was about to head downstairs when a shadow from the hall caught her eye. The house was exceptionally large and modern compared to most on the beach and the upstairs was in a bit of a horseshoe pattern, the view from the "bend" open to the living room below. On either side, the hall wrapped around a corner. Lisa followed the shadow, expecting to find some person she didn't know snooping around her aunt's place. This was exactly why Lisa didn't like the idea of letting strangers into the home of her relative.

Puffing up and ready to do battle, she rounded the corner and stopped short.

Ashley jumped, obviously startled by Lisa's sudden appearance. She pressed a hand to her chest and her expression of shock softened into something…different. "Lisa. Hi."

"Hey," Lisa said, surprise stealing any other words she may have been ready to say. She apparently had no control over her own eyes as they raked over Ashley's body, from her head down to her toes and back up again. Slowly. Ashley watched it happen, and Lisa saw her throat move with a hard swallow, saw her eyes darken.

"I'm sorry. I don't mean to snoop." Ashley seemed to have a hard time pulling her gaze from Lisa's, but she did it and gestured to the wall of framed photographs in front of her. "I was just…looking at the pictures." She cleared her throat and glanced down at her feet. Lowering her voice to just above a whisper, she added, "And hiding."

"Hiding?"

Ashley nodded with a grimace.

"From?"

"Mr. Breckenridge?"

Lisa nodded, not trusting herself to speak over the onslaught of unexpected emotions that simple name conjured up inside her.

"Um…" Ashley turned toward the wall and pointed. "Is this you?" She was obviously uncomfortable and wanted to change the subject. Lisa let her—momentarily. She stepped forward to look at the picture. It was front and center in a wall collage of eight framed photographs, and showed Aunt Joyce at maybe forty holding a toddler on her lap. Neither faced the camera. Rather, they sat face-to-face and both were in the obvious throes of full-on laughter, their smiles huge, their eyes crinkled in similar fashion. This shot never failed to bring a smile to Lisa's face.

"Yeah, that's me. I think I was two or three?" she said uncertainly.

"And that's your aunt? The one who owns this house?"

Lisa nodded. "My Aunt Joyce. Yes."

"Look at how adorable you were." Ashley smiled, her eyes seeming to take in every detail of the photo. "That big smile.

And look at those chubby little thighs," she added, pursing her lips and talking through her teeth.

Lisa laughed. "Yeah, some things never change."

Ashley paired her scoff perfectly with a roll of her big blue eyes. "Please. Um, no."

Their gazes held for a moment longer than was comfortable and Lisa broke away first, needing to put space between them, even the miniscule bit she settled for as she leaned her back against the wall and folded her arms across her chest. "Can I ask you something?"

"Sure." Ashley let her eyes roam over the other pictures, but she seemed to find them less interesting than the one of Lisa.

"How come you're avoiding Clark Breckenridge? Has he been given you problems?"

"Oh." Ashley straightened a bit, spared a glance at Lisa standing a mere six inches away, then shifted her eyes back to the photos. Her cheeks flushed a sexy pink. "No. No, of course not. I mean, don't get me wrong. He does seem to…find me wherever I go." She gave an adorable little snort, but looked back at Lisa with a grimace. "I know he gives the shelter lots of money, so I don't want to rock any boats or anything. You know? It's fine." She rubbed at her eye and it occurred to Lisa then that Ashley might be just a little bit tipsy. "He's super nice to me and says really nice things. He's asked me out twice now. It's just that he's…" Her voice trailed off and she swallowed audibly.

"Not your type?" Lisa supplied, remembering what Tammy had said.

A relieved bark of a laugh popped out of Ashley's mouth and she quickly covered it with her hand. "Wow, that was loud." She smiled and nodded. "But, yes. Exactly." She shook her head, eyebrows rising toward her hairline as she said, "*So* not my type. Not even close."

Lisa studied her, watched her shift her weight from foot to foot in what seemed to be nervousness, even as she pretended not to be, watched her eyes skim over the photographs, her small hand lift to a frame, trace a fingertip over an unknown face forever frozen in black and white. She had a softness about her, a general relaxed demeanor and that, combined with the embarrassment over her laughter, told Lisa that Ashley had definitely had a bit to drink. Ashley was usually pretty relaxed, but now? She was more so; she seemed more at ease than her normal self, her cheeks still flushed a pretty pink, a small grin pulling up one corner of her full mouth. Lisa liked the whole package and continued to watch her as she perused the photos. It was when she caught her bottom lip between her teeth that Lisa felt that long-dormant flutter in her stomach and she knew she was going to ask the question only a split second before it came out of her mouth, barely a whisper. "What is your type, Ashley?"

Ashley stopped what she was doing, her hand in midair, as if they were playing that old outdoor game of Statues, she'd been spun and then ordered to *freeze!*

A beat passed. Two. A quiet buzzing sounded and it took a moment for Lisa to realize it was Ashley's phone, which was tucked in her back pocket. Ashley ignored it, seemed to be taking stock, but Lisa wasn't sure of what. She watched as something washed over Ashley's beautiful face, her porcelain skin, saw her throat shift as she swallowed. When she finally moved her hand again, it wasn't to let it drop back down to her side. Instead, she pulled it back from the wall, took one step sideways, putting herself directly in front of Lisa, and used that hand, those fingertips, to stroke Lisa's cheek with a touch so featherlight, it caused goose bumps to erupt along Lisa's bare arms. She inched closer until they were breathing the exact same air, their lips only millimeters apart. Lisa was sure Ashley could hear the pounding of her heart, but she couldn't formulate a sentence of any kind. She could only stare at Ashley's mouth, so close to her own. Neither of them said a thing as Ashley pushed up slightly on her toes and pressed her lips softly to Lisa's.

Time seemed to stop and the air stilled.

How is it possible for one woman's lips to be this soft?

Lisa couldn't get the thought out of her head as Ashley pulled back a little bit and looked into Lisa's eyes. Lisa wondered if hers had gone as dark as Ashley's, if her own desire was as obvious. She didn't wait for an answer; she grabbed Ashley's face in her hands and kissed her again. Less gentle this time. Less tentative.

And Ashley kissed her back.

Hard.

And Lisa never wanted to stop. It was a thought that zipped absently through her mind, and it should have shocked her silly, but it didn't. She grabbed Ashley's shirt and held on for dear life, pulling her closer, pushing into her, letting Ashley push back. Senses blurred for Lisa until there was nothing but red-hot eroticism. *Good God, this woman could kiss...*

They made out like teenagers on prom night, Lisa trapped between the wall and Ashley's warm, soft body, tongues battling, breathing ragged, the tastes of beer and each other mingling into a sensual potion Lisa couldn't get enough of. Only when hands started to wander was she yanked cruelly back to her senses and remembered where exactly they were, remembered they were surrounded by work colleagues, any of whom could stumble upon them at any moment, which would make for a very large pile of awkward. It wasn't easy, but she caught Ashley's wrist as her hand closed over Lisa's breast and she wrenched her mouth from Ashley's. They stood for a moment, forehead to forehead, each woman trying to catch her breath. Before Lisa could say anything, Ashley took a small step back from her and planted her palm against Lisa's sternum. While her fingertips gently stroked Lisa's visible collarbone, Ashley looked up at her, those blue eyes light and sparkling.

One corner of Ashley's mouth quirked up in a half-grin as she whispered, "Does that answer your question?" With a quick stroke of her thumb across Lisa's lips, she grinned and then was gone.

Lisa stood against the wall for long moments, breathing like she'd just sprinted up the stairs, flushed as if she'd been sitting in a sauna, and more turned on than she'd been in…as long as she could remember. Slowly, she lifted her hand and touched her fingers to her own lips, still sizzling from Ashley's. Her legs felt weak and rubbery and she didn't trust herself to stay upright on them, even as she rolled her eyes at how ridiculous that was. Still, she didn't move until the sound of footsteps approaching had her both excited about and dreading the possibility of Ashley returning to her.

"There you are," Aunt Joyce said, her words only slightly slurred despite the amount of wine currently coursing through her system. Lisa was continually amazed by the fact that a woman as small and birdlike as her Aunt Joyce could put away so much alcohol and not simply fall over incapacitated. And besides that, she was perfectly coherent as she squinted her eyes at Lisa like she was reading something right off her face.

"What's going on? Why do you look like you just did something bad, but you really, really want to do it again?"

Lisa's eyes flew open wide.

~⊷⊶~

"Oh, my God, you have to get me out of here." Ashley grabbed Tammy by the elbow, her eyes darting around in a panic.

"All right, all right," Tammy said and excused herself from the conversation she was having with another volunteer. "I said we'd go whenever you were ready and…" She ran her eyes over Ashley's form. "You're obviously ready. Why are your cheeks so red?"

"Never mind that," Ashley said as she grabbed her bag from the coat closet by the door and spun in a circle to make sure she had everything she'd come with. "I should not be allowed to drink. Like, ever. I do stupid things when I drink."

Tammy gave her best look of befuddlement and parked her hands on her hips.

"I'll tell you in the car," Ashley said, just this side of exasperation. The image of Carly's face suddenly ripped through her mind.

Oh, God. Carly…

It was too much to deal with right now, and she shook her head, shoved the thought away. "Please, Tammy. You have to get me out of here."

Holding up her hands in surrender, Tammy said simply, "Okay. Let's go." She waited until they were in the car and had driven nearly a mile in total silence before finally saying, "All right. What the hell happened? What is going on with you? You look like you just robbed a bank and I'm your getaway driver."

Ashley inhaled a deep breath and blew it out very slowly. She closed her eyes, covered her face with her hands, and said quietly, "I kissed her."

Tammy did a double take. "You what? Who? You kissed who?"

Ashley swallowed audibly. "Lisa." When she spared a glance at Tammy, it was as if her entire face had drooped south. Her jaw fell open. Her eyes widened. She laid a hand on one cheek, inadvertently pulling it downward.

"Holy shit."

"I know."

A beat passed. "Holy shit," Tammy said again.

"*I know.*"

"How…what…how…?"

"Sam Adams, that's how. That bastard is a terrible influence." Ashley shook her head as she gazed out the passenger side window. "I get way too brave when I drink. I have few inhibitions when beer is involved."

"But…did you just walk up and kiss her? I mean, give me some background here. Did you plan it? Paint me a picture."

"No, I didn't plan it. I don't plan things like that." Ashley shook her head at such an idiotic idea. "I was hiding out from Clark Breckenridge. God, I wish he'd back off. I told him I had to use the ladies' room, and I did. So I went upstairs and took care of things. But when I was done, I just couldn't stand the thought of dealing with him again and I had a feeling he was hovering near the bottom of the stairs just waiting for me. So… I stayed upstairs. I was wandering a little bit, just looking at the pictures on the walls, minding my own damn business. And Lisa found me."

"Okay. Then what?"

"I asked her about one of the pictures, one of her as a toddler with her aunt. She got this sort of dreamy, soft look on her face and...God, Tammy. She was beautiful. I've seen glimpses of it before, when she's not aware of it. She can be so goddamn gorgeous."

Tammy nodded. "She can. She is. I've seen it, too. The woman is stunning."

"Right? I mean, it's not the first time I've noticed. It's hard not to. But...I know where the lines are. Usually." She groaned in frustration. "It was an innocent conversation, I swear. She asked what I was doing and I told her I was avoiding Clark because he's not my type. And then we talked about the photograph on the wall and then she asked me what my type was."

Tammy's eyebrows flew up into her hairline. "She did not!"

"Swear to God. And then..." Ashley dropped her face into her hands. "And then I got all brave and stupid and I kissed her, and when we were done I asked her if that answered her question. Oh, God, I can never show my face at the shelter again, can I? I have completely lost my mind. Completely."

"Wow," Tammy said, a grin on her face. "You will absolutely show your face at the shelter. And no, I don't think you've lost your mind at all. I think that was damn smooth of you." She turned to look at Ashley's stricken expression. "Did she kiss you back?"

Ashley's vision went a little hazy as she brought her fingers to her lips, sure she could still taste Lisa on them. With a subtle nod, she said softly, "Oh, yeah."

Tammy's grin widened. "Fantastic. I think you need to stop worrying and let her make the next move, because you way outdid yourself. That was, like, romantic comedy good. Nicely done, my friend. Nicely done." A moment passed as they drove in silence before Tammy said, "Although...can I ask you something?"

Ashley sighed. "Sure."

"What about Carly?"

Ashley flinched at the realization that she hadn't once thought about Carly the entire time she was alone with Lisa. What did that say about her? She turned to look out the window as her eyes welled. *I am a horrible person.*

"You're going to have to do something there." Tammy's voice was gentle. "You know that, right?"

Ashley nodded, her focus still on the passing trees.

Tammy reached over with one hand and squeezed Ashley's knee. "Hey, come on, kiddo. It's gonna be okay. I promise."

Ashley just shook her head, still in disbelief, confused about what had happened...more confused about why. Remembering suddenly that her phone had buzzed, she pulled it out, knowing full well who it was. A missed call. And six texts.

All from Carly.

Ashley dropped her head down, closed her eyes, and groaned.

CHAPTER EIGHT

"DAD?"

Lisa entered the kitchen of her father's house and set down the two heavy grocery bags with a relieved grunt. A cereal bowl, coffee mug, and lone spoon sat neatly in the dish drainer. The counter was shiny and clean.

"Dad?" she called again as she opened the refrigerator and deposited the milk, eggs, and lunchmeat she'd purchased.

"In here, honey." Her father's voice came from the direction of the living room. Lisa finished putting away the perishables, then followed the sound. Will Drakemore sat in his usual recliner, pretty much the only piece of furniture he ever occupied. On the TV tray next to him sat the remote for the television, the cordless phone, an opened bottle of Coors Light, and a half-eaten bowl of potato chips. The television showed a baseball game, as usual for this time of year. In the fall, it would be football. In the winter, hockey. Will was nothing if not a sports enthusiast, at least from the comfort of his La-Z-Boy.

He turned kind brown eyes in Lisa's direction and the corners crinkled when he grinned at her. "Hi there, beautiful girl. How's tricks?"

Lisa smiled back and bent to kiss him on the cheek. "'How's tricks?' What are you, 85?"

"Some days, it feels like I'm not that far away from it."

Lisa scoffed at the remark. In reality, her father was only fifty-nine. Admittedly, though, he was not aging well, and Lisa knew it had almost everything to do with his horrifically unhealthy diet and utter lack of anything even remotely resembling exercise. He'd been a handsome man once, in pretty good shape. But in the years since the divorce, he'd put on weight and seemed to lose an alarming amount of hair, so that now he resembled Ned Beatty a bit, complete with a doughnut of snowy hair around the perimeter of his head and a protruding belly that rivaled Santa Claus's. He looked a good ten years older than he was.

Another thing to blame on her mother.

He caught Lisa eyeing his bowl of chips. "Don't start. I'm just having a few." He kept his voice light. He didn't like conflict and Lisa knew it. Part of the reason for the divorce…he avoided instead of dealing with something uncomfortable.

"I'm not starting anything," she said, holding her hands up in supplication. "I have no problem with you eating chips if you've had something decent first."

Her father turned back to the game. "I had eggs for breakfast."

She wanted to ask if that meant scrambled with some vegetables or fried in a boatload of butter (his preferred way), but she just wasn't in the mood to be that person today. "Good. I will accept eggs." She took a seat on the couch. "I bought you some more."

Will looked at her. "Lisa. I appreciate it a lot, but you don't have to buy me groceries. I'm a big boy." His smile took out any sting his words may have carried.

"I know. I just like to make sure you've got food. I got you some salad stuff and some bananas, too. And that coffee creamer you like."

He shook his head good-naturedly. "You take good care of your dad."

"It's my job," she replied with a bit too much enthusiasm. He gave her a look, seemed about to say something, but apparently changed his mind. "What's new?" Lisa asked him.

He waited for the pitch before answering, which used to drive Lisa crazy until she realized there was nothing in the world she could do to make things any different. She would never understand the fascination with watching baseball on television. Being in the ballpark and seeing a game was totally different and something she enjoyed, but watching baseball on television was like how she imagined it would be to watch her own hair grow: boring and endless.

The pitch was a strike and the batter called out. "Damn it," Will muttered under his breath. Then he turned to his daughter. "Not much is new. Work's the same. The house is the same." He shrugged. "Oh. Your brother got a promotion."

"Eric? Yeah, I heard." *Not from him*, she almost said, but didn't want to get started down that road, as it would only depress her to know how low she ranked on her brother's list of important people. "He's doing so well there. I'm amazed."

"Me, too. How are the animals?"

It was always the way he asked about her job and she smiled in response. "The animals are good. There are too many of them, but I doubt that will ever change."

"It won't change until humans stop being assholes."

Her father had lots of quirks, but he tended to tell it like it was.

They sat for a while, alternating between watching the game and partaking in small talk. The sound of the back door caught their attention and a voice boomed through the house.

"Where are you, old man?"

Lisa recognized Eric's voice and watched with mixed emotions as her father's face lit up.

"I'm in the living room, boy," he responded and soon Eric filled the doorway.

Even on a Saturday, he was dressed so neatly it was almost comical. Khaki pants with a sharp crease down each leg, dark brown loafers, navy blue polo shirt with the Ralph Lauren logo on the breast pocket area. His light hair was trimmed precisely and neatly combed. He was clean-shaven and smelled of a light musk—the same aftershave he'd used since college. His bright brown eyes landed on Lisa and he grinned, dimples just like her dad's becoming visible.

"Hey, Lise. How's it going?"

"Fine," she replied as she got up to give him a hug. When she pulled back, she looked him in the eye and said, "Heard you got a promotion."

He caught the meaning behind her words immediately—*but I didn't hear it from you*—and scrambled to do damage control. "I did. Listen, I meant to give you a call and then I got waylaid in the office and it slipped my mind. I'm really sorry."

He did a good job of sounding sincere, so Lisa let him off the hook even though she didn't quite believe him, and even though it stung to be so insignificant to him as to "slip his mind." She patted his shoulder and said simply, "Good for you. I'm proud of you."

He had the good sense to flush a light pink, so Lisa was pretty sure her subtle guilt trip had struck home. She had a flash of satisfaction…and then she felt bad. Shaking it off, she sat back down and proceeded to listen for the next twenty or thirty minutes as her father and brother chatted on and on.

"So, you gonna do financial planning for corporations now?" Will asked.

Eric nodded, pride obvious on his face. "Yup. That's a big chunk of what this promotion means."

"Like, retirement and stuff?"

"Annuities, 401(k)s, IRAs. Things like that."

They talked a bit more and Lisa had the sudden need to be part of the conversation. "Um…we don't have very many full-time employees, but I could talk to Jessica, see if we could use your services."

Eric's smile was wide. "You'd do that?"

"Of course. No promises, though."

"I'd like that. Thanks, Lise."

Lisa nodded as Eric and her father picked back up as if they hadn't missed a beat. A smile tugged at Lisa's lips and she suddenly found herself enjoying their banter. She listened for a while longer, tossing in a comment or question here and there, but finally stood to go.

"Already?" her father asked, surprised. She had to give him credit. His reaction seemed genuine.

"Afraid so. I've got a few things I've got to take care of today."

"Well, okay." Will stood up and opened his arms to his daughter. "I'm glad you stopped by, honey. It's always good to see you."

She stepped into his embrace and allowed herself that short burst of feeling safe, like she had in her dad's arms when she was a little girl.

"Thanks for the groceries."

"You're welcome," she said.

Eric took his turn and wrapped her up in a hug as well, something that surprised her. She forced herself to relax and let her little brother hold her. It was weird. And nice. And weird. But nice.

On her way home, Lisa stopped by the garden store. Often, when feeling stressed or confused or too much in her head (an all-too-common scenario for somebody who spent the majority of her time with animals), she liked to combat it with some kind of mindless busywork. So she bought pots, dirt, and some vegetable plants and decided she'd work on the patio garden she'd promised herself last summer. The sun was shining, the air was warm—it was the perfect day for gardening. She was elbow deep in potting soil and tomato plants when her cell rang. A quick glance at the screen had her smiling, and she peeled off her gardening gloves quickly so she could answer.

"Hey, stranger," she said by way of greeting.

"Back atcha, gorgeous," Grace McKinney replied. "Long time, no talk."

Lisa plopped down in a lawn chair. "How's life on the other side of town?"

"Not gonna lie, it's pretty great."

Grace and Lisa had been friends since high school, and Grace was one of only a small handful of classmates Lisa still kept in touch with. She was also one of the few people on earth who knew Lisa better than she knew herself. She'd been around during Lisa's parents' divorce, through Lisa's various attempts at therapy, and she was the only other person besides Aunt Joyce who could tell it exactly like it was. And Lisa would actually listen. Being very aware of all these things didn't always help, because Lisa also knew she couldn't really hide anything from Grace; the woman would see right through her.

"I'm glad to hear it. And Ella? Work? The house? Everything okay?" She listened to Grace update her on things, a smile on her face. As Grace spoke, Lisa went inside the house and poured herself a Diet Coke.

"And what's new with you, my friend? It's been too long since we talked. Catch me up."

Lisa sank into the couch, dangled her feet over the upholstered arm, and spent several minutes artfully sharing the parts of her life that didn't include kissing a certain cupcake-scented volunteer in the upstairs hallway of Aunt Joyce's house. She concluded the heavily edited version of her life by detailing her visit with Dad earlier in the day.

"How is the old man?" Grace asked. "I haven't seen him in years."

"Oh, you know. Same shit, different day. At least his house is neat; he hasn't fallen into bachelor messiness. But he's got to be lonely. All he does is watch sports."

"Yeah, but he likes sports. Has he dated at all? I mean, it's been what? Ten? Twelve years since the divorce?"

Lisa sighed and shook her head, even though Grace couldn't see her. "I don't know. I do think he's gone on a date or two, but nothing serious. Honestly? I think he still is, and always will be, hung up on my mom."

"That's so sad," Grace said, her voice sympathetic.

"Isn't it? He's still got pictures around the house of all of us. As a family. I got rid of most of mine."

"You did?"

Lisa furrowed her brow at the surprise in Grace's tone. "Of course I did. Why would I want to be reminded of a family that no longer exists?"

"Um…because that's where you came from? I mean, just because your parents are no longer together doesn't mean they didn't love each other once. And love made you and your brothers. Right?"

She made it sound so simple and Lisa squinted at the ceiling as she absorbed the words. "I suppose."

"Okay," Grace said with a gentle chuckle. "I get it. Shutting up now. Tell me about Junebug Farms instead. What's new there? Anything?"

"Again, same shit, different day."

"Well, how about with you, then? Any dates recently? It's been a long time since you made out with somebody, Lise. Or at least since I heard details of you doing so. Give me some dirt."

Ashley's face flashed into Lisa's mind, without warning. Not for the first time, and not just her face. Her eyes. Her hands. Her mouth. *That mouth.* Lisa relived—again—Ashley's ambush kiss in the beach house, how easily Ashley had won her over, how quickly she'd taken Lisa's control away, how amazing a kiss it was.

And how she'd avoided Ashley like a rabies-infected raccoon ever since.

She should tell Grace.

Grace would have advice.

Guidance.

No. She couldn't tell Grace. She couldn't tell anybody. Well, she'd told Aunt Joyce. She hadn't had a choice; the woman was relentless. But she couldn't tell anybody else. She couldn't. It shouldn't have happened and it wouldn't happen again. "No dirt, I'm afraid. Unless you count the dirt on my back patio in which I'm planting tomatoes, peppers, and basil."

"Lame," Grace said. "You disappoint me. How am I supposed to live vicariously if you don't go off and do something wild and crazy once in a while? I'm settled down now. I can't do wild and crazy anymore."

Lisa snorted a laugh. "Yeah, like you ever did wild and crazy when you were single. You're one of the most level-headed people I know."

"Shh! Don't let that get around. Ella has no idea."

Lisa laughed louder. "Ella knows *everything* about you."

Grace offered up an enormous sigh. "She does. Damn it."

They talked for a few minutes longer before signing off. Even then, Lisa stayed on the couch, cell phone in hand, as her thoughts drifted back to the day at Aunt Joyce's beach house. It had been nearly two weeks, but her mind couldn't seem to stop hitting the replay button on that kiss. Over and over again she found herself staring off into space, lost in that moment. The memories were still fresh. Still hot. Still caused Lisa to flush with the pleasant heat of arousal, caused her heart rate to pick up speed, caused her to forget whatever it was she happened to be doing at the time.

Without thinking, she pushed the buttons on the phone. It rang once.

"You missed me already?" Grace's amusement carried across the line.

"I kissed somebody," Lisa blurted.

Silence.

"Excuse me?"

"At the volunteer picnic. Over Memorial Day. At my aunt's beach house." She swallowed past a tight throat. "I kissed somebody."

"Okay, okay. Back the truck up, skippy. I have three very important questions. One, whom did you kiss?" She emphasized the word "whom," as an English teacher would. "Second, how and why did this kiss come about? I want all the details. Spare nothing. And third, was it awesome?"

Lisa took a deep breath, knowing she couldn't back out on the story now, and feeling simultaneously regretful about and relieved by that fact. She started from the very beginning, from the first day she met Ashley some time in January, through the fundraiser. She included Ashley's crying jag in the break room and Lisa's offer of comfort—*"Looking back now, that might have sent a few signals," she told Grace, who replied with a smarmy, "You think?"*—She told Grace about Clark Breckenridge's creepy near-stalking of Ashley, and the unpleasant weirdness Lisa still suffered whenever he got too close to her. She ended with the volunteer picnic and the ambush kiss, leaving out no detail.

"Wow," Grace said after a beat of silence. Another beat passed and she repeated, "Wow."

"I know," Lisa said, inexplicably exhausted after telling the story. "Also, I think she might have been a little tipsy."

"Understandable. Maybe she needed a little liquid courage to do something she'd been thinking about doing for a while."

Lisa shook off the suggestion. "Oh, I don't know about that."

"And where do things stand now? Are you guys dating?"

"Things are nowhere." Lisa braced for the scolding. It came immediately.

"What? What do you mean they're nowhere? Did you ask her out? I mean, you've had your tongue in her mouth. Call me crazy, but I think buying her dinner is the next logical step."

"I don't know if it's a good idea."

"Why not?"

"Because we work together?" Lisa made a face at the questioning tone of her own voice.

"No, you don't. She's a volunteer. Next excuse?"

Lisa sighed.

"Lisa. What's the problem?"

Lisa let a beat pass. Two. The smallness of her voice when she spoke embarrassed her, but she spoke anyway. "I'm nervous. It's been a long time for me, Gracie. And you know me; I'm not big on relationships. I've seen how they crash and burn. Also, I suck at them."

Grace did not make fun of her—one of the reasons Lisa adored their friendship so much. Grace knew when *not* to make a joke. "You do not suck at relationships. You're just… overly cautious to the point of…ridiculousness. You've got to put yourself out there, you know? Hell, if I can do it, you can do it." They chuckled together. "Look where it got me."

"I don't want to take care of anybody else." A succession of images flew through her brain: her father, her brothers, her animals, her job. "I've done enough of that in my lifetime already."

"This is true. But who says you'll have to take care of her?"

Lisa said nothing. She couldn't imagine.

"You're projecting and you know it."

She sighed. "You're right. I do know it. It just feels so… risky."

"It is. I completely get that. Believe me, I do. But…listen, just because your parents' marriage didn't work doesn't mean you shouldn't try to be with somebody."

Lisa scoffed, mentally patted herself on the back for such a good performance. "I know that, silly."

"Whatever," Grace said. "I know you and I know that's what you're thinking." Grace paused a moment, then said, "You can't just sit by and be passive in your own life, Lise. You have to...*take part*. You have to *make* things happen, not wait for them to happen *to* you."

Lisa said nothing. Grace was right, but that didn't make Lisa any more ready.

A sigh of defeat carried across the line. Finally, Grace said, "Okay, I really have to go." She lowered her tone and added, "Seriously, Lisa, you deserve to be happy. I'm not sure why you seem to think otherwise."

"An analysis for another time, my friend," Lisa said, before they exchanged goodbyes.

With a huge groan, Lisa hauled herself off the couch and back out onto the patio to finish her planting, taking Keeler with her this time. She clipped his chain on him and he plopped down on the patio with a relieved groan.

"Me, too, buddy. Me, too."

It was blissfully quiet—her neighbors apparently out for the day—and she tried to focus on her task...the feel of the plant's delicate root system between her fingers, the earthy, woodsy smell of the potting soil...but Grace's words kept coming back to echo through her head:

Just because your parents' marriage didn't work doesn't mean you shouldn't try...

This wasn't news to Lisa, obviously, this uneven line she mentally drew that went from her parents' divorce to the likelihood of her own. She'd been to therapy...

Well, okay.

She'd been "to therapy" three times. When the probing questions grazed nerves and struck sensitive areas, she'd decided she was cured and stopped going. She shook her head as she dug a hole in the middle of the potted dirt for the tomato plant. Admittedly, quitting therapy so easily probably hadn't been the smartest move of her life. But did it really matter? She was just fine.

"I am *just fine*," she said aloud, as if trying to reassure herself. When she heard her own voice, she closed her eyes and shook her head slowly back and forth.

But what if...?

It was a little voice inside her, the one she'd spent years tamping down and wrestling into submission. It was back and it was scratching at her brain now.

What if what? she thought, with no small amount of anger and stabbed her trowel into the pot of dirt. *What if* what?

Suddenly, she stopped what she was doing and glanced up. Peering around, she searched for the source of...that smell.

That scent.

That oh-so-familiar aroma...

Keeler raised his head and studied her, clearly puzzled by her actions.

She held his gaze and said simply, "Cupcakes."

Keeler cocked his furry head to the side, as if trying to understand.

"Yes," she said with conviction, even as Keeler's head swiveled inquisitively to the other side. "I feel like making cupcakes."

CHAPTER NINE

FOR NEARLY TWO WEEKS, Ashley had thrown herself into every aspect of her life except Junebug Farms. Oh, she didn't stop going completely; she was a volunteer, after all, and she'd made a commitment she intended to honor. Plus she couldn't bear to stay away from the dogs for that long. But avoiding Lisa was a matter of prime importance, and she'd done a commendable job. Exhausting, but commendable. It involved crucial timing and lots of darting in and out of doorways or around corners like a spy. But it had worked. Avoidance. As long as she avoided Lisa, she didn't have to deal with that kiss. Didn't have to talk about it, didn't have to explain it, didn't have to deal with it.

"If I never bring it up, and I avoid Lisa so she can't bring it up, then it never happened." She stared at herself in her rearview mirror as she sat in the parking lot of Junebug Farms and wondered when exactly she'd become such a prime example of insanity. With a groan of frustration, she shoved her way out of the car and headed in, scanning the lot for Lisa's car as she walked. *Relax,* she told herself, forcing her attention to the world around her.

The weather had been beautiful all week, seasonable for mid-June, and Ashley took in a deep breath of outdoor air. That it happened to contain remnants of hay and manure from the horse barn and the field across the street didn't bother her at all. She loved the country. In fact, one day down the line, she hoped to have a house with some acreage, some space to breathe and walk and enjoy nature. She'd always lived in the city, but she was a country girl at heart.

Inside was quiet, but that was typical for a Friday in the late afternoon. Ashley waved furtively to Bill Tracey, who absently waved back as he hurried off to fix some mysterious issue, tool belt slung low on his hips and a furrowed-brow expression on his face. She rasped a cautious greeting to Maggie, who would close the gift shop at four, as Friday in the summer was her early night. Hoping for an easy, incognito evening of walking the dogs and not having to deal with a lot of details, Ashley pushed through the doors of the dog wing.

And collided with Lisa Drakemore.

She knew who it was before she even saw her face, before she even reached out to maintain her own balance and catch Lisa to keep her from falling. She knew because she could smell her...that intoxicating perfume or lotion or soap. Whatever it was that Lisa used each day, Ashley could smell her, knew if she was nearby, knew if she'd been in the room first. It was disconcerting. And wildly erotic.

"Sorry," Ashley said at the same time Lisa said something similar. She didn't know what it was because every bit of sound seemed to stop—or she'd gone spontaneously deaf—and all she could focus on was Lisa's mouth.

Lisa extricated herself from Ashley's grip, avoided eye contact, and was through the double doors and out into the main part of the building before Ashley could think. Instead, she stood there, a cacophony of barking permeating the air, and wondered what exactly had just happened. It hit her very quickly after that thought: was Lisa avoiding her as well?

It made perfect sense, didn't it? Ashley found her clipboard and scanned the list, picked up a leash, all of it second nature by now. *What did you think would happen? You kissed her in her aunt's house in the middle of a work function. Of course, she's avoiding you. Duh.*

She should do something. Shouldn't she? It was true they had successfully avoided each other for nearly two weeks, but… was that practical? Could they keep it up? Should they? Ashley supposed she could keep track of Lisa's work schedule and only sign herself up for times when Lisa wasn't around, but that could prove to be tricky. Plus, Ashley liked coming in right after she left the bakery, which was generally early afternoon. It worked for her. But it also meant that it was still normal work hours for most people, including Lisa.

So. She was going to have to apologize.

With a heavy sigh, she headed down the aisle, weighing in her mind exactly how she'd word things. Two other volunteers were working the dog wing and Ashley nodded and smiled at both as she opened cage twenty-three and clipped the leash on an enormous black Lab who was so happy to see her, he almost knocked her over.

"Okay, buddy. Okay. Relax." Across the aisle was a beagle that had been barking nonstop since she arrived. He continued with his baying howl until Ashley turned to look at him. "I'll take you next, I promise."

Junebug Farms had several paths that were used for walking the animals. One led to the barn. One circled around it, wove through the woods for a short stint, then wound back to the main building. One went in the opposite direction of the barn, along the parking lot, past the goat pen and toward the woods on the other side. Ashley liked the path that circled the barn the best because it was a little longer and she got to see the horses and burros as she went by. The Lab was a bit overenthusiastic, but she wound the leash snugly around her hand and held tight and after a few minutes, he eased up, seemed to understand that Ashley was in charge.

Footsteps on gravel crunched behind her and she turned to meet the glass-framed eyes of Jason Reed. "Hey, Ashley. I thought that was you," he said as he jogged the last few feet to catch up to her. He wore ripped jeans, work boots, and a little bit too much cologne. In his arms was a bundle of what looked to be plastic poles.

"What are you up to?" she asked him, gesturing to his load with her eyes.

"Oh. Agility. I'm helping Jamie set up the course."

"And those are for?"

"These are weave poles. They get lined up and the dogs have to weave through them, one then the other." He moved his hand sideways, back and forth, like he was indicating the path of a very curvy road.

"I've seen that on TV," Ashley said with a nod as she stopped to let the Lab sniff a tree. "Very cool."

"Yeah, we have a good-sized class tonight." Jason used a finger to push his glasses up the bridge of his nose.

Ashley squinted at him. "You out of school already?" She glanced at her watch. "It's barely three."

"I just have finals left," he said. "I had calculus this morning."

"Ugh. Just the word gives me heart palpitations."

Jason grinned at her, his eyes twinkling. "Math isn't your thing?"

"Numbers hate me," Ashley said. "The last math class I took was trigonometry, and I'm lucky I passed. I cried in the classroom on the daily."

"I love math."

"I'm not surprised." Ashley smiled at him as they reached the barn. "How'd you do on your test?"

"I aced it."

Ashley barked a laugh at his confidence, then said, "Good for you." He grinned back at her.

"Well," he said as they passed the barn door. "This is my stop." He gave the Lab a pet on the head and waved at Ashley. "See ya."

Ashley watched him go, thinking not for the first time that he was a good kid. Awkward, but a good kid.

They circled around the barn and were headed back toward the main building when Ashley saw Tammy striding toward her from the parking lot.

"Hey there," she said as she met up with them, squatting to give the Lab some love. "I saw you walking with Jason. That boy has such a crush on you."

Ashley shrugged. "He's sweet."

"Look at you, a boyfriend *and* a girlfriend at work. You multitasker, you." She bumped Ashley with her shoulder to soften the joke.

"Ha ha. Very funny."

"Do you want me to let you know if I see Lisa so you can dive behind a tree or something?"

"Oh, and she gets even funnier." Ashley shook her head, but couldn't help but smile. "No, I've had enough of this avoidance thing. It's exhausting."

Tammy nodded her agreement as they approached the back door of the main building. She pulled it open and held it for Ashley and the dog. "You gonna talk to her?"

"I think I have to. I don't know what else to do." She and the Lab stopped in the aisle and Ashley grabbed Tammy's elbow, suddenly nervous. In a whisper, she asked, "Any advice?"

Tammy cocked her head and raised her eyebrows. "Yeah. Don't kiss her."

Over an hour went by before Ashley was able to catch more than a glimpse of Lisa, solidifying her suspicion that Lisa was avoiding her. She felt stung. *What was that saying? Turnabout is fair play?* She reminded herself of this and continued on with her tasks for another ninety minutes before working up the nerve to approach Lisa, sitting behind her desk doing computer work.

"Hi," Ashley said softly, aware that she was shifting her weight slowly from one foot to the other, but unable to stop herself.

"Ashley. What do you need?" Lisa asked the question without looking up and she continued to punch keys on her keyboard. Ashley smothered a sigh of frustration.

"I need to talk to you. Just for a minute. In private."

The keystrokes stopped for a good three seconds before Lisa looked up at her, green eyes guarded.

"Please," Ashley added softly.

Lisa glanced at her watch. "I'm leaving for the day soon. Meet me in the break room in ten minutes."

"Okay." She stood for an awkward few more beats until she realized nothing more was forthcoming. Feeling her face flush hotly, she turned and walked down the aisle, no destination in mind other than "away from Lisa's desk." She shook her head in wonder, but was interrupted by Mark before she could think about it.

"Hey, Ashley. Nice to see you."

Because his full-time job was at night, Mark generally volunteered in the mornings, so it was a rare day that he and Ashley ran into each other. They'd met at a volunteer orientation meeting because they'd started the same week, but other than that, they'd been in the building together only a handful of times. Which was too bad because Ashley liked him. "How've you been?" she asked as she hugged him. He smelled like spicy aftershave.

"I'm great. You? How's the bakery?"

"It's good. Busy. Very busy."

"Wedding season, right?" His brown eyes crinkled at the corners when he smiled. His dark hair was super short and he had a habit of running his hand over the top of his head when he spoke.

"Exactly. Then the Fourth."

"They keep you on your toes, don't they?"

"You know it. How are the kids?"

They fell into conversation for several more minutes, Mark filling her in on a couple of new dogs that had been brought in that morning. Abuse cases.

"God, I'm glad I wasn't here," Ashley said with a shake of her head. "Those cases just break my heart."

"I know," Mark said. "I just don't understand what kind of person beats on a dog that weighs ten pounds. Luckily, they're both in okay shape and will recover. Hopefully, they'll find homes."

"Fingers crossed," Ashley agreed, then noticed the clock on the wall behind Mark's head. "Shit."

"What?" Mark looked over his shoulder, lost.

"Nothing. Just me being me," she said with disgusted self-deprecation as she stepped around him. Clapping him on the shoulder, she said, "So good to see you, Mark. Take care." She hustled off at a near-run. She was supposed to have been in the lounge to meet Lisa almost ten minutes ago. "Story of my life," she muttered as she pushed through the door, fully expecting to not see Lisa waiting.

She was wrong.

"I know. I know," Ashley blurted the second her eyes fell on Lisa, who was waiting in front of the Keurig, watching her coffee trickle into her travel mug. The scent of hazelnut filled the air of the lounge. "I'm sorry."

Lisa doctored her coffee as Ashley watched. A generous serving of half-and-half from a container in the fridge (interestingly, not the fake creamer that everybody else used). No sugar. She stirred it with a spoon and took a tentative sip and only then did she look up at Ashley and raise her eyebrows expectantly.

"Oh. Right." Ashley cleared her throat and walked the rest of the way into the room. She pulled out one of the four chairs around the round table in the center of the room and gestured to it. "Sit. Please."

Lisa studied her for a moment, then surprised her by doing as she was asked.

Ashley took a seat in the chair across from her. Folding her hands, she set them on the table in front of her and blew out a breath. "So…"

Lisa watched her with those eyes, and Ashley did her best not to squirm like a guilty criminal in the interrogation room on *Law & Order*. She was pretty sure she failed miserably.

They sat looking at each other for what felt like ages. Ashley had rehearsed her apology in her head a dozen times in many different forms.

I'm so sorry I kissed you.

I had no right to put you in that situation.

That kiss was out of line and inexcusable, not to mention inappropriate.

I would totally understand if you want me to resign, but I'd really like to stay.

I am terribly embarrassed and so incredibly sorry.

"So," she repeated.

"You said that already." Lisa sipped her coffee.

"Yes. I did." Ashley scratched the back of her head, looked off to her left. "I guess I just wanted to say that I'm sorry."

"For?"

Ashley gaped at her. Really? She was going to make her say it? Wow. That was cold. *Okay, I got this.* "For kissing you."

"For kissing me."

"Yes."

"At the picnic."

Ashley arched an eyebrow. "Yes. At the picnic." Had they kissed elsewhere and Ashley had forgotten?

Lisa was quiet for a moment. A long one. She sipped again and this time when she looked up at Ashley, there was something else in her eyes, something Ashley couldn't quite define, but she'd seen before. Lisa gave a slow nod and stood up. Ashley slid her chair back and rose to her feet.

"Okay," Lisa said quietly.

Ashley waited for her to say more, but nothing followed, so she gave a nod of her own and echoed Lisa. "Okay." Uncertain what more she could do, she turned and walked toward the closed lounge door.

"Wait." Lisa's voice stopped her in her tracks and when she turned to look at her, Lisa was walking toward her. This time, that something in her eyes was easy to define. Obvious. Blatant. *Desire.*

As Lisa rapidly approached, Ashley backed up until she hit the door with a soft "oof." And then Lisa was right there, right in her personal space and before Ashley could utter a word, Lisa's mouth came down on hers. No preamble. No warm-up. Just a kiss. A deep, hot, wet, thorough kiss with lips and tongues and—oh, my God, Ashley was sure her legs were going to just fold beneath her and drop her on the floor like a sack of flour. To prevent that, she grabbed the front of Lisa's shirt and held on as the kiss took everything from her. Her willpower, her control, all coherent thought. Gone. There was nothing but Lisa's mouth. And what Lisa's mouth was doing to her mouth.

And just like that, it was over. Ashley blinked her eyes open, stunned by the sudden absence of Lisa's lips on hers. Lisa's green eyes were dark, gorgeous, as they focused on Ashley's. Her warm hands closed over Ashley's shoulders and gently moved her away from the door, as if they were doing a dance step. Then she swiped a fingertip along the corner of her own mouth in a move that was somehow ridiculously sexy, leaned close to Ashley, and said on a whisper, "I accept your apology."

And then she was gone, the only signs that she was ever there in the first place being her mug on the table and the sexy aftershocks rumbling through Ashley's body.

Hand out, as if she were blind, Ashley made her way back to the table and plopped down into a chair before her knees gave out completely. Lifting a shaky hand to her swollen lips, she realized with shocking clarity that her life had become *so* much more complicated than it had been five minutes ago.

⊷

"You okay?" Carly asked as she took a bite of her burger.

Ashley glanced up from her barely-touched food. "What?"

"I asked if you're okay. You've been really quiet tonight." Carly dunked a French fry in the huge puddle of ketchup she'd squirted onto her tray and then popped it into her mouth. Her eyes stayed on Ashley the whole time, and Ashley was sure she could feel them boring into her skin, making her feel squirmy and uncomfortable.

"Sorry. I'm fine. Just tired." *Also, I made out with a woman at the shelter. Twice now. And both times were amazing. I've never been kissed like that. Ever. Otherwise, just another regular day. No big deal.*

Carly nodded, but it was clear she wasn't buying the "I'm tired" story. They ate in silence a bit longer and Carly said, "That new Sandra Bullock movie opens this weekend. Want to go?"

Ashley chewed on a fry, her sour stomach wanting nothing more than to reject it the second it hit home, but she held it down. "Sure."

"Great. I'll find out times and let you know." More silence. More chewing. Then, "Hey, guess what. I think I landed that contracting client I told you about."

"Yeah?" Carly was a sales rep for a computer equipment company. "That's fantastic. Congratulations." Ashley did her best to inject her words with some modicum of enthusiasm. *Guess what I did. I made out with somebody at work!* She squeezed her eyes shut in an attempt to block out the voice that had been teasing her sarcastically since Lisa left her in the break room.

"Are you sure you're okay?" Carly's face was clouded with concern, which only made Ashley feel worse.

"Maybe I'm coming down with something. Do you mind if we call it a night?"

"Not at all, babe." Carly reached across the table and laid a hand against Ashley's forehead. "You're a little flushed, but you don't seem warm." She began clearing their table, tossing her unfinished burger and nearly Ashley's entire meal onto one tray, then taking it to the trash can. Back at the table, she held out her hand. "Come on. I'll take you home."

They drove in relative silence, but Ashley could feel Carly glance at her every so often. She felt terrible for the lie, but she couldn't sit across from Carly making small talk when all she could think about was earlier in the afternoon. She needed some time alone. To think. To analyze. To beat herself up a little bit. Or a lot.

Sliding the car into Park in the parking lot of Ashley's apartment, Carly turned to her. "Want me to come up and take care of you?" Her expression was so kind and sweet that Ashley thought she might vomit from guilt right there in the passenger seat of the Prius.

"No. I'll be fine. I think I'm just going to go to bed. But thank you."

"All right. If you're sure."

"I am. Thanks for dinner."

"Next time, we'll actually eat it." Her smile was tender and took any sting out of the words. Then she leaned in and kissed Ashley softly on the lips.

It took every ounce of energy Ashley had to keep from flinching away. Carly's kiss was nice, but Ashley's brain immediately tossed her a flashback of Lisa's, her mouth hot, her tongue demanding. Ashley's body flushed and she pulled back from Carly with an uncertain grimace. "I don't want to get you sick." She pawed at the car door until her fingers snagged the handle and she practically threw herself out onto the pavement.

Carly ducked down to catch her eye. "I'll call you later to check on you."

"Okay. I'll probably turn my phone off, so if I don't answer, that's why." God, when did she become so good at lying?

"Well, just take it easy, okay?"

"I will. Bye." Ashley slammed the door shut before the conversation could continue. She turned and quickly went up the walk, unlocked the lobby door, and tossed a wave back to Carly. *I am a horrible person. I am a horrible, horrible person.* She'd been—was being—so unfair to Carly. *Because I am a coward.* She was stringing Carly along, leading her on, and Ashley knew it, was fully aware, but was too much of a weakling to do something about it. "Goddamn it," she muttered closing the lobby door. She practically flew up the stairs to her second floor apartment where she shoved her way in, slammed the door, and fell back against it, sucking in air as if she'd just escaped a horde of zombies.

Of course, leaning with her back against the door only reminded her of the last time she'd been in that position. How was it that a woman who was normally more removed than friendly, more aloof than approachable, could suddenly be the hottest, sexiest thing in Ashley's world right now? She felt like her brain was scrambled, like she couldn't grab onto a clear, rational thought no matter how hard she tried. They spun around her head like pieces of paper in a tornado.

"Jesus Christ," she whispered to her empty apartment. "What the hell am I gonna do?"

CHAPTER TEN

THE SHELTER WAS BUSY, phones ringing off the hook, and—if it was even possible—the dogs seemed louder today. Not that Lisa hadn't already had a splintering headache when she'd arrived. She had. Thanks to the crazy, unstoppable thoughts about kissing Ashley in the break room and *what the hell had she been thinking?*

Pressing the fingertips of one hand into the base of her skull, Lisa turned back to her desk and grabbed the ringing phone. The call was quick and as she hung up, she saw Tammy bringing one of the Lab mixes in from his walk, then clip her leash to the next dog on her list. Swiveling back to the monitors, she scanned them, then the cages. All the dogs were accounted for except the one Tammy had just taken. So… where the hell was Ashley?

Scrubbing her hands over her face, Lisa reminded herself of two things. One, she wasn't even sure she wanted to see Ashley in any way other than from afar. And two, Ashley was a very responsible volunteer. Lisa shouldn't be worrying about her blowing off her shift. It was true that Lisa didn't have a lot of control over the work ethic of the volunteers. Sure, she could suggest they're maybe not a good fit for Junebug. And in once instance, she did have to ban somebody from the facility for stealing, but overall, the volunteers were there because they wanted to be and Lisa rarely had issues with any of them. And certainly not with Ashley. Well. Not with her *work…*

Her phone buzzed where it sat on the corner of her desk. Lisa glanced at it, saw *Mom* on the screen, and groaned. No. She was not in the mood for small talk with her mother.

Forcing herself to chill, she pulled open the desk drawer, tossed the phone inside, and pulled out a bottle of Motrin, her headache showing no signs of abandoning her for quite some time. Four pills in her hand, she headed to the employee break room for some water. The door was slightly ajar and something about the sound from inside made her stop in her tracks. Hand flat against the wood of the door, she stayed out of sight and strained to hear the conversation happening just on the other side.

"I'm pretty sure you've been feeling the same thing I have." It was a male voice, a raspy almost-whisper that Lisa thought she recognized, but wasn't certain.

"I'm sorry, but I don't think so." This was Ashley. She was speaking quietly as well, but Lisa knew that voice. And right now, it had a slight tremor to it. "You have the wrong idea here —"

"Do you know who I am?" The male voice took on a slight edge and Lisa knew right then that it was Clark Breckenridge. Her nostrils flared with irritation as she heard him say, "I don't get the wrong idea. I always have the right idea." There was the sound of a long intake of breath and then he added, "God, you smell delicious."

"Please, Mr. Breckenridge, you're making me really uncomfortable."

"I told you to call me Clark. And we can change that very easily. Come back to my place with me. I'll make sure you're *very* comfortable."

"I don't—"

"Do you know how much money my family gives to this place a year?" The edge was back and much sharper than before. "Do you? A lot. A ridiculous amount because my sister has a soft spot for animals. Frankly, I don't care one way or another about them, but it's my money that keeps this place afloat. So if I want a little bit of a thank you from somebody on the staff…" He let his voice trail off and Lisa's heart began to pound. "That's what I get."

Ashley whispered, "Please," but it was laced with fear and humiliation, not desire, as Lisa was sure Clark expected. Red-hot fury flooded her system like adrenaline. She pushed the door open quickly so there would be no time for a cover story of any kind.

Clark had backed Ashley into the corner behind the door, his considerably larger form pinning her there with one hand braced against the wall next to her head, the other gripping the back of her neck. He'd planted his foot between hers, one knee poised to push between her legs.

Lisa had trouble ripping her eyes from the sight.

She said nothing. She didn't trust herself to form words. She simply glared at Clark Breckenridge, one eyebrow arched in question, and waited.

"Lisa. Hey." He took a step backward, away from Ashley, then another, and Lisa felt the fist that had gripped her heart loosen slightly. Clark gestured to Ashley. "We were just… having a little discussion. About…stuff."

Lisa continued to glare at him, mostly because she was trying her best to burn a hole through his skull with her eyes, but also because she was afraid to look at Ashley, afraid of the mortification she'd probably see. She felt her, though. Felt her move away from the wall and come to stand next to Lisa, her body heat apparent in the two inches of space between them.

Clark fidgeted, ran a hand along the back of his neck, and at least had the good sense to look slightly embarrassed…only slightly. He pointed to the door. "I'm just…I'm gonna…head home. It's about that time." He took half a step, then seemed to realize that, in order for him to leave, Lisa would have to move. She didn't. For a long moment, she stood there, staring him down, until he began to subtly shift uncomfortably from one foot to the other. Finally, she took a small step sideways, her hand moving out to grasp Ashley's forearm and nudge her in the right direction. She didn't let go.

"So, I'll…" He gave a ridiculous wave, looking as ashamed and nervous as he should have. "I'll go. See you later. Have a good night." With that, he nearly sprinted out the door. Lisa and Ashley stood quietly until the slap of his very expensive loafers on the tile floor could no longer be heard.

Finally, Lisa turned to regard Ashley and realized she still held on to her arm. Letting go quickly, she asked, "Are you okay?"

"Yeah." Ashley's face flushed a deep red and she stepped toward the door. "That guy is such a caveman," she said quietly.

"Were you just going to stand there and let him do whatever he wanted?" Lisa didn't mean to sound as accusatory as she must have, which she could tell by the zap of hurt and disbelief that shot across Ashley's face.

"No, I was…I just…" She shook her head, then left the room before Lisa could say another thing.

Lisa stood staring at the door, her emotions racing, bouncing around from anger to sympathy to disbelief and back to anger. Determination suddenly settled over her and she stomped out of the break room, up the hall, through the lobby, and down another hall until she stopped at a closed wooden door sporting a placard that read, *Catherine Gardner, Accounting.*

Not stopping to wonder if there might be a good reason the door was closed, Lisa rapped on it with her knuckles, then turned the knob.

Catherine blinked up from her desk in surprise, glasses perched on the end of her nose. Anna St. John whipped her head around quickly to meet Lisa's eyes, her own brimming with unshed tears. She cleared her throat, said to Catherine, "We'll finish this later," and left the room without another word, Lisa watching her exit with surprised embarrassment.

"I'm sorry," Lisa said to Catherine. "I didn't mean to interrupt."

"It's fine," Catherine said, gesturing to the two chairs in front of her desk. "That needed to be interrupted."

Lisa shut the door and moved to the chair.

"Is there something I can help you with?" Catherine asked, her voice tired.

"Yes. There is," Lisa said in a firm tone. She sat in one of the chairs across from Catherine's modest desk, and took a moment to school the fury out of her pounding temples by glancing around. The office was utilitarian at best; neat and tidy, but not fancy, not elegant. It was part of Jessica's design to make sure the accountant's office didn't look too well appointed. Nobody would give money to an establishment that didn't look like it needed funding. The desk was an old metal one that Lisa could imagine one of her teachers in high school sitting at. The chair she occupied was metal and vinyl. A couple rickety shelves lined the walls, holding various books, and Lisa knew the heat register on the wall behind Catherine's chair would grind and groan in the winter when the heat kicked on.

In fact, the only thing in the Catherine's office that looked classy and put-together was Catherine herself. Today's outfit was a black pantsuit with a bright electric blue cami underneath the jacket, which did a spectacular job of bringing out the blue in Catherine's eyes, even with her glasses on. Her chestnut brown hair was partially pulled back and she reached up with a manicured hand to pull the glasses off her face. "Tell me."

"You can do something about Clark Breckenridge."

With a put-upon sigh, Catherine slid her glasses back on and shifted her gaze to the computer monitor on her desk.

"Catherine. I am serious here. I just caught him…*harassing* Ashley, and I don't think it was the first time."

Catherine blew out a breath and looked back at Lisa. "Define harassing."

Lisa cocked her head to the side in a way that said *Really?* but then answered. "He had her pinned up against the wall and was telling her how important he and his money are to Junebug and that means he gets what he wants from staff and volunteers alike. Not in so many words, but that's pretty close. And his tone was definitely threatening."

The glasses came off again. "Lisa…" As she cast about for the right words, Lisa interrupted.

"Don't, Catherine. Don't you dare tell me this is how he is and boys will be boys and he does this all the time, but he gives us a ton of money so we just need to let him have his fun because *he's really just harmless.* He *does* do this all the time and he's *not* harmless. You should have seen Ashley's face. She was humiliated." Lisa stopped to take a breath, then said in a softer tone, "It was worse than that, though. She was scared, and with good reason. I don't know what would have happened if I hadn't gotten there when I did. He was…intent. You need to talk to him. Please. It's not always about the money. The safety of the female volunteers is more important."

Their gazes held for a bit until Catherine finally relented. "All right. I'll talk to him."

"Thank you." Lisa tried not to sound too grateful. This wasn't a decision that should be questioned at all. A situation like this should be handled swiftly and with zero tolerance. But not-for-profits had their own way of doing things…most often whatever way preserved the money. Lisa stood, then pointed at Catherine. "I'm holding you to that."

Catherine waved her away. "I said I'd talk to him. I will."

Lisa nodded once, then headed back to her dogs.

Ashley managed to avoid her for the rest of her shift, and though Lisa wanted to corner her and apologize for being so harsh, she also worried that she might make it worse by pointing out the incident again. So, she left her alone.

She watched carefully, but left her alone.

>—◆—<

Ashley was pissed.

No, she was furious.

"Were you just going to stand there and let him?" she sneered as she waited for the mutt she was walking to do his business. She'd pointedly avoided Lisa for the remainder of her shift. Now it was growing dark, and she was ready to go home, but her mind replayed Lisa's voice in her head, the tint of blame in her tone. Blame! Unbelievable. "No, Lisa. For your information, I was not going to just stand there and let him."

Was I?

She shook that thought away. She'd been scared. Terrified, even. She had never before been forced into that position. Clark Breckenridge had a lot of nerve. He was also rich and powerful and large. And strong. *So strong.* She could still feel the imprint of his enormous hand on the back of her neck. The fact that he could have quickly and easily overpowered her inside of ten seconds made her knees go weak with fear and her body break out in a cold sweat.

A shiver shook her entire body, which irritated her and brought her back to anger. Which was good. Anger was way better than fear.

Or hurt.

Were you just going to stand there and let him?

Yes. Lisa's words had cut deep.

Locking the last walker back up and signing off on her clipboard, Ashley looked around. There was nobody else in the dog wing except Lisa, who sat at her desk poking at keys on her keyboard. Ashley strode up to her before she lost her nerve and stopped in front of her desk.

She set her clipboard down on the desk. "I have something to say to you." She leaned forward, bracing herself on the desktop with her hands.

Lisa rolled her lips in and bit down on them, and it was a beat before she looked up at Ashley with expectation. Those damn green eyes of hers snagged Ashley and she had to fight to hold on to her anger. She ran through all the lines she'd practiced while walking.

You had no right to talk to me like that.

Thank you for stepping in, but what you said to me was out of line.

I was handling things just fine. I didn't need your help. (Which was a lie.)

But what came out of her mouth was none of those. Not even a variation. Instead, she said simply, "Would you have coffee with me? Sometime?"

The two of them sat there, twin expressions of surprise on their faces, and blinked in silence for a beat. Two. Three. Ashley dropped her head down between her shoulders, wondering who the hell had jumped inside her skull and hijacked her brain. Pushing herself to standing, she turned away and blew out a breath. She had officially lost her mind. She was sure of it.

"Okay." Lisa's voice stopped her in her tracks.

Ashley stayed perfectly still, uncertain her ears had heard correctly. When she finally gathered enough courage to turn back, Lisa was looking at her intently. "I'm sorry...did you say... what did you say?"

"Did you ask me to coffee?"

Ashley nodded.

"I thought so. I said okay."

"You said okay."

"Yes."

"Okay."

"Yes."

Ashley was shocked and could do nothing but nod for what felt like a year, but was surely only a second or two. "Okay, then." She turned to leave Lisa's office, but spun back around. "Incidentally—"

"What I said was out of line," Lisa interrupted, her tone soft and laced with regret. "I didn't mean it. And I'm sorry."

They stared at each other in silence for several moments before Ashley turned and walked as quickly as she could to the break room where she grabbed her stuff. Then she exited the dog wing without looking back, kept her gaze on her feet as she left the building and headed across the parking lot to her car. Once safely inside, she pulled her phone from her pocket and texted Jenna.

I did something totally stupid. Help me.

It only took a few seconds for a reply.

I'll need details before I offer my valuable assistance.

Always the smart-ass. Ashley sighed and typed.

Long story.

Not surprisingly, her phone rang in her hand.

"Hey," she said.

"Tell me what's going on," Jenna ordered.

There was no way around it, Ashley knew. If she wanted Jenna's help—and she did because Jenna was very wise about things like this—she was going to have to give up the whole story. As of this moment, the only person she'd told about the kiss was Tammy. And she'd sworn her to secrecy. "No judgment, Jenna. I mean it."

"None. I swear."

Taking a deep breath, Ashley dove in, telling Jenna everything, starting from the ambush kiss at the picnic and ending with the invitation to coffee. When she was done, there was silence on the other end of the phone. Ashley held her breath, waiting.

"Well," Jenna finally said, sounding as if she'd just finished a difficult math problem. "I have some comments."

"I bet," Ashley muttered.

"Hey. Relax, Ash-hole. We'll get to the big thing later. First of all, I am amazed."

Ashley pulled the phone away from her ear and squinted at it. "You are?" she asked when it was back against her head.

"Are you kidding me? You made a move, my friend. *You. You* made a move. You never make a move. And not just any move. A *major* move. You kissed her. Out of the freaking blue, you kissed her. I'm shocked."

"I was a little tipsy."

"Doesn't matter. It still counts. I am hugely impressed with you right now."

Ashley couldn't help the tiny grin that turned up the corners of her mouth. "Thanks."

"And then she kissed you? A second time? You know what that means, right?"

"She likes me?" Ashley said in a small voice.

"She *wants* you. Different thing totally."

The idea of Lisa wanting her—like that—sent a pleasant shudder through Ashley's body, ending with a flutter in her stomach.

"And asking her out to coffee? Classic."

"I had no plans to do that, Jenna." Ashley was adamant. "I don't know where that came from. I was mad at her for the comment she made. I was going to confront her about it."

"Yeah, that was a douchey thing to say."

"Right? So, believe me, I was as shocked as she was when the coffee invitation popped out."

"Classic," Jenna repeated. Ashley could hear the smile in her voice. "Now, the fact that you asked, she accepted, and then you ran like a greased pig in a hog-catching contest before ironing out any details is…slightly problematic. What were you thinking?" She said it gently and with a slight chuckle, which gave Ashley completely mixed emotions…a little levity, a little mortification.

"I don't know. I panicked." She leaned her forehead against the hard plastic of the steering wheel. "What is the matter with me, Jenna? I don't understand myself."

"You have made a bit of a mess, haven't you?" Jenna's voice gentled, but Ashley knew exactly what she was saying.

"Carly."

"Yep."

"What am I gonna do?"

"It's okay," Jenna said. "You got this. Listen to me…"

⊷

"What the hell was I thinking?" Lisa muttered to herself as she steered her car out of the Junebug parking lot an hour later and headed for home. "Seriously. What?" She shoved a hand through her hair, replaying the scene in her head as she drove. Ashley was mad at her. That much she got from her stance and the determined expression on her face. And she had every right to be; Lisa had been cold. She'd been ready to take what Ashley dished out and apologize.

But that's not at all how it had gone down.

It seemed to her that Ashley was as surprised as she was by the coffee invitation, which was actually kind of adorable now that she thought about it. And she'd seemed even more surprised when Lisa had said yes (probably not as surprised as Lisa herself, but whatever). *That* was adorable, too.

And before she could stop focusing on "adorable Ashley" and lasso her mind into submission, it tossed her a flashback of that kiss at the picnic.

God, that kiss.

Her body immediately flushed hotly at the memory. She recalled the uncharacteristic boldness with which Ashley had trapped her between the wall and her body, how she hadn't even hesitated a second before taking the reins. It was so unlike Ashley, so not what Lisa would have expected from her. It was forward. It was brazen.

It was hot.

A small, guttural sound escaped from Lisa's throat as she braked for a light. Thank God it was Friday. She wouldn't be back at Junebug Farms until Monday, which meant she had two full days get her shit together, maybe visit with Aunt Joyce, possibly see what Grace and Ella were up to—anything to occupy her mind, which was preoccupied with replaying her kiss with Ashley, over and over and over. And when she was done with that one, she flashed on the *other* kiss. God. Had she ever kissed anybody who kissed back as well as Ashley? As thoroughly? As sexily? She closed her eyes and shook her head, didn't open them until an impatient honk sounded from the car behind her, and she realized the light had turned green.

Kissing Ashley was breathtaking.

Seriously, was anybody else's mouth that soft? Did anybody else taste as good as Ashley did? Was it suddenly oppressively warm in this car? Lisa hit the button, and her window slid down, letting the early summer breeze cool things off. She turned on the radio, cranking the volume in the hopes of drowning out any thoughts of sexy women who smelled like cupcakes and kissed like nobody's business.

Once home, she felt a bit more grounded. Focusing on her animals always helped her to put things into perspective. This was real. These creatures needed her and somehow, she needed them as well. Everybody got extra hugs and kisses as she murmured her love to each of them, then fed them dinner. Once the kitchen was quiet except for the various sounds of munching and crunching, Lisa stood in front of the refrigerator with the door open, trying to decide on something for the human in the house to have for dinner. That's when she heard her phone beep with a text notification.

Reaching into the fridge, she chose some romaine lettuce, celery, and half a remaining cucumber from the crisper. From the cheese drawer, she snagged a bowl of crumbled blue cheese. She dumped it all on the counter, opened a cabinet, and found walnuts and dried cranberries. With a satisfied nod, she retrieved her phone from a side table to check the text before settling in to chop up the salad ingredients.

The text was from Ashley.

Lisa stared at the entry for a long time, finger hovering over the Read button. Wetting her lips, she braced herself, touched her fingertip to the screen and read.

I'm sorry I'm such a dumbass. I didn't expect you to say yes and I had a minor freak-out (obviously). But you did say yes and I am really happy about that. I think we could use some time to talk. Away from work. Not sure of your schedule. How about tomorrow at Beans? 3pm? Let me know if a different time works better. Or if you've changed your mind completely...

The emoticon at the end was a grimace face and Lisa couldn't help but smile, as she could almost picture Ashley making it. That slight self-deprecation was kind of cute, really. She could admit that. And come on, it was just coffee. It could be fun. Worth going, even if nothing came of it but friendship. You can't really have too many friends, right?

Friends. She snorted a laugh. Who was she kidding?

She texted back: *Sounds good. I'll meet you there.*

CHAPTER ELEVEN

AT PRECISELY 2:35 ON Saturday, Ashley accepted her mocha latte from the barista at Beans and looked around for the best table. She was intentionally early—the only way she'd been able to accomplish that was to trick her mind into believing she was meeting Lisa at 2:30—for two reasons: one, she wanted to give herself a chance to settle in, get comfortable, and for quite possibly the first time in her life, not be late. This felt too important, though she couldn't put her finger on why. Two, she needed to get the hell out of her apartment before she tried on every last piece of clothing she owned. There was a fine line, she decided, between overdressing for this occasion and looking far too casually weekend-ish, and she was not walking it well. Finally choosing a pair of black capris, a summery orange short-sleeved button-down shirt, and black sandals, she was sure she was perfectly decked out for the late-June weather. Of course, she hadn't counted on Beans having their air conditioning blasting like they were in the tropics. She was already freezing.

The coffee shop wasn't terribly busy at this time of day, which was partly why Ashley had chosen it (the other part being that Jenna had actually chosen it). Her eyes fell on a corner table and she snagged it quickly, sitting with her back to the wall so she could watch the door. Wrapping both hands around her cup to keep warm, she scanned the other patrons as she willed her heart to stop pounding quite so vehemently in her chest.

What would they talk about?

Lisa wasn't exactly chatty, so Ashley knew that, by default, she'd most likely need to start the conversation—and possibly keep it going. She ran through various safe subjects in her mind.

The weather.

Beans.

Work.

Only then did she come to understand that what she really wanted to talk about was Lisa. She wanted to know more. More about her, about her life, about her thoughts. It was a strange, invigorating feeling and it caught Ashley off guard. She could not, for the life of her, pinpoint when her views of Lisa had changed. Sure, she'd always found her extremely attractive —anybody would. The woman was gorgeous. But she'd always been a bit standoffish, removed, clear about keeping her distance from people. She was abrupt. A little cold, even.

But sweet baby Jesus, she kissed like a goddess.

Ashley sipped her coffee, enjoying the slight chocolate flavor of it as well as the warmth it tracked into her body, though she knew it wasn't the only reason she was suddenly warm inside. Maybe it was that day in the lounge...the day Ashley had become a blubbering mess over Jax being adopted. Lisa's support then had been so...unexpected. And warm. It was then that Ashley had seen her in a slightly different light, saw that maybe she wasn't cold and unfriendly.

Of course, then there was the accusatory comment about her letting Clark do whatever he wanted.

Maybe she *was* cold and unfriendly.

Maybe she was just...intensely private.

Or something.

She shook her head, not wanting to drive herself crazy before her date even arrived. Shifting her focus, Ashley studied the coffee shop. It was a large, open space with the coffee bar in the center, like a theatre-in-the-round. Above, a second level circled the entire shop with an open balcony, and the walls were painted a pumpkin orange. There were chairs and tables and couches up there, too, and you could look down onto the rest of the shop. The open, airy feel and the décor of stainless steel and glass made the whole place feel modern and large. The delicious smell of freshly ground coffee beans was simply a bonus.

A few people milled around on the second level. One couple cuddled and laughed on a loveseat. Three others sat at separate tables with laptops open, looking very much like the working college students they probably were, as summer sessions had just begun. On Ashley's level, two baristas worked behind the counter, one a man who looked to be maybe twenty-five and sported a ponytail and a neck tattoo. The other was a woman in her forties, her brown hair short and her smile very pleasant and nurturing. They laughed together when they had nobody to wait on, and Ashley thought being a barista might be a fun job. She was just trying to decide on what kind of specialty drink she'd invent when she saw her.

Lisa looked stunning, and it was momentarily confusing for Ashley. Lisa always looked amazing; she couldn't not. But at Junebug Farms, she was always dressed for work and that usually meant simple, functional clothing like khaki pants or shorts and T-shirts or polos.

That's not what she wore today.

Today, she wore a bright yellow sundress with light green flowers. The short sleeves showed off arms tanned a golden bronze that shocked Ashley (how had she not noticed such gorgeously colored skin?). Her sandaled feet revealed toes polished a deep plum, and she had a small, rectangular purse dangling from one shoulder. The sun shining through the many windows of Beans made Lisa's hair seem to sparkle with gold highlights, and she lifted one hand to remove her sunglasses and tuck a lock behind her ear.

Ashley's mouth went dry.

Those breathtaking green eyes scanned the shop before landing on Ashley, who smiled and gave a little wave, amazed she was even able to move her hand after being paralyzed by such a striking woman. "Oh, my God," she breathed out quietly as Lisa held up a finger to let Ashley know she was grabbing coffee and would be over shortly. "I am *so* out of my league..."

Time seemed to stand still as she waited for Lisa to get her order, and the butterflies in her stomach became belligerent, causing almost-nausea as her nerves doubled, then tripled. Finally, she gave herself a little mental pep talk. *Relax. It's Lisa. You know her pretty well. And this is just coffee. Chill. Be yourself. Smile. Oh, my God, here she comes!*

"Hey," Lisa said with a grin as she pulled out the chair across from Ashley and took a seat.

"Hey to you. You..." Ashley swallowed and cleared her throat. "You look amazing." She was rewarded by the slight coloring of Lisa's cheeks.

"Thank you," Lisa replied, looking down at her cup and running her fingertip around the rim.

"So. You made it. Have you been here before?"

Lisa shook her head and looked around, up, behind her. "I haven't. I've heard a lot about it, and my townhouse isn't far from here, so it's kind of surprising that I haven't come here. I may have to change that now. I like it."

"Me, too." Ashley sipped and Lisa followed suit. "What did you get?"

"I got the French roast."

"You like strong coffee."

"I like *bold* coffee. There's a difference." Lisa winked and Ashley felt a tightening low in her body.

"No sugar?"

"Just cream."

Ashley feigned a horrified gasp. "*No* sugar? But then it just tastes like…coffee."

Lisa laughed. "Exactly." She gestured with her eyes to Ashley's cup. "What's in there?"

"Sugar. Chocolate. Cream. Did I say sugar? And maybe a tiny bit of coffee."

Lisa laughed again and Ashley decided right then that she wanted to make her laugh as often as possible. It was a beautiful sound, slightly musical and very feminine. "You like sweets."

"I work in a bakery. It's kind of a requirement."

Lisa propped her elbows on the table and set her chin on her folded hands. "Tell me about that."

"The bakery?"

A nod. "How you got there, what you do there, do you like it?"

There was something about having those green eyes focused entirely on her that Ashley found intensely erotic and she tried to be subtle about the hard swallow she took.

"I started working there when I was in high school." Ashley took a small sip of her coffee. "I have always liked baking, I've always baked with my mom and my grandma." She held up a hand, traffic-cop-style. "I don't like to cook. I like to bake."

"What's the difference?"

"Cooking is a lot of winging it. I don't like that. I don't wing it well."

Lisa grinned teasingly. "Not a fly by the seat of your pants kind of girl, are you?"

"No. Not at all." *Which is why it's so completely bizarre that we're even here,* she almost said, but managed not to. "I like rules. And with baking, you have to follow the rules or it doesn't work."

"I see." Lisa sipped her coffee, her eyes never leaving Ashley's face, something Ashley found simultaneously unnerving and a complete turn-on.

"I wasn't a great student in school. I mean, I did fine, but I didn't enjoy it, and the thought of college just filled me with... angst. Plus, I liked working at the bakery, so I just...stayed."

"Can you, I don't know, move up? Is there a career path for you there?"

"I don't really think about it. I guess there is. It's just...I like it. I'm comfortable there."

Lisa gave her a look she couldn't quite define.

Instead of pursuing it, Ashley changed the subject. "What about you? How did you end up at Junebug?"

"That's a long story."

"I like long stories."

Lisa held Ashley's gaze for a beat, then glanced down at her cup. She took a sip, looked toward the large windows that showed the street and began to talk. "I knew Jessica through softball. She's a little bit older than I am and I always..." She hesitated slightly before settling on, "I always looked up to her."

Ashley arched a knowing eyebrow. "Is that code for 'had a crush on her'?"

Lisa blushed attractively. "It might be."

"Just checking. Does she play on our team?"

Lisa gave a quick nod. "So we've been friends for a while. I was working at a vet's office when Jessica's grandma died and left her Junebug Farms."

"I always wondered how somebody as young as she is ended up running such a large business."

"She and her grandma were very close. Did you know her grandma's name was June? And that Jessica's grandfather called her his little Junebug? That's where the name came from."

"Aww. That's a sweet story." Ashley sipped her coffee, perfectly content to listen to Lisa talk.

"Anyway, Jessica took over and pretty much cleaned house. She loved her grandmother very much, but said she was a terrible manager of people, that she didn't hire well, but then couldn't bring herself to fire anybody. Jessica was a business major in college and she can be really tough. So, she came in, got rid of almost everybody, and then hired a bunch of people she had faith in."

"My dad would caution her against hiring her friends, but it seems to have worked in this case."

"It has. Which doesn't mean there haven't been issues." The tone of her voice told Ashley there likely was one of those issues now, but she didn't ask. "But overall, it's been good."

"So…who works there that was her friend first?"

Lisa gave her a half-grin. "Pretty much the entire board. Me. Catherine and Anna and David. Maggie has known her since Jessica was a kid. The rest, she hired once she took over."

"Interesting. And you enjoy adoption and intake?"

walled up inside her? This sudden, burning desire to know everything she could possibly know about Lisa? The need to inhale her scent on a near-constant basis? The necessity of shoving her hands into her pockets so she wouldn't just randomly touch Lisa any chance she got? It was all so invigorating, so exciting, and so confusing, wrapped up into one big ball of eager uncertainty.

"Tell me more about you," Lisa said as they walked.

"Me? I'm totally boring. I promise."

"I don't believe that for a second. How come you're single? When was your last relationship?"

Ashley felt a wave of panic hit as Carly's face flashed before her eyes. She could hear the concern in Carly's voice when she'd called this morning to see if Ashley was still feeling crappy. She'd even offered to come over and play nursemaid. Ashley pasted on a smile and looked off to her right, away from Lisa. "Just haven't found the right one yet, I guess. But you know what I love? Volunteering at the shelter."

She hoped she hadn't given Lisa whiplash with the sudden change of subject, but Lisa only hesitated for a minute before saying, "Okay. We'll shelve the relationship talk for the time being. Tell me why you wanted to volunteer at Junebug."

"Well, for starters, I love animals. Love them. I really want to have a dog of my own, but my schedule at the bakery can be crazy and I don't think it's fair to a dog to leave him home alone for hours and hours and hours. I will have one some day, but not yet. I watched the telethon last year," Ashley went on, referring to the yearly fundraiser Junebug Farms did in partnership with a local television station. "They talked about how volunteers were always needed and I thought that'd be a good way for me to get my animal fix without actually getting an animal. The fact that Junebug is no-kill was a huge factor for me. There's no way I could handle dogs being put down." With a self-deprecating laugh, she said, "Hell, I could barely handle Jax getting a new home. Imagine what a mess I'd have been if he'd been put to sleep." She'd spoken it all rather fast, hoping Lisa wouldn't notice that she was babbling.

"Ashley." Lisa stopped walking and touched her arm. Ashley stumbled to a surprised halt at the sound of her name in such a tone. It was very unlike Lisa, who was usually no-nonsense. Now, her voice was firm yet gentle, and a little sexy. Okay, it was a lot sexy. "Please don't be embarrassed by your reaction to that. You have no reason to be."

Ashley glanced down at her feet, felt her face heating up. "I did feel kind of silly." She looked up, looked into the green of Lisa's eyes. "You helped, though. You helped a lot."

"I'm glad."

They had reached the park, which was well populated by dog-walkers and families pushing strollers, a few guys tossing a Frisbee, and a smattering of sun worshippers on blankets. Ashley pointed out an empty bench and they claimed it and sat quietly for long moments. Lisa crossed one leg over the other and turned her body slightly so she faced Ashley.

"So," she said, then said nothing more.

"So?" Ashley responded, eyebrows raised.

Lisa pulled in a deep breath and said, "This is going well. Don't you think?"

"This?" Ashley asked. Waving a finger between the two of them, she said, "You mean…this?"

"Yes," Lisa smiled while making the same gesture. "This."

"I think so, too."

"I honestly had no idea what to expect when you asked me to coffee."

"No? Well, I honestly couldn't believe I actually asked you to coffee."

"Yeah, you were mad at me."

"Yes, I was."

"I'm sorry about that." Lisa grimaced and glanced off at the park. "I shouldn't have said what I did."

"Lisa?" When Lisa looked back at her, Ashley leaned in and kissed her gently. Not hungrily or demandingly, but softly, sweetly. When she pulled back, she whispered, "I accept your apology."

Lisa's cheeks flushed a pretty pink as she grinned and nodded and said, "Well played."

CHAPTER TWELVE

THURSDAY TURNED OUT TO be a disaster of a day. It was hectic and long, and by the time two p.m. rolled around, Lisa felt like she'd been at Junebug Farms for three days straight. The medical suite was booked up all day doing spays and neuters—which was a good thing, as it meant all the animals being operated on had been adopted—but it took a lot of coordination and timing. The animals recovering from surgery had to be monitored. The ones about to have surgery had to be monitored (no food or water since midnight the previous night). Five different veterinarians and their technicians rotated shifts at Junebug, and today was Mark Jackson. He was good. Competent. Lisa liked him. He was quick and no-nonsense, but also showed a tender side to the animals, which she found to be all-important. Lisa only had two actual paid employees and both were part-timers. These were the days she realized how important her volunteers were. Ashley and Tammy were both on this afternoon, as well as Bobby Griffin, one of the part-timers. Bobby was good, a vet tech in his late twenties who was amazing with animals and people alike. Lisa wanted nothing more than to hire him full-time, but she couldn't match what the animal hospital he worked for was paying him and he and his wife had a baby on the way, so it just wasn't in the cards.

To make matters worse, Animal Control had called and was bringing in three more dogs seized during raids on a suspected dog fighting ring. Lisa normally had to work hard to school her features, her thoughts, to go into what she called Robot Mode. No feelings. No emotions. Just do the paperwork, get the dogs situated, show them kindness and love (if they'd accept it) and hope Jamie could work some of her magic.

As would typically happen on a crazy day, one dog was ready to come out of recovery, another needed to be prepped for surgery, and Animal Control showed up at the back door all at the same time. To make matters worse, Ashley had arrived at 2:45 and was her usual, sweet self, but Lisa didn't have time for pleasantries. The chaos at the back door was loud, and Lisa moved Ashley out of her way so she could get by and jump into the fray. After a few moments of trying not to scare the dog any more than it already was, Lisa glanced up to see Ashley standing in the same spot, riveted, eyes wide with fear. Lisa caught Tammy's eye and gestured to Ashley with her chin. "Get her out of here. For God's sake, send her to medical. She's not going to be any help standing there like that."

A flash of embarrassed hurt flew across Ashley's face, but Lisa didn't have time to deal with it. Ashley headed off to the medical suite without looking back and Animal Control brought in the next dog.

It was a mess.

That was the easiest way to describe it in the aftermath. The dogs were ferocious—which Lisa knew actually stemmed from fear. They were beaten. They were starved. They were expected to fight to the death in order to get any kind of food. The three today showed obvious symptoms of malnutrition and abuse. Open sores. Poorly healed broken bones. Fierce aggression.

The worst part was their eyes.

Lisa always tried to gauge a dog's rehabilitation chances by looking at their eyes. Not directly, no. Direct eye contact was considered a challenge and a dog used to fighting would go for her in a second if she stared too long. But she watched as the gazes darted this way and that, from one side to the other, constantly expecting the next threat to pop up and surprise them. It was frightening. It was also heartbreaking. She could often tell by looking at the eyes if these dogs would be able to be re-homed or...not.

In this trio, she thought only one had possibilities.

She hoped she was wrong, but she'd been at this for a few years now. She knew her way around.

Once the three were into their cages—no easy feat and not done as gently as she liked, due to the new guy at Animal Control. Jeff? Jack? Jerk? Yeah, she liked Jerk. He yanked the dogs around by the leash pole and used a loud, threatening voice. He was much rougher, much angrier than she liked. Jerk's partner, Kevin, was much more seasoned and he caught the looks Lisa tossed his way. He did his best to redirect the new guy, but this was going to take some time. It took longer than normal to do the usual intake procedures, and once the dogs were caged and somewhat settled, Lisa's adrenaline flowed away and she was left with anger, exhaustion, and sorrow, her emotions too raw, too close to the surface.

She knew what she had to do.

⚬

Ashley felt like she'd been run over by a steamroller. A check of her watch had shocked her by letting her know it was after six. She had no idea how nearly four hours had flown by in what felt like forty-five minutes.

Bobby Griffin was sitting in the lounge chatting with one of the vet techs when she went in to get herself a cup of coffee. She was actually grateful they were in the midst of a conversation she wasn't a part of, as she had no desire to talk to anybody at the moment.

Not even Lisa.

Her comments had stung. So, Ashley froze. So what? It was a lot to take in. Yes, she should have taken some initiative or at least tried to help in some way, but…nothing she could do about it now.

She popped a cup into the Keurig and waited for her coffee to brew. Her phone, tucked in the back pocket of her jeans, buzzed, and she pulled it out to glance at the screen. A text from Carly. A sweet one.

I miss you. Dinner soon?

Ashley sighed quietly and tucked the phone back in her pocket without responding. She had never moved so slowly with anybody in her life. Intentionally, she knew. She hadn't even slept with Carly, and that was all Ashley's doing. Carly would be sleeping over every night if it were up to her. But Ashley kept the brakes on. And Carly let her.

Ashley hadn't seen Lisa in more than half an hour, and though the noise had settled to a somewhat less ear-splitting level, it was still loud. So she'd simply grabbed a dog to walk and allowed herself to get away from the dog wing for a little while.

She'd never seen an abuse case before. And today, there were three brought in at the same time. The dogs were loud and ferocious and so terribly scared, it broke her heart. And she did not like the way that one guy handled them. He was mean and far too enamored of the power he had over them. It made

145

her extremely uncomfortable to watch him, and despite being stung by Lisa's dismissal, she'd been glad to get away from the whole thing.

Coffee in hand now, she left the lounge and wandered around to look for Lisa. She needed to apologize for freezing. She wasn't anywhere in the dog wing or the medical suite (surgery was done for the day). Ashley even went out into the lobby, checked down the hall near Catherine Gardner's office, peeked into the gift shop. She walked out the front door and looked toward the goat pen. She'd been to the barn during her walk and had seen no sign of Lisa there. With a sigh, she turned and went back into the main building.

Bill Tracey was coming out of the gift shop carrying a long fluorescent bulb that Ashley assumed was burnt out. When he smiled a hello at her, she asked him if he'd seen Lisa.

"I think she went down to the basement," he said matter-of-factly.

"There's a basement?" This was news to Ashley. "I've worked here for almost five months and I had no idea there was a basement."

When Bill laughed, his eyes squinted and looked exponentially smaller behind his huge, out-of-style glasses. "Oh, yeah. There's a basement. Not many people go down there besides me." He explained where the door to it was and she was surprised to note that she'd walked right past it every day she'd volunteered.

She thanked him and headed toward the door.

It wasn't exactly dank and creepy, like lots of basements, but it was nothing special. Ashley descended the narrow flight of stairs to the bottom where she could smell an interesting mix of earth, damp, and dog food. The lighting was dim, limited to several bare bulbs spaced out along the rafters on the ceiling. To the left was a wall of shelving covered with various boxes and plastic storage containers, most neatly labeled. Reading the neat writing, she could see inventory for Maggie's shop, Christmas decorations, and various printed forms used at the front desk. Along the right wall stretched more shelving and then a small workbench. She assumed the bench was Bill's domain, judging by the tools, various slabs of scrap wood and pieces of small electronics. On those shelves sat bags and bags of dog food, cat food, and kitty litter.

Ahead of her loomed a hallway, and she headed in that direction, passing a couple alcoves too small to be called rooms. More bags of food along with stacks of blankets and towels, probably from public donations, lined the walls. As she perused the piles, a sound registered in her ears. She wasn't sure what it was, a smacking sound of some sort, like slapping or something. Ashley cocked her head and just listened for a moment. It was fairly steady—*smack, smack, smack*—and she followed the sound down the hall to the end.

There wasn't so much a doorway, as the hallway simply opened into an enormous room. It was still very much a basement, with cinder block walls and a concrete floor. It was darker on this end by just a bit, and she squinted to make out the scene in the far corner.

Hanging by a chain from the ceiling was one of those things boxers worked out on. A heavy bag? Ashley thought maybe that's what it was called. That wasn't the surprise, though. The surprise came in the form of the sweating, punching figure with her back to Ashley.

Lisa had changed into tight-fitting, capri-length workout pants, a gray T-shirt, and sneakers. On her hands were not boxing gloves, but some kind of padded protection in black and pink. She'd hit a rhythm and her punches, combined with the shuffling of her feet, made it look more like a dance than anything else. A darker V was visible on the back of her T-shirt where she'd worked up a sweat, and Ashley could see the matted hair at the base of her neck, perspiration making it look darker than its usual gold.

Ashley watched for a long moment, mesmerized by the movement, the rhythm, and strangely, a shockingly raw sensuality. Lisa's arms glistened with sweat, the veins standing out, the muscles shadowed and defined. Ashley wasn't really one for solid muscle on a woman—she liked soft and feminine —but there was something undeniably sexy about watching Lisa beat on the bag. After a few more moments, Ashley opened her mouth to let Lisa know she was there. Before she could make a sound, though, something else happened and she snapped her mouth shut.

Lisa stopped punching.

She wrapped her arms around the heavy bag, panting with exhaustion, leaned her forehead against it.

And then she started to cry.

Ashley's eyebrows rose in surprise as she realized what was happening. She pressed a hand to her heart, feeling actual pain as she witnessed Lisa's.

Lisa held onto the heavy bag and sobbed. After a second or two, she slid to the floor and sat there, sobbing quietly, her back to Ashley. With a bend forward, she covered her head with her arms as emotion poured out of her.

Ashley was torn. She wanted nothing more than to go to Lisa, to wrap her arms around her, to cradle her while she cried, murmur soft words to her, stroke her hair, simply hold her. But she also understood what an intensely private moment this was and somehow, she knew if she made her presence known, Lisa would be mortified, embarrassed beyond belief, and she did not want to be responsible for that.

Soundlessly, she backed away from the room, quickly and quietly retraced her steps, and went back upstairs.

Lisa felt better. The muscles in her arms and shoulders felt like wet noodles, and her knuckles sported a few broken capillaries marked by some red spots, but her head was clear and her anger had dissipated. She'd used her key to get into Jessica's office where there was a full bath and showered off the sweat and the emotion, then changed into a spare outfit she kept at the shelter for emergencies. When she'd first started working at Junebug, she'd been surprised by the bathroom. Turns out, Jessica's grandma June used to spend the night at the shelter on occasion and needed to be able to clean herself up in the morning, so Jessica's grandfather built her a bathroom. There were rare occasions when Lisa had a late intake to deal with, or sometimes David was in the midst of a fundraising push. Jessica had given each board member a key so they could take advantage if need be.

Her upper body would pay the price tomorrow, but she kind of liked that version of soreness, so she'd relish it. Feeling fresher, rejuvenated, Lisa headed back to the dog wing where the barking was still constant, but not as loud as earlier. It was after seven, and things seemed to have calmed down—at least a little. Thank God.

She had just taken a seat at her desk when Ashley came in the back door walking a border collie/Something Undefinable mix. The dog was super friendly and lovable, so Lisa had high hopes for its adoption. Whatever the "something undefinable" was, it tempered the energy level from the border collie side. Her gaze locked with Ashley's and she grinned, thrilled when Ashley smiled back at her.

"How is she on the lead?" Lisa asked.

"Not bad," came Ashley's reply as she unclipped the dog and put her back in her kennel. "She pulls a little, but listens well…until we saw a rabbit."

"That's to be expected. She probably wanted to herd it."

Ashley locked the cage and strolled down toward Lisa. "How're you doing?" she asked.

She looked amazing and Lisa almost laughed at the thought because Ashley would be mortified to hear it. She'd come to the shelter from the bakery and she smelled like cupcakes, as usual. But the ponytail sticking out the back of her hat was one big corkscrew curl, her cheeks were rosy, and Lisa couldn't help but notice—even during the height of the intake ruckus—that Ashley's jeans seemed to *love* her ass.

"I'm good," Lisa replied. "You?"

"I'm okay. Look, I'm sorry I froze earlier." Ashley's voice was soft and she avoided eye contact.

"Froze?" Lisa furrowed her brow.

"Yeah, when you yelled at me." Ashley met her gaze now.

"Oh. I didn't yell." Lisa cleared her throat, realizing with a start that she'd hurt Ashley's feelings. "I'm sorry you felt like I did. It was just…a little crazy around here, as you clearly saw."

Ashley gave a slow nod. "Okay." She inhaled slowly and said, "Well, I'm gonna hit the road. Good night." And with that, she hurried away, leaving Lisa looking after her in confusion.

What had just happened?

Lisa shook her head, slightly annoyed by feeling forced into playing mind games. Ashley obviously hadn't liked her dismissal earlier, but what was Lisa supposed to have done? Ashley had been just standing there. In the way. But not even that, so much. She'd looked…horrified by the scene unfolding in front of her, and that was no good for anyone. Maybe Lisa could've dismissed her in a gentler tone, but hell, she had been in the middle of dealing with vicious dogs and a jerk of an Animal Control Officer. Right then, it hadn't been about Ashley. You'd think that would be obvious. With a shrug and another shake of her head, Lisa went back to her paperwork. She'd deal with this later.

It was another hour before she got home, a longer night than she'd expected and Keeler relieved himself for what seemed like ten minutes when Lisa took him outside. "Sorry, buddy," she whispered, then kissed him on the head. "Got caught up with some dog fighting victims." Keeler looked up at her with his big brown eyes as though he completely understood and she kissed him again even as she shook her head and tried to dislodge the three pit bulls from her thoughts.

It was one of the hardest parts of her job: leaving work at work. And part of her didn't mind that she kept thinking about the animals long after she left the shelter; what would it say about her as a human if she didn't? But she was usually able to at least turn the volume down a bit so she could focus on her home life instead of only work. That being said, now and then something just stuck in her brain and wouldn't completely let go. Today, it was Kevin's partner at Animal Control. She was going to have to say something because that man should *not* be handling animals.

And on days like this, the heavy bag in the basement was a godsend.

It had been David's idea. About eight months ago, there had been a particularly horrific example of animal cruelty. The abused animals were collected from the home of the accused and dispersed among the local shelters. It had been horrible. Beaten, starving, terrified animals. Some were diseased. Some were beyond repair psychologically or physically or both and had to be put down. It had taken its toll on several of the workers at Junebug—a dark handful of weeks, indeed. On one particular day, Lisa had been so angry that she snapped at every single person she crossed paths with, the majority of whom did not deserve her ire. David had been walking by at a moment when Lisa was about to shred some poor volunteer to ribbons and he'd simply closed his huge hand around her elbow and steered her away without saying anything other than, "Come with me."

She'd gone without argument, as David was huge and imposing and wouldn't have redirected her without cause. Plus, deep down, she knew she was being unreasonable and unfair and she also knew exactly why she was so frustrated. When they'd reached the heavy bag in the basement, she cocked her head in surprise. David had simply pointed at it and said, "That's the abuser. Give him what he deserves."

Lisa had blinked at him.

David pointed at the bag again. "He starved and abused nearly twenty-five animals, Lisa," he said loudly, his voice taking on an angry edge.

Lisa looked at the bag, threw a timid punch.

"Really? That's your best shot?"

She leveled a look at him, her anger building back up.

"I'm not the one you're pissed at," he said, a valid point. He gestured to the bag again. "It's that guy."

This time, she balled her fist and threw a real punch.

"Now you're talking. Again."

She obeyed him as he egged her on until she was throwing punch combinations and sweat ran down her back. It didn't take long before a pained cry worked its way up from her lungs and escaped from her throat. That was all it took. She continued to beat on the bag even as tears ran down her face and sobs ripped out of her. She threw punches until she could barely lift her arms any more. When she finally stopped and dropped her arms to her sides, feeling spent and blessedly empty of the rage, she turned to look at David. His expression of sympathy was something she'd never forget.

"Feel better?" he asked softly.

And she had....

Back in the townhouse, she fed Keeler and the cats, made herself a turkey sandwich, and sat on the couch with her dinner and a glass of wine. She clicked on the TV and was twenty minutes into the latest episode of *Castle* when her phone beeped with a text. From her mother.

Hi, sweetie. Just thinking about you and wanted to say hello. What are you up to tonight?

Lisa paused the television show and reread the text. She sucked in a big breath and blew it out loudly enough to scare Clyde, who was perched on the back of the couch. She typed back.

Hi. Long day at work. Just got home.

Her mother's response only took a minute.

Just now? That IS a long day. Eat something decent for supper, okay?

The mixed emotions Lisa felt when her mother said something like that were hard to deal with, because her first response was always warmth and happiness that her mother cared about what she was eating. It didn't last long before that first response was bulldozed by the second response, which was always anger and irritation and she had to physically set the phone down, out of reach, to keep herself from typing back, *Now you want to make sure I'm eating something decent? What about when I was twenty and trying to feed not only myself, but your sons? Where were you then?* It never failed and Lisa always wondered why she hadn't simply grown used to it. She gave herself a few moments to let the second response pass before she retrieved the phone and typed something sane.

Turkey sandwich. I'm good.

Lisa absently pet Tiny, who was curled up next to her thigh, as it occurred to her that the contact from her mother seemed to be getting more frequent. And were Lisa's responses slightly less snarky? "Well, let's not go *that* far," she muttered aloud. She didn't want to analyze this. Analyzing it meant actually thinking about it and she didn't want to do that either. She'd grown very comfortable and familiar with her anger toward her mother. There was no desire to poke at it. She picked up the remote and started *Castle* up again.

This week's red herring character was blonde, chipper, very cute, and reminded Lisa of Ashley, which was slightly ridiculous as the actress didn't really resemble her physically in any other way but the color of her hair. And thinking of Ashley brought her back to the earlier conversation, the look of hurt on Ashley's face.

She probably should have handled that differently. Better, somehow. But honestly, in that moment, she hadn't had time to worry about somebody who froze in horror during a crisis, somebody who needed her hand held. They'd all been horrified, but they still had difficult work to do, and right then, Ashley had been the only one not up for the job. Too harsh? Maybe. Or maybe it was just reality, and reality could sometimes sting. She liked Ashley. Liked her a lot, in fact. Thought they might possibly be able to have something good together.

But she was not going to take care of her.

No, she wasn't going to take care of anybody ever again.

CHAPTER THIRTEEN

"THIS IS GOOD," ASHLEY said, forcing a smile as she took another bite of her barbecued chicken.

"Thanks." Carly's smile was wide. "I don't cook a lot of things, but I can grill and I have a few go-to dishes. This is one of them." She studied Ashley's face as they ate. "I'm so glad you're here. I didn't think you were ever going to let me cook you dinner."

Ashley shrugged as she chuckled. "If I'd known it would be this good, I'd have come sooner."

Carly's house was kind of adorable, small but the space was used very functionally. She seemed partial to green, as the walls in the living room and kitchen were both an inviting sage. The hardwood floors were white oak and a thick, soft area rug pulled the entire open floor plan together. Ashley had been impressed when she walked through and out the sliding glass door to the small deck. A bistro table was set for two, and Carly had poured her a glass of Pinot Grigio and told her to sit and talk to her while she grilled the chicken and vegetables.

Now, they sat across from each other in the lovely Sunday evening sunshine. Carly had her portable speaker sitting on the railing playing The Piano Guys softly. The wine was smooth. The food was delicious. A bird was chirping overhead. Carly looked so happy.

Ashley wanted to run.

"You okay?" Carly asked, pulling her out of her own head. "You look a little pale. Still not over that bug?"

"Not quite," Ashley agreed, mortified at how easy it had become to lie to Carly.

"Well, you need to take better care of yourself. You put in so many hours and you start so early at the bakery." Carly stabbed a piece of zucchini with her fork. "Maybe you should put the shelter on the back burner for a while. Just until you feel better."

"Maybe," Ashley said on a sigh. A week ago, she'd have been furious with Carly for even suggesting such a thing, but now? She thought back to Lisa, to the fear that Lisa thought she was weak, oversensitive. She hadn't said so. Not in so many words. But Ashley could see it. Remembered the disappointed —and irritated—look on her face when Animal Control had brought those dogs in and Ashley hadn't been able to move, the annoyed dismissal. Ashley had expected an apology later, understanding that sometimes a crisis made people say and do things they didn't mean. And Lisa had apologized...but not really.

So Ashley had gone home and waited for a phone call or text.

Neither had come.

That was three days ago.

Throwing herself into things with Carly was probably not the best course of action, in hindsight. But here she was, eating chicken on the back deck, sipping wine, and being smiled at.

It all made her ill.

And angry. There was anger, if she was going to be honest. Anger because she still wanted Lisa. After everything that had happened and everything that had been said, she still wanted Lisa.

What the hell is the matter with me?

Ashley forced herself to return to the present where Carly was talking about her job. Smiling, she nodded like she'd been paying close attention the entire time. Tipping her wineglass up, she emptied it.

"More?" Carly asked, pulling the bottle out of an ice bucket, one of those fancy modern ones with no ice. It just stayed in the freezer.

"Please." Ashley held out her glass and watched as the golden liquid filled it. Then she took a much-too-large swallow.

"Easy there, tiger," Carly said with a smile that didn't quite reach her eyes.

"What?"

"Just…maybe not such big gulps, you know?"

"No? Why not?" The anger was back. Ashley could feel it simmering in her gut. She tried to tamp it down, but it bubbled.

Carly shrugged, clearly trying to avoid an argument. "No reason. Just saying."

"That I need to be told how to drink my wine?"

Carly's eyes widened. "No. Not at all. Are you sure you're all right? You've been so…different lately."

Had she? Well, maybe that was a good thing. She inhaled slowly, managed to calm her escalating heartbeat. "I'm sorry. I'm fine. Just…tense."

"S'okay." Carly smiled, but seemed wary. "So, I was saying that I have two appointments next week with two new, really big clients…"

And we're off. Ashley felt bad. She did. But she'd had enough. She knew it right then. She wasn't sure why. What she was sure of was that the sudden horrifying vision she had of a lifetime of conversation about computer equipment and being told how much wine she was allowed was enough to shake some sense into her. She set her wineglass down and cleared her throat.

"Carly."

Carly looked up at her, chewing a mouthful of chicken. "Hmm?"

"This isn't working for me."

Carly's eyebrows rose and she looked around the table at the food and wine, obviously trying to pinpoint what part of the meal Ashley was talking about. Ashley reached across the small table and closed her hand over Carly's forearm.

"No. Carly. This." With her other hand, she gestured between them. "Us. We are not working for me."

Carly finished her mouthful of chicken in what looked like a rather painful swallow. "What? What do you mean?"

"You're awesome. You are. You're kind and sweet and attractive."

"But?"

"But it's not working for me. I think we need to stop." Ashley bit her bottom lip. "I'm sorry."

Carly sat back in her chair, sliding her arm from Ashley's grasp. With a hand, she rubbed the back of her neck, eyes wide as if trying to see something she couldn't. "Wow. I…I thought we had something here."

"I'm sorry," Ashley repeated.

Carly held up a hand. "Yeah, don't say that again."

Ashley stayed quiet.

"I just…I don't…" Carly blew out a breath. "I have so many questions, but I don't think they'll matter." She gazed off into the small backyard. "I wish you'd have told me sooner."

Ashley nodded, opened her mouth to apologize again, but closed it in time.

With a humorless chuckle, Carly pulled her napkin from her lap, wiped her mouth, and tossed it to the table. "Not exactly where I thought this night was leading."

She thought we'd sleep together tonight. The thought slammed into Ashley's brain and she knew in that moment that she'd made the right decision. "I'll help you clean up and then I'll go."

"No, it's okay. I'll get it. You can go. You're free."

The last line was dripping with sarcasm, but Ashley let it go. Sliding off her chair, she stood there for a minute while Carly carefully did not look at her. "I'll just get my keys. Bye." She felt horrible. The look of pained sadness on Carly's face was hard to bear, especially knowing she'd put it there. She let herself into the small house, marveling at the fact that it was the first and last time she'd see it, picked her keys up off the kitchen counter, and left through the side door.

Ashley had never done the leaving. She'd never broken up with somebody before. She'd always been the one who'd been left and she knew how awful that could make you feel, how crappy you could feel about yourself, how insecure. Being the person who *caused* the pain was new to her. And she was genuinely surprised to find out that it sucked just as badly, if not more.

She drove home feeling like the worst human being on the planet.

─◆─

The next morning did *not* dawn brightly and give Ashley a brand-new, fresh, clean, happy, sunny slate on which to begin the next phase of her life. No. It was gray and wet and raining.

Like her mood. A restless night had her hitting the snooze alarm one too many times, which ensured she had no time for coffee or breakfast at home and would have to grab some at work, where she clocked in with barely a minute to spare.

"You look like you got about three minutes of sleep last night," Stella commented as she watched Ashley sip her coffee like she needed it to survive.

"That sounds about right," Ashley replied, voice husky.

"You okay?"

"I will be. I think."

"Wanna talk about it?"

"I do not." Ashley took any sting out of the words by reaching to Stella and giving her upper arm a squeeze. "But thank you."

Katie Stanger took that moment to bounce into the area, a giant smile on her face. She was followed closely by Beth Carter, one of the owners of the bakery. Ashley straightened her stance and noticed Stella follow suit. A few other employees had drifted into the space and Ashley furrowed her brow, wondering what was going on.

Beth Carter was in her early sixties, but looked fifteen years younger. Her short, ash-blond hair was cut in a hip style and her glasses were funky, purple earpieces connected to silver fronts. She was small in stature, but made up for it with her huge personality and warm smile. One of those people who made you instantly comfortable, she was like everyone's favorite aunt...which was not to say she was a pushover. One didn't end up with the most successful bakery in the city by lying down and letting people walk on you.

"Good morning, my little marshmallow peeps," she said, her voice cheerful. "I have an announcement." Reaching to her left, she grasped Katie's arm. "I'd like to introduce to you our new head of ordering and delivery, Katie Stanger." The round of applause that went through the small crowd of people was polite, though a few looks of confusion were exchanged. "She'll be taking care of all the ordering of supplies as well as shipments of cookies and cakes. So if you've got questions, see Katie or myself. It's a new position, so there'll be a learning curve. But if we're all patient, we'll get there."

Katie just about glowed with excited anticipation and it was hard not to be happy for her. Still, a pit of unpleasantness sat in Ashley's stomach, making the next swallow of coffee feel like acid. Making a face, she set her cup down as the gang got back to work and Katie bounced off at Beth's side.

"Um, what just happened?" Martha asked, eyes wide.

"Tigger got a promotion," Stella informed her.

Ashley let a slight smile cross her face, but she didn't partake in the mocking. Something wouldn't let her. Instead, she shrugged and headed to the day's cookies, her mind a jumble of uncertainty.

The rest of the day was uneventful and went by more slowly than Ashley would have liked. It was hard to describe how she felt and so many words passed through her head in the attempt. Confused. Irritated. Sad. Envious. Bummed. She frosted twenty-seven dozen cookies and then helped Katie figure out how to fill out the shipping form and send them to the companies that placed the orders. Katie paid surprisingly close attention and was very appreciative of the help.

Ashley was just getting ready to pack up for the day when there was a knock on the wall near her desk. She looked up to see Beth Carter leaning against it, a gentle smile on her face.

"Hi, Ashley."

"Mrs. Carter. How are you?" Ashley had know the woman since she was seventeen years old, but still couldn't bring herself to call her by her first name.

"I'm good." She looked around as if to ensure they were alone, then she lowered her voice a little anyway. "And a bit confused."

Ashley's eyebrows climbed to her hairline. "By?"

"By why you didn't apply for any of the manager openings. I know you saw them. You're more than qualified..." Beth let her voice trail off and her own eyebrows rose in expectation.

"Oh, I..." Ashley swallowed down a sudden lump of nerves that had lodged in her throat. Searching for a response was fruitless and she felt her face flush with embarrassment as she simply shrugged.

"Are you unhappy here? You're one of my best employees. If something isn't working for you, I want to know."

Ashley could tell by Beth's tone that she was honestly worried about her and that just made her feel worse. "I'm very happy here. Very."

A flash of relief zipped across Beth's face. "Well, that's something I suppose. I just...I really thought you'd apply for one of the jobs. Any of them would have been yours." Moving in a step closer, she dropped her voice to a whisper. "Katie wasn't my first choice for ordering, but the girl has enthusiasm in spades and she reaches for what she wants, so..." She let the sentence dangle and her expression said, "Oh, well." She squeezed Ashley's shoulder and left.

Ashley stood quietly at her desk for long moments trying to absorb what she'd just learned. Again, a myriad of feelings ran through her. Sadness. Frustration. Disappointment. Embarrassment. And she couldn't just go home...though she realized that she didn't want to. She had a shift at the shelter and she had no intention of bailing on it, despite how crappy she felt right now.

She thought of the resident dogs, of Lisa, of the new dogs, of Lisa, and all of a sudden, it hit her. God, she was so stupid. Out of the blue, just like that, she got it. She laughed out loud, causing more than a couple of curious looks from nearby employees, but she just grinned and waved at them.

She got it.

Now, to do something about it.

CHAPTER FOURTEEN

IT WAS NEARING THREE o'clock in the afternoon, and things were starting to slow down a bit, thank God. The dog wing had been fairly busy with browsers for much of the day, but now only one person wandered the floor, peering into cages and scanning clipboards. The barking had died down and only occasional yaps punctuated the air, harmonizing with the whines. Lisa watched on the monitor for a few moments, then spun her chair around and focused on the intake papers for the two new dogs that had arrived this morning.

She didn't hear Ashley's approach until her hands rested on Lisa's desk and she leaned almost directly into Lisa's space. Looking up, Lisa blinked in surprise at the expression Ashley sported: flashing eyes, an arched eyebrow, full, glossy lips and flushed cheeks. It was shockingly sexy.

"You're abrupt," Ashley said without preamble.

Lisa squinted at her. "I'm sorry?"

"And you can be kind of abrasive."

"Okay." Lisa drew the word out, no idea what was happening. She tossed a glance toward the browser, but he wasn't looking so must not have heard.

"Sometimes, you're a little cold."

Lisa straightened her stance, defensiveness seeping in. "Is there a point to this…barrage of compliments?"

"There is." Ashley took a deep breath and blew it out as a slow smile pulled up the corners of her mouth. "The point is that you also make me brave."

Though she really liked that smile, Lisa was now completely confounded. "Okay, you lost me. What are you talking about?"

Ashley stood up straight and looked around as if checking to make sure they weren't being overheard. "I had an epiphany," she said, then laughed a laugh so sweet and genuine that Lisa couldn't help but smile along with her. "I don't rock the boat. I don't step out of line. It's not who I am. And most of the time, I'm okay with that. I like comfortable and familiar. It's... comfortable."

"And familiar?" Lisa winked.

"Funny. But yes. It can also be dead, dull, boring." With a self-deprecating chuckle, she scratched at her forehead and said, "You know what else I don't do?"

"Tell me."

"I don't apply for jobs I should apply for because I'm too passive."

"I see."

"Know what else I don't do?"

"What?"

"I don't kiss a beautiful woman in a darkened hallway in the middle of a work party. Ask that same woman to coffee. Kiss her again on a park bench. I don't do that stuff."

Lisa narrowed her eyes at her. "But you *did* do all that stuff."

"That's right. I did. Because *you* make me brave." Ashley leaned forward again, her excitement and enthusiasm so damn sexy Lisa had to consciously keep her butt in her chair to prevent herself from grabbing Ashley's face and kissing her senseless right there in the middle of the dogs. "Have dinner with me," Ashley whispered. "We have something here, Lisa. You feel it, too. I know you do."

She wasn't wrong. Lisa knew that much. Could they give this a try?

Lisa rolled it around in her head as Ashley's blue eyes held hers. She was uncertain. The two of them were very different, that much was obvious. There would inevitably be head-butting. And probably hand-holding—she tried to contain the grimace. Remembering that their chemistry was off the charts certainly helped. She couldn't remember that last time she'd been kissed the way Ashley kissed her, if ever. Which definitely boded well for...other things. But was that enough? The silence stretched until she saw Ashley's face flinch slightly, her confident mask slipping just a touch. What could it hurt, right? She was only asking for dinner. She hadn't proposed. Lisa glanced at the guy still perusing the dogs, then turned back to Ashley. "Okay. Dinner."

"And a movie."

Lisa quirked an eyebrow. "Demanding."

"Damn right."

"Okay. Dinner and a movie. When?"

"Saturday. I'll pick you up. Text me your address."

"Demanding and bossy. This is certainly a new you."

"You have no idea. Now give me a leash so I can get to work."

Without a word, Lisa grabbed a leash and a clipboard and handed them over. Ashley thanked her, winked, and headed for her first dog. Lisa watched her walk away, watched that gentle sway of her hips, the bounce of her ponytail sticking out the back of her hat. She was the same, but different. Lisa had no other way to explain it. What had happened? She had no idea, but it was intriguing.

Intriguing lasted for the rest of the afternoon and until Lisa got home. Once there, an insistent, thrumming panic began in the pit of her stomach as she fed her animals and sifted through her mail. The feeling was familiar, nothing new to her. She knew where it came from, knew she was hesitant around people who could hurt her, steered clear of potential heartbreak, because of her childhood. Her mother walking out on her family had shocked her, shocked the lot of them. It stopped her life in its tracks for long months. The whole issue had shaped young Lisa, taught her to tailor her life, educated her so that she learned to step carefully so as not to have anybody blindside her that way again. Ever.

She couldn't step carefully if Ashley was running the entire evening.

Before she could stop herself, she picked up her phone and typed out a text.

How do you feel about a change in plans? My house for dinner and movie instead of out?

She hit Send before she could think hard about it and caught her bottom lip between her teeth as she waited.

———

"Well, that's interesting," Jenna said, reading over Ashley's shoulder.

Ashley shrugged her off, tilted her phone from view. Pressing the pause button on the episode of *Scandal* they were watching, she asked, "What's interesting?"

"She's changing plans on you."

"So?"

Jenna sat back on Ashley's couch and studied her friend for a moment. "Wasn't the whole idea of you asking her out because you wanted to take the bull by the horns? For once? 'She makes me brave'?" Jenna made air quotes with her fingers.

"I just want to spend some time with her," Ashley retorted as she began typing a response. Somewhere in the back of her brain, a little voice was telling her to listen to Jenna, to consider what she was saying, that maybe she had a point and Ashley should stop. Ponder a bit. Instead, her fingers kept typing and she hit Send before she could prevent it. When she glanced up, Jenna was looking at her with a strange expression. It took a beat or two before Ashley realized it was pity, which pissed her off. "What?" she snapped.

It was only because she knew Jenna so well that she saw the flinch of pain flash across her face. Jenna put her hands up, palms out, like a robbery victim. "Hey, I'm just trying to help you. I don't know why you get mad at me." She picked up the coffee she'd been sipping and sat back with it in both hands. "You made some progress today, had a sort of breakthrough, and I don't want to see you backpedal. That's all." She took a sip of her coffee, watching Ashley over the rim of her mug. Then she shrugged. "You're a big girl. If you want to date a control freak, go for it."

"She's not a control freak."

Jenna simply raised both eyebrows.

"All right, she's a little bit of a control freak."

Jenna set her mug down and turned on the couch so she faced Ashley. "How long have we known each other?"

"Long time."

"Do you think I know you pretty well?"

Ashley gave a soft smile. "Probably better than anybody."

169

"I agree with that. And was I the only one sitting here an hour ago when you told me all about your crazy epiphany today? How you realized that you're kind of passive in your own life and you want to change that? That you feel like Lisa gives you courage?"

"I was here," Ashley said quietly and looked down at her hands.

Jenna wet her lips and seemed to take a moment to find the right words. "Then hold on to that. You're not magically going to become the alpha dog. We both know that. You're going to have no choice but to baby step it. But don't go backward if you can help it."

This was uncomfortable.

Ashley could admit that, and the rolling in her stomach was proof. Talking about an unfavorable personality trait wasn't easy for anybody, but it was especially hard to talk about it with somebody who's known you for so long, somebody who already knows this aspect of you. Ashley wanted to crawl under a rock and hide. But she didn't. She simply nodded.

"And you've made some huge strides," Jenna said, reaching for Ashley's forearm and gripping it warmly. "Breaking things off with Carly?" Jenna held her hands up and looked at the ceiling. "Amazing." Making a face at Ashley, she added, "Not for Carly, of course, but holy shit. That was a huge step." When she looked directly into Ashley's eyes, she must have seen something there. The embarrassment? The worry? Ashley wasn't sure. All she knew was that Jenna's voice got quiet and her expression turned tender. "I just don't want to see you get hurt. That's all. I love you. You know?"

"I do know. I love you, too."

A few minutes later, they were back to watching Kerry Washington be flawless on the television, but Ashley's mind was wandering. Jenna was right. She knew that. She was right about Ashley and she was right about Lisa.

Lisa.

What was it about her that drew Ashley so strongly, like bumblebee to an open flower? Lisa was so not her type. At all. She was cold. She was distant. She was authoritative—and not always in a good way. She was bossy and dismissive of people. But...Ashley flashed to that day in the shelter basement, of Lisa battering the heavy bag, then dissolving into tears over some abused animals...she was also sometimes sensitive. Ashley's brain tossed her an image of kissing Lisa at the beach house, up against the wall, face flushed, lips swollen, eyes dark and heavy; Lisa was sometimes vulnerably sexy. Ashley recalled their coffee date, the amazing conversation, the intense interest on her gorgeous face. Lisa could be open and warm.

Is that how life worked? One day, you had somebody who was kind and gentle and sweet and wanted nothing more than to look after you? And then the next, you meet someone who is none of those things—the polar opposite, in fact—but who pulls you toward her as if she'd lassoed you with some unbreakable rope, and you have no choice but to be tugged along? And you let go of the person who has all the right qualities so you can use both hands to hold on to that rope while you follow the person with the wrong ones, the person who terrifies you? The person who could slice you open with little effort and watch while you bleed out onto the floor? Is that how life worked?

She glanced over at Jenna, who was hunkered down so her butt was on the very edge of the couch and her knees were up, feet propped on the coffee table, engrossed in the show, obviously unaware of the crazy, twisty path Ashley's brain was taking. Ashley envied her for a moment before she was submerged once again in the pool of questions.

Would she get any of them answered?

She had been so looking forward to this date with Lisa. Still was, really. But now there was a new emotion involved: fear.

CHAPTER FIFTEEN

LISA WAS NERVOUS, AND it was pissing her off.

She wasn't normally a nervous person, either. Being nervous freaked her out a bit and made her clumsy. She'd already broken a glass, stubbed her toe on the foot of her bed, torn the seam of the shirt she wanted to wear, and stepped on one of the cats, who was none too happy about it judging from the pained squeak he let out.

Standing in the kitchen, she put her palms out in front of her like a magician and just willed herself to breathe calmly, to relax her tensed muscles, to ease the rhythm of her pounding heart.

She was aware of the little panic attack that had her convincing Ashley to let her cook instead, and then they could watch a movie here. Ashley had hesitated, but ultimately agreed, and while Lisa was relieved by that, she was also slightly disappointed. Which was crazy, because why the hell couldn't she make up her mind?

Regardless, the ball was back in Lisa's court where she liked it. Except she was nervous. She knew exactly why...she just didn't want to *think* about why. Instead, she went to the refrigerator and opened it, forcing herself to focus on dinner. That would occupy her mind. She removed the Ziploc bag that held marinating chicken breasts. She also grabbed ingredients for salad. A sizzling sound caught her attention and a swear word escaped her lips as she grabbed the pot of boiling-over rice off the burner. Lowering the heat, she set it back down and gave it a stir as two different cats wove themselves between and around her ankles. A glance at the clock on the stove told her Ashley would arrive any minute.

Ashley would arrive any minute.

So many mixed emotions about that statement...

The doorbell pulled her off of that train of thought—thankfully. Lisa put a lid on the pot, smoothed her hands over her hips as she blew out a slow breath, then tucked her hair behind her ears. A quick glance in the mirror in the foyer told her things were as good as they were likely to be in the appearance department, and she wet her lips as she pulled the door open.

Lisa swallowed hard.

Ashley wore soft-looking capri-length jeans and a button-down tank top in a royal blue that made the color of her eyes pop. Her blonde hair was in a French braid down the back of her head and several rebellious wisps lined her tanned face, looking like they were intentionally curled around a finger before being allowed to dangle in front of an ear or along the side of her neck. A silver watch was clasped around one wrist and in that hand was a bottle of red wine. The other hand held a small, colorful bouquet of daisies, which Ashley held toward Lisa with a smile.

"Hi," Ashley said softly. "These are for you. Also, you look amazing. Wow."

Lisa felt herself blush as Ashley's gaze roamed from her sandaled feet up her bare legs over the skirt of her grass-green sundress with the cream-colored polka dots, stopped briefly at the peek of cleavage, then continued to move up until it settled on Lisa's eyes.

"Hi," Ashley said again.

"Hi," Lisa replied, feeling a wide grin cross her face. "Come on in." She stepped aside and let Ashley enter just as Keeler made his way from the living room. "Wow, buddy, you're a little slow on the uptake today. She's been here for a good thirty seconds, you know."

Keeler ignored his mistress, instead choosing to bathe the new arrival in love and kisses—tardy or not—which Ashley seemed to love almost as much, given how quickly she handed the bottle of wine off to Lisa and plopped herself on the floor. Lisa shook her head with affection as she closed the door and took the wine and flowers into the kitchen.

"I'm going to throw some chicken on the grill. Is that okay with you?" she asked.

"Sounds perfect," came the answer, punctuated with girlish giggles as two of the cats joined in on the love fest on the floor.

"I'm going to open this wine and I'll leave a glass for you on the counter if you want it," Lisa said in a teasing tone.

"I want it. I want it." Ashley managed to get herself back to standing. "God, don't you ever give these animals any love? They seem so neglected."

"Love?" Lisa asked, feigning a face of confusion as she pried the cork from the bottle. "What do you mean? Why would I love them? I give them food, shelter, a warm bed to sleep in. You mean I have to love them, too? Nobody told me that."

Ashley laughed as she took a wineglass from Lisa's hand and held it up. "To love," she said, and the glimmer in her eye had Lisa feeling warm and slightly panicked at the same time. They touched glasses, sipped, and then Lisa pulled her gaze away from Ashley's to get the chicken.

"Come outside with me?" she asked.

Ashley grabbed Lisa's wine and followed her through the living room and out the sliding glass door to the small patio. Lisa's shiny new grill gleamed in the fading sun and Ashley held a hand out, obviously feeling the heat from it. "Do you cook a lot?" she asked.

"I used to a long time ago. Then I sort of got away from it for a while." Lisa opened the lid of the grill and laid the chicken breasts on the rack with a sizzle. "I've been getting back into it more recently."

"You cooked for your dad and brothers," Ashley stated, obviously remembering Lisa's past.

"I did. So once I moved out, it was kind of a relief not to have to cook for three other people. I ate a lot of takeout for a while there," she added with a laugh. "It was not a good year for my hips, believe me."

Ashley shook her head with a smile. "I find it hard to believe you were ever anything but gorgeous."

Her voice was soft, her eyes sincere, and Lisa felt a tingle low in her body. She cast her eyes back to her cell phone and the timer she'd set for the chicken. "Well. I don't know about that."

"I'm sure of it."

"Thanks."

"Welcome."

They sipped, studying one another over the rims of their glasses and that was the moment that Lisa knew exactly where things would end up tonight.

"So. Tell me about your day," Lisa said as she checked the chicken.

Ashley perched on the edge of an Adirondack chair, then let her butt slide backward until she was tucked snugly into the body of it. "Oh, let's see. I went to see my mom and stepdad. I try to stop by on the weekend if I can, have a cup of coffee with them and catch up."

"Every weekend?" Lisa could hardly imagine.

"I try," Ashley said with a shrug. "Doesn't always happen."

"And you like your stepdad?"

"He's great. Treats my mom like a queen."

Lisa's phone beeped and she turned away to open the grill. "What about your dad?"

"God, that smells good," Ashley said from directly behind her, her nose so close to Lisa's neck she wasn't sure if Ashley was talking about the chicken or her. A pleasant shiver ran along her spine as she used tongs to flip each piece.

"Thank you," she said quietly, then arched an eyebrow in expectation.

"Oh, right. My dad." Ashley took a step back out of Lisa's personal space, and Lisa felt the loss immediately. "My dad is dating somebody new from what my mother keeps telling me."

"Your parents still talk?"

"Oh, yeah. They're pals. Better pals than they were spouses, actually." Ashley smiled, as if that was the most normal thing in the world to say. Lisa just blinked at her as she went on. "My dad has dated on and off since their divorce. He's even had a couple of steadies, but this one—according to my very nosy mother—is a big deal."

"Have you met her?"

With a shake of her head, Ashley said, "No, but he wants me to. So, maybe soon."

Lisa nodded, trying to imagine sitting down to a meal with her mother and some new beau. It was not an image that slid smoothly into place. At all. It was yet another reminder how different she and Ashley were. Removing the chicken from the grill to a plate, she turned to Ashley. "Hungry?"

They ate at the small table tucked into the breakfast nook, laughing and talking, and Lisa couldn't remember the last time she'd felt this comfortable with somebody. It was an unfamiliar, strangely uneasy feeling that, at the same time, had her stomach doing an enjoyable fluttering thing and had her leaning forward in her chair to better hear (and see) Ashley when she spoke.

"More wine?" Lisa asked.

"Love some." As Lisa stood to get the bottle from the counter, Ashley went on. "This is fabulous, by the way." She held up her fork with a piece of chicken on it.

"It's just chicken, rice and salad. Not terribly complicated." Lisa topped off each glass. "But thank you."

"Well, I don't cook much, so…thank *you*."

When dinner was done, they stood together, but Ashley held up a hand. "No. Sit. I got this."

Lisa shook her head. "It's okay. I'm used to cleaning up."

"Lisa." Ashley's tone stopped her in her tracks and she met kind blue eyes. "Please," Ashley said softly. "Sit. You cooked. Let me take care of this. All right?"

Much to her own surprise, Lisa felt herself sinking back into her chair. "And what should I do while you're cleaning?" she asked.

"Sit there and look pretty." Ashley held her gaze and a sensual sizzle ran between them. Lisa sipped her wine and, after a few moments of uncertainty, allowed herself to sit back and enjoy the view, which was ridiculously sexy, she had to admit. The soft-looking denim of Ashley's capris hugged her backside closely, and Lisa had an almost unstoppable urge to slide her hands into the back pockets. The tank left Ashley's shoulders bare, a smattering of freckles visible on each one, the smoothness of the skin apparent even from where Lisa sat. She felt her heart rate kick up a notch as Ashley glanced over her shoulder and smiled. Lisa sipped her wine to distract herself.

It was nearly nine o'clock when they carried their glasses into the living room and made themselves comfortable on the couch while discussing movie options. Ashley kicked off her shoes, as did Lisa, and put in her vote for a critically acclaimed independent film, a romantic dramedy. Lisa agreed with the choice and pushed the necessary buttons on the remote. When she sat back, Ashley's arm was up, offering the space beneath it to her. Surprisingly unhesitant, Lisa snuggled in against her and asked, "Is this okay?"

"It's very okay," Ashley replied with a smile. She gave Lisa a squeeze and then tucked her hand against Lisa's side. Keeler somehow fit his not-terribly-small body between the couch and the coffee table, so both women propped their feet up on the table. Three of the four cats found spots on the couch as well, Groucho next to Ashley's thigh, Tiny on Lisa's lap, and Clyde along the back. Ashley started to chuckle.

Lisa hit the pause button on the remote and craned her neck to look up at her. "What?"

"I just had a flash of Snow White. You know, with all the animals circling around her? I'm waiting for these guys to start singing or something."

Lisa grinned. "They might. You never know."

The movie was good. At least, Lisa was pretty sure it was. She'd lost the ability to concentrate about a half hour in when Ashley's fingers began to move against her skin, trailing a delicious path from her elbow up to the top of her shoulder, circling, then traveling back down. Up and down...up and down...so slowly and sensually that goose bumps broke out along her entire body, and the gentle throbbing between her legs made it hard to focus on the television screen. Swallowing hard, she furrowed her brow and did her best to ignore what her body wanted and concentrate on the film.

Her mind would not allow it, however. Instead, it insisted on taking in every single thing about Ashley that it could. Her scent—still vaguely like cupcakes, but also fresher: soap, coconut, a little musk. The softness of her hands as they moved along Lisa's skin. Warm, velvety, with just enough length to her nails for Lisa to feel the gentle scratch. The color of her hair, which Lisa could scrutinize from her vantage point of being on Ashley's shoulder. So many different shades of gold...lighter on top where the sun could have its way, darker underneath, and several varying colors in between, the waves curling around on themselves.

Yanked suddenly out of her reverie by the words, "Don't you?"

Lisa looked up at Ashley, whose beautiful blue eyes sparkled in amusement.

Lisa cleared her throat and spoke. "I'm sorry. Um...what?"

"Are you even watching this movie?" Ashley asked, her voice low and husky.

Lisa shook her head slowly.

"Oh, good. Then it's okay if I do this." Finger under Lisa's chin, Ashley tipped it up and brought her mouth down slowly, inch by inch, until only scant millimeters separated their lips. Her eyes searched Lisa's and Lisa held her gaze, every fiber in her body as taut as a rubber band stretched to its limit, waiting, anticipating, preparing...

When their lips finally met, it was like a jolt of electricity, hot and bright. Ashley had the softest mouth in the world, Lisa was certain, and she savored the feel of it. The taste. "God, why do you taste so good?" she asked, not realizing she'd posed the question aloud until she felt Ashley chuckling.

"Obviously so that you'll keep kissing me," Ashley replied. "Is it working?"

Lisa responded by grabbing the back of Ashley's neck to pull her closer.

Tiny and Groucho both decided they'd had enough at this point and abandoned ship, followed shortly by Clyde, which was fine by Lisa, as it allowed her to get closer to Ashley. She pushed forward and tossed her leg over Ashley's thigh. Then Ashley pushed back and they played that delicious game for a long while, that push and pull, their mouths never parting.

The movie played on unwatched. When Lisa shifted to straddle Ashley's lap, her bare foot brushed Keeler's back, and the last animal evacuated the living room.

Lisa grinned as she watched him saunter off, then turned her gaze back to Ashley's and settled her weight down against the denim-clad legs. Ashley moaned as she slid her warm hands along the sides of Lisa's bare thighs, under her dress.

"I am a big fan of lap sitting," Ashley said with a grin. "FYI."

"I'll make a note." Lisa grinned back, but became serious again when she looked into Ashley's eyes, their bright blue dark now with desire. She leaned close until they breathed the same air.

"You are so beautiful," Ashley whispered, and that was all Lisa needed. She took Ashley's face in her hands and crushed their mouths together in a blistering kiss that stole the breath from both of them.

Sensations blended together at that point. Lisa knew Ashley's hands were on her, felt them skim along her thighs, over her bottom, and up her back, but it seemed like they were everywhere at once. She knew they were kissing, could feel Ashley's mouth melding with hers, knew Ashley's tongue was pushing against her own, but she couldn't differentiate between her lips and Ashley's. It was all sensation—hot, wet, thrillingly erotic sensation that seemed to go on for hours.

It wasn't until Ashley's warm hands cupped her bare breasts that Lisa had any inkling at all her bra had been unclasped. But it had been. And Ashley was zeroing in on her hardened nipples in a way that sent pinpoints of pleasure zipping through her body from her breasts down to her center. She wrenched her mouth from Ashley's long enough to let, "Oh, my God," escape from her lips. Ashley took that moment to lift Lisa's dress up over her head and off. The unclasped bra followed and Lisa was left in Ashley's lap wearing only her white bikinis.

Ashley was quiet, but her expression made Lisa's face heat up. It was reverent. It was admiring. It was hungry.

Bringing her hand up to Lisa's sternum, Ashley trailed her fingers lightly downward, between Lisa's breasts and down her stomach to the elastic waistband of the bikinis. She dipped one finger under it, slid it from side to side.

"I need these to come off," she whispered, and it was as if it took her great effort to pull her eyes from Lisa's bare torso and look her in the face. "I need to see all of you. Can we go to your bedroom? Please?"

The idea of taking things slowly went right out the window for Lisa, as did her desire to keep the upper hand. Ashley was everything right now. Ashley owned her and the realization was alarmingly erotic. There was no way Lisa was going to stop this. She was too hot. Too ready. She too badly wanted Ashley's hands on her. Immediately. She slid backward off Ashley's thighs, stood, and held out a hand.

"Oh, my God, that's the most beautiful sight I have ever seen, right there," Ashley said as she remained in place, moving one finger up and down in front of Lisa's nearly naked body.

Lisa made a come-hither gesture with her fingers. "Let's go. You have clothes on that need removing."

Ashley wasted no more time and put her hand in Lisa's. Lisa pulled her to her feet and tugged her toward the stairs. Lisa couldn't remember the journey; they were suddenly standing in Lisa's bedroom. The moon was full and cast a bright bluish light onto the paisley spread of the bed, and the ambiance was so shockingly romantic and sensual that Lisa didn't even think about turning on a light. Instead, she faced Ashley and reached for her top.

"You are ridiculously overdressed," she said quietly as she worked on the buttons, a little disconcerted by the trembling in her fingers.

Ashley covered them with her own, looked Lisa in the eyes, and gave her a tender smile. Then she grabbed the hem of her shirt and pulled it up and over her own head. "There," she said, dropping it on the floor. The bra followed and Ashley stood before Lisa, naked from the waist up, her small nipples standing at attention under Lisa's gaze.

"Oh," Lisa whispered, drawing the word out as her eyes took in Ashley's gorgeous body. Her breasts were not big and not small; they were perfect. Freckles peppered her shoulders, and Lisa's gaze skimmed over them, across her chest, down to her stomach then back up. Reaching a hand out, she pulled the band holding the French braid together and dug her fingers in to loosen it. A cascade of golden hair fell across those mouth-watering shoulders and Lisa took a moment to simply feast her eyes. Moving her hand down, she touched that perfect skin, found it just as smooth as she'd expected, velvety and soft. She ran her fingertips along a collarbone, took a step closer. With both hands on Ashley's torso, Lisa pulled her in until they stood breast to breast, skin to skin, face to face. Lisa's nose was only an inch higher than Ashley's, and she couldn't wait any longer. She dipped her head down and captured Ashley's mouth with her own.

There was no more preamble.

The kiss was hard and demanding, almost bruising in its intensity. Lisa grabbed Ashley's face with both hands and pushed herself as far into Ashley's mouth as she could, still feeling like it wasn't enough. Her body took over then, completely shutting her brain out of the situation. Her hands grabbed at Ashley's jeans, unfastened them and pushed them down her legs, revealing a pair of black lace bikinis. She felt Ashley's hands on her shoulders briefly, for balance, as she stepped out of the pants. Lisa was interrupted by the creamy white legs and stopped what she was doing long enough to put her mouth on that skin, trail her tongue along those thighs. A small gasp sounded from above and she looked up at Ashley's face, at her dark eyes and her parted, swollen lips, and swallowed hard.

"Do you have any idea how beautiful I think you are?" she whispered.

Ashley's expression softened as she looked down. "I...don't know," she said with uncertainty.

In one quick movement, Lisa stood, grasped Ashley by the shoulders, and spun her toward the bed. One gentle push later and Ashley was on her back, Lisa sliding her bikinis down her legs and baring her completely.

Lisa wanted so badly to stand still and just look, just let her eyes roam over the tantalizing body laid out only for her, but the desire to touch was much stronger. She needed her hands on that flesh, on Ashley, right now. She couldn't wait another second. Lisa crawled onto the bed and lowered herself onto Ashley, tandem moans escaping each woman at the contact. They kissed hungrily and Lisa could feel Ashley's hands on her back, then lower, cupping her ass inside her bikinis. A finger dipped down and between her legs from the back, forcing a gasp from her.

"Off," Ashley demanded, tugging at the offending garment. Without waiting for a response, she pushed them down and over Lisa's ass, dragging her finger again through the hot wetness and causing a second gasp. Ashley made a sound then, one Lisa hadn't heard before. A cross between a moan and a growl, and it was sexy as hell and unquestionably hot, and every muscle in Lisa's lower body tightened at it. With a push, Ashley flipped their positions, and Lisa found herself looking at the ceiling in surprise. Before she could form a coherent thought, Ashley had her bikinis completely off, her thighs spread apart, and was lowering her head. Without a wasted second, she covered the entirety of Lisa's hot center with her mouth, pushing her tongue immediately inside.

A cry tore from Lisa's throat as her hips raised up off the bed at the deliciousness of the contact. Her hands found Ashley's head, Ashley's hair, and she dug her fingers in, holding on for dear life as Ashley's mouth did unspeakably erotic things to her. Again, sensations blurred and melded until they became only one: pleasure. She couldn't tell exactly where Ashley's tongue was touching her, where her lips were, what pressure may have been from teeth. It was all one big, joyous feeling of sexual bliss. Lisa's thighs dropped open as far as they would go, of their own accord, as if they had minds of their own and wanted to offer up as much access to Ashley as possible. Ashley's hands grasped Lisa's sides, pulled at her, forcing more pressure from Ashley's mouth. And when those hands then slid upward to Lisa's breasts, captured both nipples, and rolled them between thumbs and forefingers, Lisa's body could take no more.

The orgasm ripped through her like an electric shock, tensing every muscle in her body, setting every nerve ending to dancing, tearing a rather unladylike cry from deep in her throat. Her fingers clenched and she was vaguely aware that she tightly gripped a handful of Ashley's hair, but she could do nothing to stop it, nothing to ease her grip. Colors exploded behind her eyelids and she rode out her climax while half-thinking she was going to simply die of heart failure right then.

But what a way to go...

Just when she started to think a heart attack was imminent, the pulsing began to ease up. Her fingers relaxed slightly and Ashley's tongue, pressed against Lisa's hot, wet flesh, stilled. She could hear Ashley's breathing, rapid. She could feel the heat of it on her bare skin. They stayed in that position for a long moment before Ashley slowly eased her mouth away, causing a ripple of leftover pleasure that made Lisa's legs spasm. Lisa groaned as Ashley softly touched her tongue to the same spot and got the same result.

"Stop that," Lisa whispered with a chuckle as Ashley did it a third time and Lisa's legs twitched. "Come up here." She couldn't open her eyes or lift her head, so she simply crooked a finger in Ashley's direction. "Please."

With a reverent kiss on Lisa's center, Ashley whispered, "I'll be back," and then made her way up so they were face to face. Her mouth tasted musky and hot as she kissed Lisa softly and said, "Holy shit."

Lisa's shoulders shook with gentle laughter. "I think that's supposed to be my line."

"No. It's definitely mine. 'Cause, I mean, God, that was amazing, Lisa. Seriously amazing. And I have to apologize because I like to take my time." She kissed Lisa again, this time slowly. Pulling back, she looked into Lisa's eyes and said seriously, "I don't usually just dive in like that but..." Her words trailed off as she looked out into the room and ran a shaky hand through her own hair. "I don't know what it is about you." Her gaze returned to Lisa's. "I couldn't wait. I couldn't stop. I just...had to have you."

"Hey, you're going to get no argument from me," Lisa said with a smile. "That was..." Her shoulders moved in a shrug. "I have no words."

It was the truth. Lisa was usually the one with the upper hand in bed. She tended to be the one to run the show; it was safer that way. Tonight...what the hell had happened? Not only had Ashley taken over, but Lisa had let her. Super out-of-character. She wasn't quite sure what to do with that yet, so she set it aside for the moment, not ready to examine it further.

Instead, she turned her focus to the gloriously naked woman lying on top of her, all flushed cheeks and hot skin, and decided better late than never. Lisa reached up a hand and touched her fingers to Ashley's swollen lips, felt the silkiness of them, and gently brought their mouths together in a soft and tender kiss. It was only a matter of moments before things began to heat up, and Lisa was momentarily stunned by how aroused she was…again. That was also unusual. She was a one-and-done kind of girl, but…that was not going to be the case tonight from what she could tell. With a light shove, she pushed Ashley off her and onto her back, whispered, "My turn," then closed her mouth over a nipple.

Ashley's sharp intake of breath only caused Lisa's arousal to surge higher and she gently used her teeth. Ashley's fingers tightened in her hair, holding her in place, so Lisa did it again, felt Ashley squirm beneath her, heard her whispered, "God…"

That one quiet word, spoken on nothing more than a breath of air, pushed Lisa's arousal even higher, and she suddenly found herself on the very edge of frantic. She couldn't touch enough of Ashley's skin, but she tried, trailing her fingers, her palms, her mouth, her tongue over every inch of soft, hot female flesh within her reach, and when Ashley bent her knee and her thigh hit Lisa's sensitive core, she couldn't help herself; she began to rock against it. Details blurred until everything seemed melded together: sight, sound, scent. She kissed Ashley, hard and deep, as she slid her fingers into the overheated wetness waiting for her between Ashley's thighs.

Ashley wrenched her mouth away long enough to sputter out Lisa's name, but then grabbed her head and crushed their mouths back together.

Kissing Ashley was both completely new and as comfortable as if Lisa had been doing it forever. She seriously couldn't believe she'd gone thirty-two years without ever doing so, and it was also hard to believe this was only the first time they'd had sex. She felt like she knew this body underneath her, knew everything about it, every sensitive spot, every nerve ending that might cause a gasp when touched, the exact taste of each expanse of skin. How was it possible she'd never touched Ashley this way before, when it was so inexplicably perfect right now?

Pushing her tongue into Ashley's mouth at the same time she plunged her fingers into her center was more than Ashley could stand, and she arched her head back, a long, sensual moan humming up from her throat as her hips rose slightly and she came against Lisa's hand. Lisa watched with rapt fascination, changing the movement of her fingers, matching her speed and pressure to the expression on Ashley's face, the tightening of her grip on Lisa's shoulder, until everything began to gently come back down.

Ashley surprised her then by pressing her hand to the small of Lisa's back, forcing her up against her thigh more firmly. Looking Lisa in the eye, she pushed her leg against Lisa's slick center, and Lisa realized Ashley had been paying more attention than she'd realized. Quickly finding a rhythm, it was only a matter of seconds before Lisa's second climax hit her, stealing her breath from her lungs and all sound from her throat. She could feel Ashley's eyes on her even as she heard her whisper, "There it is."

Lisa collapsed, half on the bed, half on Ashley, breathless. She laid her head on Ashley's shoulder and willed her heart rate to return to normal.

Long moments went by before Ashley finally spoke. "Am I dead?" she asked quietly. "I think you may have killed me."

Lisa chuckled. "Oh, no. Trust me, you are alive and well. I can hear your heartbeat."

"Well. I suppose that's a good thing."

"It is. And if anybody killed anybody, *you* killed *me*. Oh, my God."

Ashley raised her arm and wrapped it around Lisa's shoulder, squeezed gently. "I will happily kill you again any time. That was…you were amazing." Her warm lips pressed against Lisa's forehead.

"Back atcha," Lisa said, tightening her arm around Ashley's middle. She was suddenly so tired, her body heavy in that sapped-of-energy, just-had-amazing-sex kind of way, her limbs leaden. Her eyes drifted closed just as she heard a gentle whining coming from the floor. She groaned, took a deep breath, and pushed herself up.

"What's the matter?" Ashley asked.

"I have to take care of the animals before I fall asleep." Lisa extricated herself from the tangle of limbs—regretfully—and pulled on a pair of striped pajama bottoms and a tank top. Then she grabbed the sheet and pulled it up, covering Ashley. "I'll be right back," she said quietly as she kissed her on the mouth. "Don't go anywhere."

"I couldn't move if I wanted to," Ashley said drowsily. "Good thing I don't. I'll be right here. Promise."

Lisa softly called to Keeler and they headed downstairs. She stood in a daze as the dog did his business, her fingertips against her lips, Ashley's scent still apparent on her hand. She inhaled deeply, couldn't keep the smile from her face.

In the kitchen, the cats got treats, as did the dog. She picked each feline up, snuggled it to her chest, and kissed its furry head, as she did every night. Then she got on her knees on the kitchen floor and wrapped her arms around Keeler's thick, black neck, hugged him tight, told him she loved him more than any dog in the whole world, and kissed him between his kind brown eyes. The cats went off to do whatever they did at night. Keeler followed her back upstairs to the bedroom.

She was unsurprised to find Ashley breathing the deep and even rhythm of slumber, and she stood still in the doorway, just looking. Ashley was turned slightly on her side, one leg out from under the covers, and Lisa noticed for the first time that her toenails were polished a bright blue. The sheet was draped over her behind, but the wide expanse of her back was completely exposed and Lisa feasted her eyes on it, noting that she'd have to explore that beautiful back next time. Her blond hair was draped on the pillow, tousled and sexy, and suddenly Lisa couldn't wait for one more second to be back in bed with her. She pulled her pajamas back off, then carefully slid under the covers until she was spooned up behind Ashley, who grasped her hand, lazily kissed the knuckles, and tucked it up against her chest, never opening her eyes or saying a word.

Lisa snuggled in, feeling an unfamiliar warmth and contentment settle over her. Keeler jumped up on the bed and curled up in the crook of her knees, and it occurred to Lisa in that moment that things could not be any more perfect if she'd painted the picture herself.

CHAPTER SIXTEEN

DELICIOUS.

That was the word that came to mind for Ashley as she gently floated up from sleep into the conscious world. She kept her eyes closed, hoping to take a few extra minutes to savor the pleasant soreness in her thighs and nipples, the slightly chapped feel of her lips, the dreamy signs that she'd had some damn good sex the night before. Her mind projected instant replays onto the screen inside her skull, flashes of the highlights: Lisa coming under Ashley's mouth, the blast of pleasure from Lisa's fingers pushing into her, the zero-to-sixty revving up of her arousal when they'd found each other again in the wee hours of the morning. She relished every memory for as long as she could before she felt a gentle tapping on her nose, and she opened one eye to see Tiny peering at her with his little cat eyes.

Arms reaching over her head, Ashley stretched, loosening muscles that had been overworked, then stiffened up as she slept, and was disappointed to find the bed empty next to her. She'd hoped to find Lisa sleeping peacefully—and then she wanted to wake her up. Pleasantly. Softly. Sexily.

Her morning plans disrupted, she lay quietly in the bed and listened, but heard nothing. No shower running in the bathroom. No dishes clanging in the kitchen. She smelled no coffee brewing. A glance at the clock told her it was after nine. With a furrowed brow, she got out of bed and stretched again. Groucho slinked into the room, gave her a once-over, then turned to leave, obviously unimpressed with her nakedness. She grinned, then went into scavenger hunt mode, searching the floor for her clothes.

Once dressed, she made a detour to the bathroom, where she found a tube of toothpaste and squirted a bead onto her finger, then did a makeshift brush job. Finished with that, she headed downstairs to find Lisa and give her a proper good morning.

She didn't find Lisa.

She found a note from Lisa.

Took Keeler to the park, then we're headed to my friend's. Thanks for a great night. Please lock the door on your way out.

Ashley stood in the middle of the kitchen, note in hand, and simply blinked. Just blinked. That was it? Thanks for a great night, lock the door when you leave? Seriously?

"Wow," Ashley said to the empty house. "That's cold."

And hurtful, if she was going to be honest. Not to mention, embarrassing. As if she was being observed, Ashley quickly found her things and left the house—obeying the note and locking the door behind her. Once in her car, she allowed herself to look up, back at Lisa's place, and humiliation flooded her like water in her veins, flushing her skin hotly, making her feel like a fool.

Glancing at her cell, she saw a couple of missed texts from Jenna, who knew where she would be the previous night. There was a text this morning from her.

Assuming your failure to answer me last night to mean you scored. I want to hear all about it!

Ashley quickly texted her back, then keyed the ignition and backed out of the driveway.

"So wait. Let me get this straight." Grace filled Lisa's mug with rich-smelling coffee, then got the cream from the fridge. She sat down at the table across from Lisa, wrapped both hands around her own mug, and stared at her friend. "You just left her there?"

"I just—" Lisa stopped at Grace's upraised hand, halting her speech.

"She told you that you made her brave. She said those exact words to you."

"Yes." Lisa had the good sense to look a little chagrined at the statement.

"The sex was good?"

Lisa's eyes went wide. "The sex was outstanding. The sex was…" Her voice trailed off, speaking volumes.

"And you left her there. Alone. In *your* house. With a note."

Lisa swallowed, the coffee suddenly feeling as if it was burning a hole in her stomach. "Yeah."

Grace's head tilted to one side as she looked at her friend in what could only be described as disbelief. "You suck. You know that, right? You suck in a big, big way."

Lisa dropped her head down between her shoulders with a groan. "I know!"

Grace blew out a breath and Lisa knew she'd frustrated her. They sat quietly for a long moment before Grace said, gently now, "What were you thinking?"

"I was thinking that I didn't want to have to make breakfast and small talk and plans for the day and—"

"Why not? I got the impression you liked this girl. Don't you?"

The sound Lisa made was unfamiliar to her, sort of a cross between a groan and a whimper. "I do," she whispered, mortified to feel her eyes well up.

"Lisa." Grace reached across the table, closed a warm hand over Lisa's arm. "Talk to me. What's going on?"

Lisa shook her head, her mind a jumble. This morning had been a bizarre combination of amazingly wonderful and frighteningly awful. She'd woken up to a delightfully relaxed body, pleasantly sore muscles that hadn't had that kind of a workout in ages. She'd glanced over at Ashley's sleeping form, so peaceful and gorgeous, and she'd simply...panicked. Even as she was leaving that ridiculous note for Ashley, even as she was leashing Keeler and loading him into the car, she wasn't sure what she was doing, what was driving her, why she felt such a surge of apprehension. She still didn't. "What's wrong with me?" she asked quietly.

"Oh, sweetie, nothing's wrong with you." Grace made a face. "I'm sorry I said you suck. You don't. Well...what you did sucked, but you don't. You're one of my very favorite people. You know that?"

Lisa sniffled, nodded.

Grace took a deep breath as she studied Lisa, then seemed to come to a decision. With another squeeze of her arm, she held Lisa's gaze and said, very gently, "It's not your job to take care of everybody. And not everybody needs you to take care of them." She waited, raised her eyebrows as if waiting for a sign that Lisa understood what she was saying.

Lisa kept her eyes on her coffee as she heard soft footsteps. She could smell new perfume in the room and knew Grace's wife, Ella, had come in. Almost able to feel the exchange of glances, Lisa looked up in time to see the sparkling sheen of love that crossed over Grace's features, and her heart warmed.

She wanted that.

She wanted the devotion, the connection, the certainty that Grace and Ella shared.

She wanted that. Badly.

A warm hand landed on her shoulder and a gentle kiss was pressed to the top of her head. Then Ella left the room, Grace watching her go with such reverence on her face that Lisa nearly burst into tears. Turning back to Lisa, Grace smiled and picked up where they'd left off. "You know what I mean?"

Lisa nodded and sipped her coffee. Oh, yes. She knew exactly what Grace meant.

She just didn't know how to fix it.

—◇—

"You've got to be kidding me. What the fuck?" Jenna's hand flew to her mouth as she glanced around the diner. Then she shrunk down in her seat, lowered her voice to a whisper. "What. The. Fuck?"

Ashley shook her head as she scooped a forkful of scrambled eggs into her mouth, not really hungry, but knowing she should eat something. Having spent the past ninety minutes nothing more than stunned by the morning's events—or lack thereof—she really could think of nothing to say.

"Seriously, Ash-hole. Answer me. What. The. Actual. Fuck?"

The waitress warmed up Jenna's coffee and Ashley watched as she spooned enough sugar into it to bake a small cake.

"That was a total guy thing to do."

Ashley shook her head. "No. Don't generalize. I know a lot of guys who'd never do such a thing. I just…" She gazed out the window of the diner, watching the people out for a Sunday morning stroll on Monroe Avenue. "There has to be a reason."

"Yeah, maybe because she sucks?"

Ashley gave a humorless chuckle. "But that's just it. She doesn't." She could feel Jenna's eyes on her and she waited a beat before turning to her expectantly. "What?"

Jenna shrugged, took a bite of her toast, and chewed it while she held Ashley's gaze. Finally, she said, "Why are you defending her? I don't get it."

It was Ashley's turn to shrug. "I just think…you don't know her, Jenna. I'm not being stupid about this. There's a reason. There has to be."

"Was the sex bad?" Jenna made a face that said she was sorry to ask such a sensitive question, but Ashley didn't mind.

"No. In fact, it was kind of incredible."

"For you?"

"For me and for her."

"You're sure?"

"You know, normally that question would have me freaking out with insecurity, but not today. Which is weird. Yes. I'm 150% sure."

"Then, one more time, because I have yet to get an answer: what the fuck?"

"I don't know," Ashley said quietly, again gazing out the window.

Jenna grimaced. "So…I guess suggesting you back away from the hot chick with intimacy issues is out of the question, huh?"

Ashley gave her friend a sad smile. "You're the best, Jenna. You know that, right?" She'd texted Jenna from Lisa's driveway, crushed, and asked if she could meet her. Sunday mornings were devoted to Jenna's yoga class, and she looked forward to it all week. But she hadn't thought twice about bailing. She'd arrived not five minutes after Ashley, decked out in capri-length yoga pants and a form-fitting neon yellow tank, ready to offer whatever Ashley needed. Which, in this case, ended up being lots of questions with the F-word in them.

"I do know that. But thanks for telling me." Jenna winked. They sat in silence for long moments before Jenna softly asked, "What are you going to do?"

Ashley gazed back out the window. A young couple strolled by hand in hand. An older man walked a golden retriever, who stopped to pee on the large pot of flowers near the curb. A woman jogged by pushing a three-wheeled stroller, her baby sound asleep inside, apparently lulled to slumber by the ride.

People moved along.

Life went on.

She turned back to Jenna and said, simply and with determination, "I'm going to get to the bottom of it."

CHAPTER SEVENTEEN

"SO? HOW ARE THINGS with Ashley the Ambush Kisser?"

Lisa could do nothing but shake her head in wonder at the bluntness of her aunt. Sitting out back on the patio with Keeler on a chain next to her, she pet his silky fur with one hand while holding the phone to her ear with the other. The afternoon was sunny and warm and Keeler panted gently, his pink tongue lolling over his bottom teeth.

"You don't beat around the bush, do you?" she said with a chuckle, then lay her head back against the hard surface of the Adirondack chair. She had a quick memory of Ashley sitting there the night before, all flirty eyes and flushed cheeks. When she'd returned an hour ago, she'd been both relieved and disappointed that Ashley hadn't still been there, waiting for her.

"Which doesn't answer my question," Aunt Joyce scolded.

With a sigh, Lisa said, "Can we please talk about something else?"

"*That* answers my question. Not so good, huh? What happened?"

"Okay, since you obviously don't understand the phrase 'can we please talk about something else,' it actually means we should talk about something else."

"Oh, fine, then." Lisa could see her aunt waving a dismissive hand in the air, annoyed by having been shut down. "In other news, I'm having a family dinner. Next weekend. My house. You'll be there."

"Who's coming?" Lisa asked, having an inkling of where this was headed.

"It's a family dinner. Family is coming."

"What if I have plans?"

"Lisa." It was that stern tone, which Aunt Joyce seemed to be using on her more and more often of late. "Come to dinner with your family."

Texting was one thing. Cutting phone calls short was along those same lines. But sitting at the table for hours with her mother and having to play nice-nice...it drained her just thinking about it.

"Six o'clock," her aunt went on. "Bring that delicious red wine you brought to my last jewelry party. You know the one I mean?"

"I do." Lisa spoke, then looked at her phone and made several crazy faces of frustration at it before bringing it back to her ear. She closed her eyes in resignation.

"Bring the Ambush Kisser with you if you want."

"I don't think so." There was no way in hell she'd subject Ashley to the discomfort of a family dinner. Not to mention, she'd probably killed any possibility of that relationship going anywhere but in the crapper by acting like a complete, uncaring coward this morning. She rubbed her fingertips along her forehead, feeling the dull throb of an impending headache.

"Well," Aunt Joyce said, and Lisa could actually hear disappointment in her voice. Then it softened, as if her aunt knew things she couldn't possibly know. "If anything changes, she's more than welcome."

They made some small talk for a few more minutes before saying their goodbyes. Lisa set the phone down and tried to relax. One arm dangling, she returned to petting Keeler, stroking the soft fur on top of his head. As she gazed out onto the small berm of trees behind her complex, birds flitted from branch to branch and squirrels foraged, while her mind went off in the same direction it always did when it came to matters of the heart. Family. Relationship. Didn't matter, the question was always the same.

What is the matter with me?

She posed the inquiry to herself no less than once a week, yet she never seemed able to come up with an answer. Was she selfish? Maybe. Was she damaged by her past? Most certainly, but who wasn't? Was she afraid?

Definitely.

But, afraid of what? That was the real question and she knew it. Yet, she tended it like a giant pothole on the road of her life. Just swerved around it and kept on going. She knew it was there, could see it from a mile away, but when she approached it, just *swerve!* Avoided. No need to deal. Moving on.

This was different, though.

Today was different.

Because Ashley was different.

Lisa had run like a coward this morning. She knew that. She could admit that. It hadn't started like that, though. It had started with her opening her eyes to the most beautiful sight she'd seen in years. Ashley was sleeping peacefully on her side, up against Lisa, her arm tossed carelessly across Lisa's stomach, her forehead pressed to Lisa's shoulder. Her knees were bent and Lisa's thigh was warm where they touched her. Ashley's blond hair was tousled, splayed across the pillow and Lisa. Her eyelashes seemed impossibly long and the tiniest of smiles tugged at the corners of her mouth while she slept. A shaft of golden yellow sunlight crossed the smooth skin of Ashley's face, and honest to God, Lisa had never seen anything more gorgeous in her life.

What had happened after that?

Lisa was uncertain. All she knew for sure was that she suddenly started thinking about how passive Ashley could sometimes be, how she froze during that abuse intake recently, how she'd just stood there while Clark Breckenridge sexually harassed her, how Lisa'd had to take care of her both times. And once that seed of doubt started to sprout in her mind, it hadn't mattered that Ashley had kissed her senseless at her aunt's beach house, that she'd stomped into the shelter and brazenly asked Lisa on a date, that she claimed Lisa made her brave. None of that mattered because all of a sudden, all Lisa could see was how much work she'd have to do, taking care of Ashley all those times in the future when she couldn't take care of herself.

She felt her mind slipping into the dreaded abyss of useless, circular thought, clawing desperately at the muddy sides, digging in with its fingertips, and at the very moment it felt resistance was futile—her doorbell rang.

She was quite literally saved by the bell.

Keeler lifted his head and gave a half-hearted bark, then turned to peer through the screen as if he had X-ray vision and could see straight through to the other side of the front door. Lisa shook her head free of the crazy train that had been chugging around her skull and went inside. She could not have been more surprised when she opened the door, but had no time to react as Ashley pushed past her and into the foyer with a quiet, "What the hell, Lisa?"

With a hard swallow, Lisa gazed at the floor as she slowly closed the door, then turned to face Ashley.

The very first thing Lisa had noticed was how wonderful she smelled. Not like cupcakes today, but just as sweet. Peaches, maybe? She wore denim shorts that showcased her tanned legs, legs Lisa'd had her mouth all over the night before. A jolt shot through her as that thought hit, but she tamped it down. A pink graphic T-shirt with the words Paris Or Bust printed across the front in black highlighted the outfit. But the most noticeable thing about Ashley was the flash of her bright blue eyes. Lisa had seen Ashley in many phases: sad, alarmed, frightened, aroused.

She'd never seen her quite this pissed.

They stood in the foyer, face to face, not more than two feet between them. Keeler nudged Ashley's hand with his nose and she absently pet him, never taking her eyes off Lisa. Her arms lifted out to the sides a bit in question, then dropped back down against her body as she waited Lisa out. They stood quietly for long moments.

"Why can't you just talk to me?" Ashley asked quietly.

"What do you want me to say?" Lisa countered, feeling her frustration building. She didn't like being cornered, especially in her own home. But, this anger she was feeling? She recognized it as her own cowardice in disguise.

"I want you to tell me what happened this morning." Ashley studied her and Lisa could see by her expression that she was making an effort to hold on to her temper. After a beat or two, Lisa had to look away, the intensity of Ashley's gaze too much. "Correct me if I'm wrong, but I was pretty sure last night was kind of awesome. For both of us."

Lisa cleared her throat and nodded. "It was."

"Okay. Good. We agree on that." When nothing more came, Ashley pressed her lips together and slowly shook her head. "A note? Seriously? What is this, an episode of *Sex and the City*? You blow me off with a piece of paper?"

"I wasn't blowing you off."

"Really? That's certainly what it looked like from where I sat. In your bed. Naked. Alone." With a humorless chuckle, she added, "I didn't even get a cup of coffee as a send-off."

The acid in Lisa's stomach churned. "What do you want me to say?" she asked again, louder this time as her frustration grew. Other emotions pushed to the forefront, vying for attention: anger, embarrassment, and that big daddy of them all…fear. The shock of the realization stunned her silent, as if she'd been slapped.

She was afraid.

No.

Not afraid. She was terrified.

Instead of the explosion of angry confusion she expected from Ashley, she got even quieter. With a step forward, Ashley put her hands on Lisa's upper arms, rubbed them gently up and down. "This is what I know. One, I like you. A lot. I'm not always sure why…" She grinned to show she was kidding. "But I do. Two, you like me. And I don't think that happens to you often, so this is a special accomplishment on my part. Three, I'm not sure how you do it or what it means, but you make me stand up. You make me speak up. You make me a better person. And you know what I want to be most in the world? A better person. And four, you're afraid."

Lisa's lips parted as a small gasp escaped her.

"Yeah. I can see it. And I don't want you to be afraid with me. There's no reason." Ashley gave a small shrug and made a face so adorable Lisa wanted to pull her into a hug and forget everything. All of it. Just stay locked in Ashley's embrace for the rest of time.

Except that would solve nothing.

And Lisa realized right then, right at that very second, that she wanted nothing more than to solve things, to fix them, to give this thing with Ashley a real shot, put some genuine effort into it, because Ashley felt…right. Despite her own misgivings, her worries, her penchant for projecting things onto Ashley, Ashley felt right. And *that* scared the hell out of her.

Before she could figure out a way to tell Ashley that she was a disaster, broken beyond repair, that Ashley would do herself a huge favor by walking out the door and never looking back because Lisa absolutely was not worth the time or effort, Ashley slid her hands down Lisa's arms and linked their fingers.

"So. Here's what we're going to do. We're going to go out to dinner. On a real date. We're going to talk about things people talk about on a date. We can table this whole thing for the time being, but I will tell you right now, it's gonna come up again soon, and we're going to deal with it. Then, after dinner, we're going to go to a movie, a continuation of our date. After the movie, I will drop you off here and I will go home, so as not to complicate things with the crazy amazing sex we'd most likely have, possibly on the living room floor."

Lisa couldn't help but grin at that.

Ashley smiled, too, then continued, her voice softer. "And we're going to do that type of thing—go on dates—until you realize that it's okay to talk to me, that you're safe with me, that I'm not going anywhere, that we're really, really good together."

"I already know we're good together," Lisa said with a feigned scoff, trying to lighten the mood.

"Well, good. One down then."

Lisa looked at Ashley then. Really looked at her, in the eyes, held her gaze, and saw nothing there but a gentle kindness that put a lump solidly in her throat. It took her a moment to swallow it down before she was able to ask one simple thing. "Why?"

Ashley smiled so tenderly, the lump came back in full force. "Because I happen to think you're worth it, Ms. Drakemore. Now. Finish your afternoon. Go beat up a heavy bag if you need to." At the shocked look on Lisa's face, Ashley grinned. "Yeah, I know a lot of stuff. Do what you need to do, and I'll be back at 6:30 to pick you up. Okay?" She squeezed Lisa's hands, then released them and reached for the doorknob.

Lisa watched her and when Ashley turned back to give a little wave, Lisa tipped her head to the side, and just looked at her. Nobody had ever done that—taken charge. Never in her life. Not her father. Not her brothers. None of her past girlfriends. Nobody. The one in charge had always been Lisa. And when she pushed somebody to make them leave, they left. Plain and simple. This was different...so very different. *Ashley* was different. Different and new. And...interesting.

As Ashley turned and walked out into the summer air, Lisa leaned against the door and said simply—and mostly to herself, "You're right. You *are* brave."

⊶⊷

Dinner had been shockingly enjoyable. Ashley had been right about taking the deeper, harder part of their issues out of the equation for the time being, because doing so seemed to relax Lisa exponentially. Smart choice. Oh, it was still there, at least for Ashley it was. She had to believe it was floating around in the back of Lisa's mind as well, but when Ashley had said they wouldn't talk about it tonight, she wasn't kidding. A pact was a pact. Instead, they talked about everything else two people on a date would talk about: the shelter, their years in school, their siblings. It was very much like that first coffee date, enjoyable and relaxing. Lisa looked shocked when nearly two hours had gone by and Ashley said they needed to get moving if they were going to make the movie.

They'd agreed on a romantic comedy, neither of them in the mood for anything too intense or emotional.

"Nope," Ashley said, waving away Lisa's money for popcorn, just as she had for the tickets and at the restaurant. "I got this. Tonight is on me." When Lisa protested, even throwing in a pathetic little pout for good measure, Ashley couldn't help but laugh. "Seriously. It was a good week in the cookie business. You get the next date, okay?" The way Lisa looked at her then, a combination of gratitude, hope, and a little bit of sex appeal, made Ashley all tingly and her stomach flip-floppy.

The old theatre nearest Lisa's house had been in a constant state of renovation for the past year, trying to keep up with technological advances that were nearly impossible to keep up with.

"The best upgrade by far, in my opinion," Lisa said, "is the new seats. They're ridiculous. You can recline in them, raise your feet. It's crazy, like watching a movie in bed." They headed down the aisle, popcorn in hand. "You can't come here if you're at all tired," she said as they wandered until they found a suitable seat. "You'll drop off like an infant."

Ashley laughed, and the second she sat down, she was astonished by the comfort. "Oh, my God. This is unbelievable."

"Told you."

The button on Ashley's armrest begged to be pushed, so she fiddled with it and raised her footrest. Then lowered it. Then raised it. Up, down, up, down.

"Speaking of infants," Lisa said with a grin. She adjusted herself into her own chair and seemed to notice the armrest was loose. When she tugged on it, she and Ashley realized at the same time that they had inadvertently chosen a loveseat instead of two separate seats. Their eyes met and held, and by unspoken agreement, they each scooted a bit toward the center so their hips and thighs were touching. Lisa held the popcorn bag so it sat between them. As Ashley reached for it, Lisa lightly slapped her hand away.

Ashley blinked in shock. "What was that?"

The lights dimmed. "Not until the movie starts," Lisa whispered as the first preview began.

"Seriously?"

"Seriously."

"Man, you've got a lot of rules," Ashley said with a shake of her head. But the truth was, she didn't mind. Lisa kept her guessing and that was…exciting.

A moment later, Lisa tapped on her hand. "Hey, Ashley?"

When Ashley turned to look, Lisa was smiling at her. "Hmm?"

"I'm having a really great time."

That smile was one of the best things Ashley had seen all evening…and it had been a pretty damn good evening. "Me, too," she said quietly.

A packed theatre made for an even funnier comedy, as everything was more hilarious in a crowd. Once the popcorn was gone, Lisa snuggled in closer, tossing a leg over Ashley's lap and linking their hands together. Lips at Ashley's ear, she asked, "Is this okay?"

Her warm breath sent an erotic shiver along Ashley's skin. Ashley turned, caught Lisa's eye, and wondered if the woman had any idea how turned on she was just from Lisa's warm breath tickling her ear, wondered if she could see, in the shadowed theatre, in the dark warmth of their cozy seat, how badly Ashley wanted her. With a hard swallow, Ashley simply nodded and squeezed her hand.

Stop it. You took sex off the table. You can't change your mind now.

It was the right thing to do. Ashley was sure of it. They weren't just good together in bed, they were a bonfire. They were fireworks. They were fluidity and pleasure and rhythm. Everything that could possibly be good about sex? They were it. Sex was not the problem for them. Their problems were internal. And if, in order to figure out and work through all that internal crap, they had to remove the possibility of sex for a while? Then damn it, they would.

Yes, Ashley realized the only person she was trying to convince with this long-winded explanation of her own decisions was herself, which made exactly zero sense at this point. *God, just shut up and watch the movie.* Which she did, happily and successfully, until the love scene came on and she surreptitiously glanced at Lisa out of the corner of her eye.

Mistake.

Because Ashley would swear on a stack of Bibles and anybody's eyesight that she'd never seen a sexier image, a vision more beautiful. Lisa's eyes were wide, rapturously watching the film. Her face was bathed in light blue from the screen, her lips parted slightly and glistening with the gloss she'd stroked on once the popcorn was gone. Her small chin led down to that sensual throat and it took every ounce of willpower Ashley possessed not to lean over a few inches and run her tongue along that warm column of flesh.

It wasn't until Lisa looked down at their linked hands, then up at Ashley and gave her the sexiest grin on the planet, that Ashley realized she'd been squeezing.

Oh, very subtle, Ash. Way to play it cool.

Pulling herself together, she managed to relax and make it through the movie. When the lights came up as the credits rolled, neither of them made a move.

"I am really, really comfortable," Lisa said, her voice a little dreamy. She leaned her head on Ashley's shoulder.

"Me, too," Ashley replied.

They stayed in place until the credits finished. "Can we just stay right here?" Lisa asked.

"Well..." Ashley glanced around at the various theatre employees weaving through aisles and picking up left-behind detritus. "Maybe..." When an acne-covered young man got to their row and looked at them with an expression that said he couldn't be less impressed by them, Ashley sighed. "Okay, okay. We're going," she told him, and they slowly, reluctantly, gathered their things.

The ride home was quiet, the air inside the car supercharged and heavy, and Ashley realized three separate times that she was gripping the steering wheel so tightly her knuckles had gone white. Forcing herself to relax, she said, "This was a fun night. You think?"

Lisa smiled. "It was great. Really great." She turned to look at Ashley and Ashley could feel her gaze, the intensity of it, the heat, without even turning her head. "Thank you."

Ashley nodded and breathed a quiet sigh of relief as she slid the car into a parking spot in front of Lisa's townhouse. She'd made it through the evening without crossing any of the lines she'd drawn. Points for her.

Shifting into Park, she said, "I'll see you tomorrow at the shelter."

Lisa cocked her head ever so slightly as she asked, "Walk me in?"

"Sure."

Pocketing her keys, Ashley followed Lisa up the walk, enjoying the view of her black capris hugging her perfect ass and providing an unobstructed view of her toned calves. Her eyes roamed the line of Lisa's back from one shoulder to the other, the way her body moved under the red button-up blouse with the cap sleeves. While Lisa keyed the lock, Ashley tried not to stand too close as she quietly inhaled, taking in the heady scent combination of Lisa's perfume, Lisa's shampoo, and Lisa.

The door pushed open and Lisa glanced at her, then whispered, "Come in here for a minute."

Not about to disobey an order handed to her by a beautiful woman, Ashley followed her in. It was dim, the only light in the townhouse being the subdued one above the stove in the kitchen. The animals made their way to the foyer, much slower at night than they had during the day, but Ashley had little chance to even notice them before Lisa grabbed her by the lapels of the boyfriend jacket she'd thrown on over her T-shirt and hauled her up against the wall.

"I have wanted to do this all night," Lisa said, then crushed her mouth to Ashley's.

Pinned between the solid surety of the wall and the soft, warm sexiness of Lisa's body, Ashley's head was spinning as she grappled for some kind of purchase. Lisa roughly pulled the jacket off Ashley's shoulders to reveal the V-neck of the T-shirt underneath, which gave her better access to Ashley's neck. Which she took, closing her hot, wet mouth over Ashley's pulse point. A moan hummed up from Ashley's throat as her eyes drifted closed and she lifted her chin just a bit. As if they had minds of their own, her hands slipped around Lisa's waist, down past the small of her back, and closed over her ass, gripping it hard and pulling Lisa closer as Lisa's mouth found hers once again and she pushed her tongue inside.

The darkness ratcheted up the eroticism and Ashley was shocked by how quickly she'd become so turned on. Not that she hadn't had a head start, but God, she'd never gotten so hot so fast in her entire life, and she wanted nothing more than to grab Lisa's hand and lead her up to the bedroom. Like, *now*.

Lisa's warm hands were under her shirt now, she realized belatedly. When they slid up her stomach and cupped each breast, Ashley wrenched her mouth from Lisa's so a small cry could break free. In a move so smooth Ashley could barely follow it, Lisa pushed her shirt up, dipped a hand into the cup of Ashley's bra, pulled her breast free, and closed her mouth over the nipple, tearing yet another sound of joy from Ashley's throat.

"God, I love your breasts," Lisa whispered with reverence as she treated the other breast to the same attention.

Listen, the feeling is mutual, Ashley thought as she dug her fingers into Lisa's hair and held her head tightly, never wanting Lisa's mouth to leave her skin. At the same time, a niggling thought scratched at the back of her skull.

When Lisa looked up at her, Ashley said, "Wait...wait." She paused, breathless. "We took sex off the table. Remember?"

Lisa responded by running her hands down Ashley's bare stomach and then grasping the button of her jeans. "Good thing we're not on a table then." She flicked the button open, pulled the zipper down, and pushed her hand into the heat that waited. This time, the moans were tandem as Lisa pressed her forehead against Ashley's, closed her eyes, and whispered, "Oh, my God, you're so wet for me." Her fingers never stilled and Ashley could do nothing more than hold on for dear life, knowing she was not going to last long.

"We weren't going to do this," Ashley whimpered feebly even as her hips picked up Lisa's rhythm and they rocked together.

"We were always going to do this," Lisa countered before covering Ashley's mouth with her own once again.

Though not unexpected, Ashley's orgasm still seemed to come out of nowhere and take her by surprise as it tore through her body. She dug her fingers into Lisa's back and muffled her own cries against her shoulder as she held on and rode the most delicious of waves, Lisa's other hand at the back of Ashley's head as she murmured encouragement in her ear.

Breathing began to even out after several long moments. That's when Lisa refastened Ashley's jeans, kissed her on the forehead, and smiled. Ashley looked up at her, bleary-eyed.

"That was incredible," Lisa said, then rubbed her thumb over Ashley's bottom lip. "Thank you for indulging me."

Ashley gave an exaggerated shrug. "Oh, hey, no problem. Anything you need, I'm here for you."

Lisa chuckled, kissed her sweetly on the mouth, and took a step back, putting the most space between them that there'd been since they entered the house. Ashley righted her bra, pulled her shirt down, and picked her jacket up off the floor.

"You wasted no time," she said with a grin as she pushed an arm into a sleeve. "My legs feel like Jell-O."

Lisa shrugged as Keeler sauntered up next to her and she laid a hand on his big head. "I thought we'd try it with the jeans on. See what happened."

"I'd say that experiment was a rousing success."

"Me, too. I've made a note." They held one another's gaze for a beat before Lisa reached a hand out to stroke Ashley's cheek. "Thank you for tonight. I'll see you at the shelter tomorrow?"

"You will. And we'll plan our next date." Tipping her face up, she kissed Lisa softly. "Bye."

The door clicked quietly behind her as Ashley walked down the front walkway to her car, legs still feeling a little weak. But in a delightfully sexy way. Nobody had ever just… *taken* her like that. She blew out a breath as she dropped into the driver's seat, knowing she would be subjected to hot and sexy flashbacks for the rest of the night. Maybe the rest of the week.

There was still the issue of the kiss-off Lisa'd given her that morning, but after tonight, Ashley felt they were at least moving in the right direction. And she was going to see Lisa again tomorrow.

She couldn't wait to find out what would happen next.

CHAPTER EIGHTEEN

"HEY, DAD." ASHLEY TOOK a bite of her tuna sandwich as she sat in the break room of the bakery. Stella gave her a wave as she exited and Ashley focused on the call as she chewed.

"What's new, butter ball?" Her father's voice held a smile. Again. She was really digging this new positivity coming from him.

"Yeah, I'm almost thirty. You can stop with that nickname."

"No way."

Ashley laughed. "Not much is new since the last time I talked to you. Which, weirdly, wasn't that long ago. What's going on with you?"

"What, can't a man call his daughter from time to time?" He played it off as casual, but Ashley could detect a tiny sting in his tone, so she backed off.

"He absolutely can and his daughter would love it. How are you?"

She listened to him talk about mundane things, but found herself really enjoying it. Ashley and her dad had a perfectly fine relationship, but they'd never been terribly tight. When one parent leaves a relationship and the kids stay with the other parent, Ashley was pretty sure it was inevitable that the kids would end up closer to the parent they lived with. It didn't mean she didn't love her dad. She did. A great deal. It just meant that they weren't what you'd call close. But now, with this new relationship, she'd seen a change in him.

"And maybe this weekend, I can come over and fix that pipe in your bathroom," he was saying.

"That'd be great."

"So, how's my daughter's life?" His voice was gentle and genuinely curious and Ashley found herself answering before she'd thought about it.

"I'm seeing somebody."

"Yeah? That girl Kelly mentioned? Carrie? Something like that?"

Ashley shook her head at her sister's big mouth. "Carly. And no, not her. That's over. Well, it never really started, to be honest."

"No? How come?"

And suddenly, she was talking to her father about relationships, something they'd never really done. "It's so hard to describe, Dad, but…it just wasn't there for me. And I didn't think it was fair to Carly to keep her hanging on while I waited to see if it ever *would* be there. Does that make sense?"

"It makes perfect sense. I'm sure it was hard to break it off, but you did her a favor, really. You have to look at it that way."

Ashley took the phone from her ear and looked at it for a beat before replacing it and answering. "You're exactly right."

"And who's the new girl?"

A flash of recall hit her at that moment and she could almost feel the solid hardness of Lisa's foyer wall against her back, Lisa's eager, skilled fingers slicking through her hot, wet —

Ashley cleared her throat and blinked quickly several times. "She's a…coworker of sorts and I'm not quite ready to go into detail about her because we're still working some things out. But, I really like her, Dad."

216

She could hear the smile in her father's voice as he said, "That's great, butter ball. I'm really happy for you."

Her cheeks warmed. "Thanks."

"Listen, though. I'm calling for a reason. Diana and I are going to McCurdy's for happy hour on Wednesday. Why don't you join us? And bring your girl. It'll be nice. Informal. Casual. We can all meet without any pressure. What do you say?"

Again, Ashley was stunned, but in a good way. Whoever this Diana was, Ashley wanted to meet her and shake her hand. "That sounds great."

A minute or two later, she hit the End button on the call, then immediately scrolled through her contacts to Kelly's name and hit Call. She wasted no time at all when her sister answered.

"I think Dad's been body snatched."

"I know, right?" was Kelly's instant response.

"What is happening?"

"It's so weird. Did you get invited to happy hour?"

"Yes!"

"Steve and I are so there. I need to meet this woman. Mom was not kidding when she said he's smitten."

"I hope we don't hate her. What if we hate her?"

Kelly laughed. "How could we possibly hate a woman who makes him so...present? Do you feel that?" Her voice held an edge of wonder. "I mean, he was never a bad father, but he was never a great one. He just kind of...did what he could manage. Now? He's called me three times since last Wednesday."

"Me, too!" They compared notes for a few more minutes. Ashley decided not to mention bringing Lisa to drinks just in case Lisa decided against going. After all, introducing her to family was a big step, and the last thing she wanted was to shake the foundation of something that was already precariously balanced. A glance at the big clock on the wall that reminded her of her high school cafeteria told her lunch was just about over. As she signed off with Kelly, Stella came sauntering in, doing an exaggerated model-like walk across the room.

"New aprons just arrived," she said as she strutted like she was on a catwalk and sang to Ashley how she was too sexy for this apron. "What do you think?"

As Ashley watched her friend sashay around the break room, hand on her hip, doing a swishy turn and sashaying back, her brain began to whir with an idea.

"Hello?" Stella said, waving a hand in front of Ashley's face. "Apron? Is it bad?"

Ashley blinked herself back to the present and looked at the apron for the first time. Black with the Carter's bread and cupcake logo in silver, it was actually quite classy. "No. Not at all. In fact, I love it."

"Okay, good," Stella said with relief, as she'd been in charge of ordering them. "You spaced out on me. I was worried."

"Sorry." Ashley stood and cleaned up the mess from her lunch. "My mind was elsewhere." And now it was racing. She couldn't wait for her shift at the shelter this afternoon.

⌐◦⌐

Lisa felt as if her mind had only been half-engaged in work all day. She was there, she was present—at least her body was. She'd sat through the entire board meeting—all ninety-seven minutes of it—and could barely remember a thing that was discussed. Jessica had given her a curious glance more than once, but neither of them had said anything. Lisa had managed to answer the phone and speak with visitors and fill out some paperwork and even do four intakes.

She could hardly recall any of it.

Instead, her mind was focused on last night. On Ashley. On she and Ashley together. On what might be happening between them. She replayed all of it in her head, over and over and over. The initial conversation when Ashley showed up at her door (which, Lisa had to admit, was impressive and unexpected coming from somebody she considered passive), and then her arrival for the date. She'd looked so deliciously gorgeous in her casual but classy outfit of jeans, a T-shirt, and a blazer with the sleeves rolled up. Totally sexy. Lisa'd had a hard time keeping her eyes—and her hands—to herself for as long as she had. Sitting in that reclining loveseat in the theatre had been simultaneous delight and torture, but Lisa was pretty sure she'd hidden it well. Even in the car ride back, she'd managed to keep control of things. That was the first time all night that she'd noticed maybe Ashley was going through the same issues. She'd been holding the steering wheel so tightly, her knuckles were white. That was when Lisa had decided to invite her in. She let her body take over after that.

And God, what a good job it had done.

Lisa had floated through the rest of the night, taking care of the animals, getting herself ready for bed. It had been like a dream, and once she was actually in bed, sensual flashbacks had bombarded her until she'd had to take care of herself to release the tension, the buildup, the delicious tightness that encompassed her entire body like a net.

And today, it didn't seem ready to let her go. Lisa was not a daydreamer, but more than once, she'd caught herself zoning out, staring off into space, completely missing the things going on around her. It was disconcerting, to say the least.

Now, it was after two and Ashley would be arriving any minute. Lisa tried to force herself to look anywhere else but at the door. When it finally did push open and Ashley came strolling through it with those big, blue eyes and smiling face, Lisa felt a warm rush of something unfamiliar, something she was not ready to deal with or analyze any further. Instead, she smiled widely.

"Hi, you," Ashley said as she approached Lisa's desk, and the expression on her face told Lisa how happy she was to see her.

"Hi back. I was just thinking about you." She hadn't meant to say it in such a husky, suggestive tone, but that's how it came out. Ashley's cheeks flushed a lovely pink in response.

"Yeah?"

"Yeah."

"Well. That makes me happy. I've been thinking about you, too."

They stayed just like that, Lisa sitting at her desk, Ashley standing in front of it, and held each other's gaze for a long, aching moment. *This is bad*, Lisa thought, but the thought made her a little giddy inside.

"Listen," Ashley said, as she finally broke eye contact and reached for a clipboard. "I have two questions."

Lisa forced herself back into stoic mode. "Shoot."

"One, if I have an idea for a fundraiser, who do I talk to about it? You?"

"You have an idea for a fundraiser?" Lisa tried to hide her surprise, but Ashley's self-conscious laugh told her she'd failed.

"I do. It might be awful, but…" She looked off down the row of cages and for a moment, it seemed like the constant barking picked up in volume. When Ashley looked back at her, there was uncertainty in her eyes. Insecurity. She gave a shrug and said simply, "I'm turning over a new leaf. Or…trying to." With that, she grabbed a leash off the hook on the wall and headed off to find her first dog to be walked.

Lisa watched her go, her stomach twisting with the knowledge that she'd stung her. Ashley was out the door with a pit bull before Lisa realized Ashley hadn't asked her the second thing. She blew out a breath and pursed her lips as she replayed the conversation in her head. Then she picked up the phone.

━◆━

"I probably should have known better," Ashley said to the dog as they strolled along the path toward the barn. He shot her a glance, then found something in the grass that was apparently more interesting. She studied his broad, muscular white back, brown spots dotting the fur, and wished she hadn't said anything to Lisa. Ashley wasn't in P.R. She wasn't in advertising. She had no idea how to raise funds for a nonprofit. That was just silly on her part.

Admittedly, she was a little hurt by Lisa's surprise, though when she thought about it, she knew it wasn't unexpected. "I'm not exactly a go-getter," she muttered to the warm summer afternoon air. "Of course she was shocked."

The pit bull looked up at her again, this time as if to say, "Are you talking to me?"

Ashley grinned at him and tugged his leash. "Come on, big guy. I've got six others who need to get some fresh air."

Back in the building, Ashley tried her best to tune out the ruckus of howls and barks, and checked her clipboard for the next dog. As she headed toward cage seventeen, she heard Lisa call her name. When she looked up, Lisa was motioning her over toward her desk.

Taking a deep breath, Ashley steeled herself. She didn't want Lisa to know she'd been hurt by the earlier remark, so she schooled her expression to what she hoped was indifference and tried not to notice that she could smell Lisa's perfume as she approached…or the erotic things the scent of it did to her.

"What's up?" she asked. *That's it. You're totally breezy. Not a care.*

Lisa took the leash and clipboard from her hands. "Go down the hallway near the front desk. You know where the offices are?"

Ashley nodded.

"The second door on the right is David's. He's in charge of fundraising. He wants to talk to you."

Ashley blinked at her. "Right now?"

"Right now."

"Why?"

"Because I called him."

"What did you tell him?" Ashley was suddenly terrified, and the crack in her voice might have given away that fact, though Lisa said nothing. Her heart beat in her chest like a jackhammer and she swallowed hard.

"I told him you had an idea you wanted to share for fundraising, and I thought he should give you five minutes."

"But you don't even know what the idea is."

"No. But I know you."

Ashley stared. She couldn't do anything but stare because Lisa had just totally made up for what had happened earlier. And also: she had to share her idea with the head of fundraising. The jackhammer launched into double-time. Her panic must have been obvious because Lisa stood up then and took Ashley's face in her hands.

"Relax. You got this. I have faith in you."

"What if it's a stupid idea?" Ashley whispered, hating that she sounded like such a child.

Lisa shrugged and just as quietly said, "Then it's a stupid idea. Who cares?" She tilted her head just a little then and her green eyes flashed with confidence. "I bet it's not, though." Stroking a thumb across Ashley's cheek, she let go of her. "Now go," she said, and jerked her head toward the door.

"Thanks," Ashley said and gave her an uncertain smile. As she moved to the door and into the lobby of the building, she felt like she was walking on rubber legs and that they might drop her to the hard floor at any moment. Cursing herself for being so nervous, she tried a mental pep talk.

This is not a big deal. It is not a big deal. It's just an idea. You have nothing to gain or lose by sharing it, so suck it up and be a big girl.

Before she had time to psych herself up any more, she was standing in the open doorway of the office of David Peters. He looked up and saw her, giving her no chance to even knock. With a huge smile filled with perfect white teeth, he stood (wow, he was big!) and held out a hand to her.

"You must be Ashley," he said, and his deep voice rumbled in the pit of her stomach. She walked the three steps to his desk and shook his hand. His grip was firm, sure. "Have a seat," he said, gesturing to the chair near her. She did. "Lisa tells me you have a suggestion for a fundraiser." He folded his big hands on the papers in front of him and gave her his full attention.

When Ashley opened her mouth to speak, what came out wasn't a voice that was shaky or questioning or uncertain. It was firm. Businesslike. Important. She sat up a little straighter and told David Peters her idea.

Lisa was thankful for the sudden rush of phone calls and visitors that happened just after she'd sent Ashley to David. It kept her from worrying. Worrying that she'd hurt Ashley's feelings and worrying that David would be less than receptive to her idea and her feelings would be hurt again. It wasn't that she didn't think it would be a good idea, it was that lots of people thought they knew about fundraising when they really had no idea. She and David had conversed many times over this exact topic.

When she finished up at cage twenty-six and answered all the questions the young man had about Frisco, the three-year-old husky/shepherd mix that had been surrendered by his family after their baby was born, she turned to head back to her desk and saw David and Ashley walking side by side toward her, talking animatedly with each other.

"Lisa," David said with a smile. "Any time Ashley says she has an idea, you have her drop whatever she's doing and come see me."

Ashley stood next to him, her smile so wide it was almost comical.

"Tell me," Lisa prompted.

"A fashion show," David said, then looked to Ashley. "You tell her."

"A fashion show. Like, with a catwalk—which we can use as a pun, obviously—just like they do for clothing. Except instead of showing off clothes, we'd be showing off animals."

Ashley was getting enthusiastic now, talking with her hands as she explained. Lisa couldn't keep the grin off her face. "So, like, I'd be walking down the catwalk…" She backed up and turned back toward them, miming having a leash in her hand. In an exaggerated announcer voice, she said, "And here we have Ashley, walking Jax, a ten-year-old German shepherd/Lab mix who's been with Junebug Farms for two weeks. He's friendly, housebroken, good with other dogs, and loves to sleep in the sunshine." She stopped walking and looked at Lisa. "That kind of thing."

Lisa couldn't decide which emotion took precedence: relief, surprise, pride. It all rolled into one ball within her.

"We won't do it right away because we'll need to iron out some details, figure it all out." David's wheels were turning. Lisa had seen it happen often enough to recognize the look. "I'll sit down with Anna and go over some options." He looked down at Ashley. "I may need you to sit in with us. Is that okay?"

Ashley beamed. "Absolutely."

"Great. Okay, gotta run. Thanks again, Ashley." With a wave to Lisa, he turned and was out the door.

Lisa waited a beat, then turned to look at Ashley. They were quiet for a beat before Ashley exploded in a squeal of delight. Lisa laughed, and it warmed her insides to see Ashley so thrilled. "Well, that went well."

"Oh, my God, that was awesome. I was so nervous."

"You obviously had no reason to be." Lisa reached out and rubbed Ashley's upper arm. "I'm proud of you."

Ashley's expression turned playfully smug. "Yeah?"

"Yeah."

"Well, good. Now, what are you doing on Wednesday?"

Lisa squinted at her. "Is this the other thing you wanted to ask?"

"It is."

Lisa looked up to the ceiling, tapped her chin with a fingertip, and pretended to be consulting her very crowded social calendar. "I think I am busy that night doing something with you, but I'm not totally certain..." She let her voice trail off and arched an eyebrow at Ashley.

"As a matter of fact, you are. You're coming with me to happy hour to meet my dad and his new girlfriend." Ashley's voice got smaller as she added, "And my sister and brother-in-law?"

Lisa stopped, blinked. A beat went by. Two. "Wow." She wasn't sure what else to say. Meeting family was kind of a big deal, wasn't it?

As if reading her mind, Ashley held her hands up, traffic cop style. "It's just drinks. Nothing big. No pressure. I promise. Casual. Easy." She studied Lisa's face; Lisa could feel it even when she wasn't looking. "Are you weirded out?"

"No," Lisa replied, and it was the truth. "I'm not weirded out. I'm just..." She searched for the right word on the wall over Ashley's shoulder. "Surprised maybe?"

"I know." Ashley's face again slipped into an uncertain expression. "But really, no pressure. It's just happy hour." Lowering her voice, she leaned in close. "Think of it as another date. That's all. Just a date. You're going there with me. Okay?"

Comfort and surety seemed impossibly far away to Lisa in that moment, but Ashley's face was so gentle, her eyes softly pleading, and she could do nothing but nod her ascent. "All right. Just a date."

"I promise." Ashley smiled then, that dazzling, infectious smile that Lisa found herself consistently drawn to. Lisa watched as Ashley retrieved her leash, checked her clipboard, and headed off to grab the next walker. Lisa watched her clip the lead on and head for the door, mesmerized by how silently Ashley called to her.

This woman...

Lisa had been so wrapped up in all of it since yesterday. New respect had entered the picture when Ashley had shown up out of the blue to hold Lisa accountable for her actions. It was so unexpected. Nobody had done that before. Ever. Well, maybe Aunt Joyce once or twice, but somebody she was dating? Never. For somebody so...lackadaisical, Ashley had shocked her. And that had earned her points.

They still hadn't dealt with the nitty gritty. Lisa knew that and she didn't relish that impending discussion. Deciding not to dwell on it, she returned to her desk and the ringing phone.

Wednesday would be nothing if not interesting.

CHAPTER NINETEEN

HAD A LATE INTAKE. Just need to change and I'll be there. Sorry!

Ashley smiled at the text. Wasn't it her job to be the late one? Then she glanced at the clock on her dashboard and realized that, technically, she *was* running late. Lisa was just running later.

"Thank God," Ashley muttered to the empty car. "All is right in the world." She slid the car into a parking spot in the half-full lot of McCurdy's and fired off a quick text to Lisa, telling her not to worry, that she wasn't going anywhere and would be waiting at the bar.

Ashley was nervous. And that was weird. It was just drinks. Just her family. But she wanted to like this new woman in her father's life. She wanted this new woman to like her. And she wanted all of them to like Lisa and Lisa to like them. "Yeah, just…everybody like everybody, okay? Make my life easier." She chuckled, realized there was nobody to hear her talking or laughing, and abruptly stopped. With a shake of her head, she got out of the car, scanned the parking lot, and saw both her father's and sister's cars. She gave herself a once-over, smoothing her hands over the thighs of her denim capris, straightening the blue, scoop-neck shirt, and pushing her arms into the sleeves of a white hoodie to ward against the air conditioning. She tucked her phone into her back pocket, shouldered her bag, took a deep, fortifying breath, and headed in.

It was 6:20 and McCurdy's bar was loud and pretty packed with a nice mix of a crowd. Blue-collar workers in overalls and dirty uniforms drank beer next to business-suit-clad office employees who sipped Scotch or martinis. The music was classic rock—Aerosmith sang about sweet emotions—and four wall-mounted televisions blared from each corner, each broadcasting a different sporting event.

Ashley craned her neck and caught sight of Kelly's head at the far end of the bar. As she approached, she could see that the foursome had commandeered a corner piece of the bar, something her father strove to do at any happy hour he attended. This way, people could sit on the stools and still see one another, rather than sitting side by side in a row. She grinned when she thought about how happy he must have been to have snagged a corner, pictured the dorky fist pump he did whenever something went his way. With a grin and a wave to Kelly, who'd just noticed her, she headed their way.

"There's my other one," Rick Stiles said with a smile as he opened his arms. He wasn't a big man. He wasn't small. Pretty much everything physical about Ashley's dad was average, and he was okay with that. She walked right into his embrace, suddenly enveloped by the scent of Old Spice, the same aftershave he'd been wearing since toddler Ashley first associated a smell with him. He squeezed her tightly, then kept an arm around her shoulders as he turned her to face the woman standing next to him. "Ashley, this is Diana. Diana, my youngest."

Diana was about the same height as Ashley, with light brown hair cut in a simple, shoulder-length style, and unique hazel eyes. She wore a small amount of makeup—some mascara and a light-colored lipstick—but that was all. She didn't really need it. Her skin was as smooth as porcelain. She shifted her glass of white wine from her right hand to her left, then held the right out to Ashley. "It's so nice to meet you," she said and her voice was unexpectedly soft. "Your father has told me quite a bit about you." Her face was unremarkable at first. Not unattractive, just…plain. But when Ashley took her hand and Diana smiled, her entire face lit up in a dazzling display of beauty.

"It's nice to meet you, too," Ashley said and meant it.

"What are you having?" her dad asked. "And where's your date?" He made a show of looking past her and Ashley laughed.

"She's running a little late. She'll be here." As her father signaled the bartender, she added, "I'll have a Cosmo."

"Girly drink," Rick scoffed, then winked at her.

"A *delicious* girly drink," Ashley amended and bumped him with her shoulder. As she waited for her cocktail, she watched Kelly chat up Diana. She knew her sister well and could tell by her direct eye contact that she was sizing up their father's new woman, trying to get the lowdown. With a grin, she silently commended Kelly, whose questions were just shy of "What are your intentions with my father?" Drink in hand, Ashley moved so she stood near the two of them and could be included in the conversation.

Diana turned to her. "So, Ashley, your father tells me you work in a bakery?"

"I do. Been there since I was seventeen."

Diana made a show of looking her up and down. "And you don't weight 350 pounds. Impressive."

"She should be running that place by now," Kelly said, looking at Ashley over the rim of her gin and tonic.

Ashley gave a half-shrug as she thought about her recent attack of mettle and wondered if it might stick. "Maybe one of these days."

"So," Kelly said, focusing her gaze on Diana. "You and my dad."

Diana had the good sense to blush when she grinned and Ashley knew right at that moment that this was an important relationship for Diana. They already suspected their father was hooked, but Diana's reaction to Kelly's simple statement made it clear the feelings were mutual.

"Yeah," Diana said, then took what looked like a nervous sip of her wine as she glanced at Rick, who was deep in conversation with his son-in-law. "Me and your dad. He's… kind of amazing."

"We like him," Kelly said.

Before she could add to the conversation, Ashley felt her phone vibrate in her back pocket. She pulled it out and saw the text from Lisa, who was in the parking lot.

Meet you at the front door, Ashley texted back, then excused herself.

Lisa looked stunning, and Ashley actually stopped in her tracks at the sight. She wore a brightly colored skirt in blues and greens that flowed around her legs like a gentle wave. On top was a sleeveless, lightweight sweater in a shade of green that both matched the skirt and accentuated Lisa's eyes. Golden highlights glimmered in her hair where a streak of sunshine came through a nearby window. When Ashley recovered herself, she walked right up to Lisa and wrapped her in a hug. "You look ridiculously gorgeous," she said in her ear.

Lisa's cheeks had pinkened when they parted. "Thanks. How's it going?"

"Great," Ashley replied excitedly. "I haven't been here that long, but I think my dad really likes this woman and she seems to like him just as much. My sister is giving her the third degree." Running her hand down Lisa's bare arm, she then grasped her hand. "Come on. I can't wait for you to meet my family."

The bar was still bustling with happy hour customers and Ashley had to jostle her way through a couple of groups, politely murmuring apologies as she asked for space to get by. "Hi there," she heard a man say and when she turned back, he was smiling at Lisa.

Can't blame the guy.

They got to the corner where Ashley's father, sister, brother-in-law, and Diana were all laughing about something. Steve and Diana had their backs to Ashley and Lisa. Ashley's dad's face broke into a wide grin as she saw them.

"Well, hello there," he said as he stepped around Kelly. "You must be my daughter's…" He paused as if he wasn't sure exactly how to label Lisa. "Date," he settled on. "It's nice to meet you."

As he held out his hand to Lisa, Diana turned around and her expression of joy slid right off her face like a greased mask as Ashley watched. In her hand, she felt Lisa's stiffen, then pull away, and when Ashley turned to look at her, Lisa's face had a very similar expression. In fact, now that they were facing each other, Ashley realized that Diana and Lisa looked very much alike.

"Lisa," Diana said, and the expression on her face was a strange combination of happiness and nerves.

"Mom," Lisa replied, answering all Ashley's questions with that one word. Rick, Steve, and Kelly all stood in silence, sporting looks of discomfort and confusion. Turning to Ashley, Lisa said quietly, "You know what? I'm going to go."

"What?" Ashley's eyes widened. "Why?"

"I need to go," was Lisa's vague and unhelpful response. She turned and headed back toward the door.

"Lisa. Wait." Ashley followed her, being much less polite this time as she pushed through groups of happy, tipsy people who seemed to have multiplied in number since five minutes ago. By the time she got to the front door and pushed her way to the street, Lisa was walking quickly across the parking lot. Ashley called her again and jogged toward her. "Wait," she said emphatically as she caught up.

Lisa pushed the button on her keychain and her car door clicked. She pulled it open.

Ashley put a hand on the door. "What the hell are you doing?" she asked, trying to keep her voice somewhat calm.

"I have to go."

"So you said. Why?"

Lisa gave her a look of exasperation. "Because that was my mother in there."

"Yeah, I got that when you called her Mom. Why are you leaving?"

Lisa closed her eyes, inhaled through her nose and blew it out slowly, as if exercising patience with a small child. "I..." She looked off into the parking lot.

"Look," Ashley said. "I know you have baggage with your mom. I get that."

"Understatement. I have an entire set of luggage."

Ashley nodded. "I know."

"Yeah, except you don't." When Lisa turned her eyes back to Ashley then, they were the same icy green they'd been the first few times Ashley had met her. Distant. Cold. "I need to go." She sat in the driver's seat and Ashley needed to move her hand or lose a couple fingers. She took a step back in disbelief as Lisa shut the door, started the engine, and pulled away, never once looking back.

Ashley stood in the parking lot for long moments, staring after Lisa's car even once it was long gone. She took a deep breath, took stock of her emotions, trying to figure out how she actually felt. She was hurt. She was angry. But most of all, she was disappointed. Folding her arms across her chest, she took in a deep, irritated breath and blew it out, then headed back into the bar.

How were there magically another fifty people in the bar since she'd left it five minutes ago? She tried not to be rude as she pushed through to where her family still stood, all of them looking at her with expectant sympathy—except for Diana, who just looked miserable.

"Everything okay?" her father asked as Ashley picked up her drink and took two, long, very large gulps of it.

"Oh, yeah. Everything is awesome."

A warm hand rested on her forearm and when she glanced up, Diana was looking at her with eyes that, now that Ashley knew who she was, were remarkably like Lisa's, aside from color. "I'm really sorry," she said quietly, and the pain on her face was obvious.

"Your daughter's kind of a pain in the ass," Ashley said with a humorless chuckle. "I'm learning her, and I've discovered that this is what she tends to do when something is uncomfortable."

"She shuts down and leaves," Diana said with a nod, then signaled the bartender for a refill. "I know. I'm sure that's my fault."

"Maybe. But she's also not twelve."

Diana nodded again, but said nothing, obviously trying to tread carefully.

Ashley wanted to scream. She wanted to shout. She wanted to throw breakable glassware and punch walls and grab the guy next to her by his shirt and shake him. Hard. She did none of those things. Instead, she sipped the remainder of her drink like a civilized person, ordered herself another, and turned to her family. She caught her father's worried gaze before he had time to wipe it off his face, and she smiled at him reassuringly.

"I think we should order some food. Anybody else hungry?"

Agreement all around was a good thing, and everybody seemed relieved that she'd broken the tension. This was good. Some calm. Some time with her family. Some good food and a little bit of alcohol. All of it was good.

And it would give her to time to think about her next move.

CHAPTER TWENTY

IT WAS 9:23 WHEN Lisa snapped the very last piece of the puzzle into place with a triumphant—albeit quiet—whoop. She knew this because Tiny was on a bookshelf he should not be on, standing near the clock. Her bare feet made no sound as she crossed the room and gently picked him up. Nuzzling his soft fur with her nose, she said, "You know better, Mister. What happens if you fall? Or worse, break something of mine I really like? Hmm?" She kissed the top of his head and set him down, then righted the knick-knacks he'd bumped out of place.

Deciding one more cup of tea might be nice—and that making it and focusing on mundane things like beverage concoction and puzzle completion kept her from dwelling on more important things—she took her empty mug into the kitchen, turned the kettle back on and waited for the water to heat up, wondering, not for the first time, if a Keurig made any sense. Her father loved his. The one at work was fabulous. She knew she could buy tea for it as well as coffee.

"I don't know," she said to Keeler, who was sprawled on the kitchen floor like road kill. "I hate the idea of all those little plastic cups ending up in a landfill. What do you think?"

Before the dog could offer his opinion, there was a knock on her door. Furrowing her brow, she glanced at the clock on the stove, assuring herself that, indeed, it was still after nine p.m.

When she pulled the front door open, Ashley didn't wait for an invitation. Like last time, she didn't even wait for a hello.

She just blew into the townhouse like a storm, which was a good analogy, Lisa realized when Ashley turned to her and she saw the mix of anger, frustration, and disappointment on her face. Definitely stormy.

Ashley paced the living room and the cats didn't know what to make of this movement. Tiny watched from the couch. Groucho stood in a corner paying very close attention to Ashley's moving feet. Hubbard was on a chair, her head moving slightly to follow Ashley's path. Clyde was near the stairs, but his one good eye was focused on the visitor. Even Keeler, who would normally want the company's attention, kept his distance as if he felt the crackle of energy in the room.

Taking a deep breath, Lisa stepped into the living room. She didn't have to wait long. Ashley stopped pacing and looked at her, then made a gesture with her finger, back and forth between the two of them.

"Is there something here?"

Lisa cocked her head. "What do you mean?"

"I mean, is there something here?" She made the same gesture. "Between me and you. Is there something or have I just been hallucinating?" Her voice was sharp and angry.

Lisa cleared her throat. "No, there's something," she said, annoyed by the tremor in her voice.

"Okay. Good. Glad we established that." Ashley looked off into space as if searching for her next words, and Lisa was surprised by how beautiful she looked. Her skin was flushed, her blue eyes flashing. She looked confident, which was unusual. She looked sexy, which was not. "Is it something you'd like to pursue? I thought we'd been pretty clear about that, but I could be wrong." Her voice was still sharp and heated, tinged with a hint of sarcasm.

Lisa felt small. Embarrassed. But she answered. "I'd like to pursue it."

"Okay. Good." Ashley turned and walked to the sliding glass door, stared out for a moment, then returned to the center of the room. Lisa was afraid to move, so she stayed rooted to the same spot. "This is the last time I'm doing this. For the record."

"Doing what?" Lisa asked.

"Chasing you when you run away like a child."

"Oh."

Ashley looked her in the face and nodded slowly. "Yeah." Then her expression seemed to soften as she said, "You're *not* a child."

"I know." Lisa reached up to fiddle with her earring.

"I have an idea."

When Lisa looked up at her, Ashley's expression had completely changed. Gone was the anger, the irritation. Instead, she saw only gentle kindness and hope. Resigned, she said, "Tell me."

"We're going to role-play."

Lisa blinked at her. "I'm sorry?"

"Yeah." Ashley moved to the chair and perched on the edge of it so as not to disturb Hubbard—who looked disturbed anyway. "I'll be your mom. You sit there on the couch and you tell me everything you've wanted to say to her all these years but never have."

The scoff was out of her mouth before Lisa could stop it. "Yeah, right."

Ashley tilted her head. "Really? Do you have a better idea? Because going on like this is not an option for me." The sharpness was back in her voice and Lisa blinked at her again, startled. "You running away and shutting me out every time something is uncomfortable? Not an option for me." Her eyes bored into Lisa. "So. Got a better idea?"

"No," Lisa said quietly.

"Okay then. Sit." Ashley jerked her chin at the couch.

Lisa did. Keeler, as if sensing the discomfort in the room, squeezed between the couch and the coffee table and sat near Lisa's feet. She dug her fingers into his fur, tried to draw strength from his solidity.

"I'm your mother. Talk to me."

Lisa sat silently, a combination of too many thoughts and no thoughts at all warring in her head. She stroked Keeler's silky fur and stared at the surface of the coffee table, absently noting that it needed to be dusted.

"I left you." When Lisa looked up at her, Ashley shrugged. "I left you and went away and never looked back. So what?"

A wave of unpleasant heat coursed through Lisa. She swallowed hard.

"I had things I needed to take care of," Ashley went on. "For me. I made a choice."

Lisa poked at the inside of her cheek with her tongue. Her knee began to bounce up and down. She swallowed again.

"Come on, Lisa. Talk to me. Stop acting like such a child."

That was it. Something inside Lisa snapped. She felt it, quite literally, in her chest and when she finally looked up at Ashley, the anger bubbled up so fast she could barely contain it. "Stop acting like a child? I *was* a child. When you left, I *was* a child. So were Eric and Ben and you didn't give a crap because you had to find yourself or whatever the hell it was you decided you needed to do instead of *raise your children*."

Ashley nodded, her expression serious, as Lisa looked at her in utter shock over her outburst. "Keep going."

Lisa shook her head, touched her fingers to her lips, looked down at Keeler. She didn't like this, didn't like feeling this way. She'd rather just tamp it all down, bottle it in. That felt much easier. Safer. "No."

"There you go again. Just like a child."

"Stop calling me that."

"Why? You're acting like one, like this is such a big deal."

"*It was a big deal!*" Lisa exploded, standing up so fast she scared Keeler and two of the cats, all of whom flew out of the room in panic. "It was a *huge* deal! What kind of mother just up and leaves her kids without a word? I had to take care of everything. Dad was a useless mess because you wrecked him. You *wrecked him.* He cried every day for months. The boys weren't sure what was going on. The house was a disaster. I was supposed to go to college. I was supposed to start living my life. And instead? I had to live yours. I was eighteen years old and I needed my mother. Instead, *you forced me to be one!*" A sob broke through and Lisa was barely aware of the fact that she was crying heavily until Ashley crossed the room, wrapped her up and sat them on the couch together.

And just like that, the wind left Lisa's sails. All the anger dissipated and nothing was left but a heart wrenching sadness. Turning her face into Ashley's chest, Lisa cried like she hadn't cried since the day her mother left.

Time seemed to cease. Lisa stayed curled up in a ball in Ashley's arms for what felt like hours. Her sobbing would subside down to little hiccups, but then the emotion would roar back up and she'd start again. Ashley said nothing, simply held her, handed her a clean tissue from the box on the end table when one was needed, and kissed her hair. Lisa couldn't remember the last time she'd felt so warm. So safe. So loved. She closed her eyes and burrowed in closer.

When she next opened them, it was dark. The living room light was on a timer set to turn off at 11:30 p.m., so she automatically knew it was later than that. The knitted afghan she usually kept on the back of the couch now covered her body and she felt cozy and warm, like she was in her own personal cocoon. One of the cats was curled up in the crook of her knees. She couldn't see which one, but judging by the gentle, familiar snoring, she assumed it was Groucho, which made a small smile tug at the corners of her mouth.

Lisa was allowed a few more moments of blissful comfort before her brain reminded her of the events of earlier. The conversation with Ashley, the role-playing, Lisa's complete and utter meltdown…it all came flooding back and the first thing Lisa wanted to know was where Ashley had gone. She sat up with a start and a small gasp, sending Groucho bolting off the couch and under a chair. She blinked rapidly, allowing her eyes to adjust to the dark and that's when she turned her head and saw her.

Big blue eyes were open, gazing at her. Ashley was on the couch, her elbow on the arm, her head propped on a fist. Bare feet on the coffee table, crossed at the ankle, her sandals on the floor. She looked decidedly comfortable and at home. And Lisa realized just then that her own head had been cushioned on Ashley's thigh.

"Hi," Ashley whispered.

"Hey," Lisa whispered back. "You stayed." The incredulity in her own voice was clear even to her.

"Of course I did. Where did you think I'd go?"

Lisa grimaced, unsure if Ashley could see it. "Anywhere but here?"

"Well, that's just silly." Ashley reached out, tucked a chunk of Lisa's hair behind her ear, and even in the darkness, Lisa could see the gentle expression, the softness of her face.

"What time is it?" Lisa looked around the room and squinted at the cable box, but couldn't make out the numbers.

"Almost one a.m.," Ashley said, after a glance at her watch.

"Do you feel like going upstairs?" Surprised by how small her voice sounded, Lisa swallowed.

"I think that's a great idea. Let's do that."

They got up together and worked side by side to take care of things. Ashley folded the blanket while Lisa let Keeler out the back door. While he did his business, Lisa cuddled each cat, one after the other, then let the dog back in. Reaching out, she grasped Ashley's hand and led her upstairs.

In the bedroom, it was as if they'd been sleeping together for years, not weeks. They left the lights off and readied themselves for bed in the dark. Wordlessly, Lisa handed Ashley a folded T-shirt from a drawer, and then pulled out one for her. They undressed quickly and quietly, donned the shirts, and crawled under the covers. Ashley lay on her back and held her arm out. Lisa simply looked for a moment, and silently thanked the Universe for sending this woman to her. She didn't know why or how it had all happened, but she did know that she was inarguably lucky. Resting her head on Ashley's shoulder, she tucked her body tightly against hers, tossed her leg over Ashley's and her arm across Ashley's stomach. Once again, she was enveloped by feelings of warmth and safety with which she was woefully unfamiliar. She snuggled in.

Yeah. I could get used to this…

❧❦❧

Ashley watched the sun come up through the window of Lisa's bedroom. It was a beautifully serene, peaceful period of time, lying there quietly and just breathing as the sky went from dark to purplish blue to pink. Just before five a.m., her eyes had opened and she'd taken stock of her location, her situation. Lisa slept soundly, still tucked up against Ashley. Ashley's arm was tingling from lack of circulation, but she didn't care. Holding Lisa made her feel amazingly content and relaxed, like she was exactly where she was supposed to be, and she had zero desire to move. At all. Possibly ever.

Instead, she pressed a kiss to Lisa's forehead and watched out the window, conveniently located across from the foot of the bed. She could see the tops of trees, a few birds flitting around here and there, and a stunning expanse of eastern sky. She was happy to have awakened first, not only because of the gorgeous view—both out the window and in her arms—but because it prevented a repeat of the last time Ashley'd woken up in this bed. The thought made an unexpected, quiet chuckle pop from her mouth, and Lisa stirred. Limbs moved slowly, a deep intake of breath, and then eyes fluttered open, revealing those heart-stopping green depths.

"Good morning," Ashley whispered to her.

"Were you just laughing at me?" Lisa asked just as quietly, her brow furrowed in puzzlement.

Ashley grinned. "Not at you, no. But I did laugh a little. Sorry."

"What was funny?"

Ashley looked down at her, gave her a kiss in the forehead. "It occurred to me that if I just make sure I wake up before you do, you'll never be able to leave me a blow-off note again."

Lisa's grin was an interesting combination of humor, embarrassment, and chagrin. "That would probably do it," she said after a beat.

They were both quiet for a long moment. "You're going to have to stop that type of thing. The running away when things get hard? Complicated? If you can't, we might as well throw in the towel on this right now because I only have so much bravery. You know?"

Lisa nodded against Ashley's shoulder, but said nothing.

"I'll help you. We can work on it together."

"Okay."

Ashley glanced down at her again. "That was convincing."

Lisa gave a sad smile. "I can promise to try, Ashley, but let's be realistic. I'm in my thirties. I've been this person for quite some time now. What if I don't know how *not* to be her?"

Ashley studied her for a moment, hearing the tinge of fear in her voice and suddenly had a tiny spark of understanding. "Oh, sweetie, is that what you think? That I want to change you?"

Lisa pushed herself up onto her elbows so she could look Ashley in the eye. "Don't you?"

"No! Of course not." Ashley gave a chuckle at the absurdity of it. "Why would I want to hook up with you only to change you into somebody else? Seems like an awful lot of effort."

Lisa looked down at her hands, toyed with a string on the corner of her pillowcase. She did not seem convinced.

Trying a different tack, Ashley said, "You know what I do want?"

"What?"

"I want you to talk to me. Instead of running. Instead of shutting down into silence. Instead of leaving me a note. I want you to talk to me."

"Tall order."

"I think you're up to it."

Lisa looked at her then…really looked at her. Those green eyes seemed to burrow in, through her skin and right into her mind. Ashley had to make a conscious effort not to squirm. "When did you get so…assertive?" Lisa finally asked, her voice barely a whisper.

Ashley smiled because that was an easy one. "When I met you." It was true. It was fact. She had no reasonable explanation. She was not a go-getter. She was not a person who stood up or raised a hand. No, Ashley Stiles was perfectly content to sit quietly, to not rock the boat, and to let life happen around her. She knew this about herself, had accepted it.

And then Lisa had come along and very gradually, something had clicked. Into place? Out of place? Ashley had no idea. She simply kept coming back to that same sentence over and over again and she said it now. "You make me brave."

Lisa gave a quiet scoff. "Well, I don't know how that could be. *I'm* not brave. In fact, I'm kind of a coward."

"You're not." Ashley said the two words with such conviction, she surprised even herself. She grasped Lisa's chin and forced eye contact. "You're not," she said again, softer this time. There was a long moment of connection then, their faces inches apart, each set of eyes boring into the other, their mouths a hair's breadth away from a kiss.

"I'm afraid," Lisa whispered, her eyes welling.

"Of what?"

Lisa blinked and a tear tracked down her cheek causing what felt like a little crack in Ashley's heart. She brushed it away with her thumb. Lisa closed her eyes as she seemed to search for the right words. "I've had a lot of anger," she began. "A lot of anger for a really long time." Ashley nodded for her to continue. "I think…I think I don't know who I'll be if I lose it." Lisa brought her gaze back to Ashley's as she asked softly, "Who am I if I'm not the angry, abandoned daughter?"

"You're you, honey," Ashley replied simply, and she really felt it was just that: simple. She put a hand over Lisa's heart. "You're you."

"How do you know?"

Ashley shrugged, having no clear answer to that question. "I just do."

"And what if you're wrong?"

"Again: silly," Ashley said with a grin, attempting to lighten the mood. When Lisa didn't smile back, Ashley said with all the surety she could summon, "Then we'll deal with it. Together. Okay?"

Their faces were still very close together, and Lisa made the move. She pushed her body the small distance left and pressed her lips to Ashley's. They kissed softly, tenderly, as the sun broke fully over the horizon outside the window, and Lisa shifted her body to cover more of Ashley's. The warmth enveloped them under the covers as Ashley ran her hands up and down the smooth planes of Lisa's back under the thin cotton T-shirt. Which didn't last long, as Ashley pulled it up and over Lisa's head, baring her lovely torso to Ashley's eyes, hands, mouth.

She easily flipped them so she was on top but it was different this time. Gone was the animalistic coupling that so often took them over. Tempered was the speed, the aggression. Ashley took her time, took the time to look, to feast with her eyes as well as her hands and mouth. She slipped Lisa's bikinis down her legs and off, then shed her own clothing. When she laid her weight on Lisa, her hips settled between Lisa's legs, a quiet moan of satisfaction pushed from her lungs and she could not recall a time when she felt more perfectly content.

Slowly and easily, she made love to Lisa, worshipped her body. Every move she made was deliberate and unhurried. She kissed Lisa languidly for what felt like hours. She spent long, long moments on each breast, tasting, enjoying. When she moved lower and finally slid her fingers inside, the sound Lisa made wasn't a cry. It was a long, low moan of what came through as relief to Ashley, and she smiled up at her before lowering her mouth and taking in as much of Lisa as she could. As she kept her movements languorous and gentle, and Lisa's orgasm grew closer and closer, one thought kept rolling through Ashley's head, warm and sweet and wonderful.

I am home.

CHAPTER TWENTY-ONE

A COMBINATION OF EMOTIONS sat on Lisa's shoulders for the next two days, and she swore she could actually feel the weight of them pushing on her. She was a walking dichotomy. She felt lighter, but heavier. She felt happier, but sadder. She was excited, but trepidatious. She was certain and she was worried.

It was exhausting.

Thursday afternoon, she sat at her desk, pen in hand, papers to be signed on the surface in front of her. And she sat there. And she sat there. Empty space seemed to hold her interest more than anything, as that's all she looked at for most of the day.

"What's going on with you?"

The voice startled Lisa on a high enough level to make her flinch in her chair. She refocused her eyes and met the squinting blue ones of Jessica Barstow.

"I'm sorry, what?" Lisa asked, mentally shaking herself.

"I said what's going on with you? You've been acting strange since yesterday morning and I can't tell if it's a good thing or a bad thing."

Lisa gave her a sad smile. "I'll let you know when I figure it out."

Jessica studied her for a long moment, and Lisa thought to herself—as she so often did—how beautiful her friend was. Today, she was more casual yet somehow still stunning, sporting a pair of dark jeans and a sleeveless button-down shirt in pink and blue plaid. Her auburn hair was pulled back into a simple ponytail and her lips were glossy. Parking her hip on the edge of Lisa's desk, she lowered her voice. "I'm here, you know."

Lisa nodded.

"Is it Ashley?"

Lisa pressed her lips together, absorbing the fact that Jessica obviously knew about them. "Um…we've tried to be subtle about that…" Her voice trailed off.

Jessica grinned. "You have been. No worries. I know you, that's all."

"Well, it's a little bit her and it's a lot of other stuff. I'm just…working through some things." She opened her hands and sort of waved them on either side of her skull. "I'll be fine."

Jessica brought a hand up to the back of her own neck and rubbed with her fingers as she looked at her friend. Finally, she seemed to relent. "All right. But you know you can talk to me if you need to. Okay?"

Lisa nodded, realizing that she'd probably stung her friend by not confiding in her, but honestly, she wasn't sure what she'd say. She was still rolling it all around in her own head. "Okay. Thanks, Jessie. I appreciate it."

Jessica squinted at the nickname, as Lisa knew she would. Nobody called her anything but her full name, and Lisa used the shortened version in a feeble attempt to lighten the mood. It worked. Jessica cocked an eyebrow as she slid off the desk and pointed at Lisa. "Watch yourself, Drakemore. I'm still your boss."

Lisa scoffed. "You don't scare me."

Jessica dropped her hand and sighed. "I know. Damn it." Then she winked at Lisa and headed toward the door.

It was good to have friends who cared. She was fortunate. Lisa knew this. But she wasn't lying; she really wasn't quite sure what was going on in her brain or what the next step would be. All she did know was that Ashley seemed to…open her up somehow. She had no better explanation for it. She was open. She had been closed without realizing it. It astonished her to understand that she didn't want to be closed any longer. Being open felt…right. It was a relief. She felt like she could take a full breath for the first time in years, and she wanted to stay this way, but in order to accomplish that, she needed to take some steps.

She reached into her purse in the desk drawer and withdrew her cell phone, then let Tammy know she was going to take a quick break and headed toward the lobby and out the front door.

It was hot out. Uncomfortably so, and Lisa felt sweat beading on her upper lip in a matter of minutes. She took a right and walked along the building, then around it to the dog-walking path that led to the barn. Once she got up next to the trees, it was shady and the temperature felt a good fifteen degrees cooler there. She slowed her pace to a leisurely stroll and dialed the number.

"Is this my favorite niece?" came the expected greeting.

Lisa couldn't help the grin. "Only if this is my favorite aunt."

"You're in luck." They both chuckled. "Hi, sweetheart. How are you?"

"I'm good. You?"

"I'm terrific. And very happy to hear from you. Unless you're calling to try and get out of dinner on Saturday. If that's the case, I'm hanging up and pretending I never got this call."

Lisa glimpsed a goldfinch out of the corner of her eye as it flew out of a tree and across the open space before her. "No, I'm not calling to bail. I promise." Deep breath in…slowly out. She cleared her throat. "I need a favor."

"Anything."

"Do you think…I mean, I need to—" A growl of frustration let loose from her throat and Lisa was suddenly angry with this whole situation. All of it. The entire past ten years and more. "God, I'm so done with this," she muttered as she felt tears closing in.

"Honey." Aunt Joyce's voice was gentle, loving. "Tell me what you need. Just talk to me."

"Can you set up a meeting with Mom? Maybe at your house? Someplace neutral?"

Her aunt was quiet for a beat. "You want to have a chat with her?"

"Yes."

"Like, a real chat? A talk? About everything?"

"Yes." Lisa could tell by her aunt's tone that she was liking this idea.

"I can do that. Tell me when?"

"Tonight or tomorrow?" Lisa said. "I need to do it before dinner on Saturday."

She could almost see Aunt Joyce nodding. "You got it. Give me a little time and I'll call you back."

"Okay. Thanks."

"You are very welcome. And Lisa?"

Lisa swallowed, her mind already racing, wondering if this was the right step. "Hmm?"

"I'm really proud of you."

They ended the call and Lisa kept walking, tried to relax by focusing on the beauty of nature that surrounded her instead of the uncertainty that swirled around in her brain. The trees were in full late-summer bloom, all lush and thick with green leaves. A gentle—albeit hot—breeze rustled them and the sound was somehow comforting. She approached the barn and walked up to the split rail fence. Four horses and two burros grazed lazily, and Lisa envied them their lack of concern. A brown and white spotted mare noticed her with one big brown eye and sauntered over to her, her strong lower jaw moving in a circular motion as she chewed. She came right up to the fence and pushed her snout in Lisa's direction. Her nose felt like velvet under Lisa's hand and she stroked it for what felt like a long while, enjoying the peace an animal could bring. This was exactly why she loved working here. The animals and their capacity to give unconditional love. They were all so special, each and every one of them. This horse seemed to know somehow that Lisa could use a little bit of love, and she'd offered it without question. It welled up Lisa's eyes, and she sniffled, then wiped away one tear that had escaped and tracked down her cheek, wondering when she'd suffered a crack in the waterworks. She'd never cried so often in her life. It was as if she'd broken a seal.

She stayed for as long as she dared before Tammy sent a search party looking for her, and the mare stayed with her, seemingly unhurried, willing to stand there and be stroked for as long as Lisa needed to stroke her. Finally, Lisa placed a gentle kiss on the horse's nose, whispered her thanks, and headed back toward the main building.

That dichotomous feeling was back, and she didn't like it, didn't like being uncertain and scared. But she was also a little bit…excited was the wrong word. She wasn't excited, but she was…cautiously optimistic maybe? Her brain knew that a frank conversation with her mother was long—*long*—overdue. But her heart was frightened, and she really did wonder what would become of her, who she would be if she wasn't Diana Drakemore's angry, abandoned daughter any longer. Would she even recognize herself?

What if she didn't?

⊷

Ashley wasn't nervous.

Was she? Well, maybe she was. But not for herself. She was nervous for Lisa and that spoke volumes about what she'd grown to mean to her. She thought about mentioning it as she rapped on Lisa's front door, but decided the poor woman was under enough stress right now. Best not to add another iron to that fire, so to speak. That was a bridge they'd cross soon enough and…she was sure she could come up with some more metaphors if she worked on it.

The door opened and Lisa looked just as frazzled as Ashley expected. She looked beautiful—all navy capris and a navy and white striped tank—but her eyes were wide and alert, like she was expecting some blunt object to strike out of nowhere and take her out at the knees. It wasn't an expression Ashley enjoyed seeing on the face of this woman who meant more to her than she cared to examine right now. What she wanted most was to take her away, to swoop her out of the path of any possible pain, physical or otherwise, to run away with her, far, far away so she'd never be hurt by anything or anyone ever again.

But, since this was reality, she simply smiled and said, "You look great."

"Thanks," Lisa responded absently as she flitted around her first floor like a very busy person. "Okay. Blinds: drawn. Lights: good. Did I feed the cats? I think I did." She moved quickly from the living room into the kitchen and inspected the cat's bowls.

"Lisa," Ashley said.

"Yes. I fed the cats. Keeler? Did I feed him?"

"Lisa."

"Did I feed you, pal?" Lisa looked down at Keeler, who looked from his mistress to Ashley and back again, his eyes speaking volumes.

"Lisa." This time, Ashley used a stern voice.

Lisa blinked and turned to her.

"You're stalling, babe."

Lisa nodded. "I am. I know." She covered her eyes with a hand and stood in the middle of the kitchen. Just stood there.

Ashley approached and gently pulled her hand away. "Hey. It's okay. It's all going to be okay. I promise you."

"You can't promise me that," Lisa said, her voice barely a whisper, her eyes wounded and terrified.

"I can. You know why? Because I'm sure of it. I *know* it." She squeezed Lisa's hand in her own.

They stood quietly, just being in each other's presence, and Ashley waited. Lisa needed time to work up to this. Ashley wasn't going to push her too hard, but she wasn't going to let her bail either. It was too important. Lisa stared at the floor for long moments before lifting her gaze to Ashley.

"Okay?" Ashley asked.

"Okay," Lisa said with a tiny nod.

No more words were spoken as they locked up the house and got into Ashley's car. They drove for a few moments before Ashley said, "So. I have some news."

Lisa turned to her and everything about her expression told Ashley she was grateful for the change in subject. "Tell me."

"I applied for a management position opening in the fall."

Lisa blinked at her. "There's another one?"

Ashley nodded. "One of the managers got a job at a different bakery. It was unexpected and it's happening really fast." She took a deep breath. "I hesitated…"

"But you applied."

"I did." Ashley had surprised even herself. Even though Beth Carter's little speech to her a while back had resurfaced in her mind, Ashley had still been uncertain. But she'd been feeling so different lately, so much surer of herself. She'd found a confidence she'd never had before. "I blame you," she said to Lisa and smiled.

Lisa laid a warm hand on Ashley's thigh. "I don't understand why, but you know what? I will take that blame and I will happily dance around with it. That blame is mine. I own it."

"You do." Ashley laughed. "So, I don't know if I'll get it. I don't even know if they'll interview me. But if they do…" She swallowed hard, a sudden lump of nerves sitting solidly in her throat at the thought of it. "Would you help me prepare?"

"Absolutely. I rock at interviews."

"Yeah?"

"Totally. We got this. Don't you worry."

Siri picked that moment to instruct Ashley to make a left and in another minute, they were pulling up in front of Aunt Joyce's adorable little bungalow. Ashley slid the car into Park and turned off the ignition.

They both sat in silence.

Ashley was pretty sure she could hear Lisa's heart pounding in her chest, a terrified staccato of dread and worry, and she reached over to close her hand over Lisa's. "It's all going to be okay. Remember? I'm going to be right there with you, every second."

Lisa turned to her then, her beautiful green eyes clouded, but wide. "At the very least, this is going to get uncomfortable. I don't know why you'd want to be here for that."

"I know exactly why. Because I love you." Ashley hadn't planned to spill those beans, not yet, not here and now, but they came tumbling out before she could catch them, so she left them to hover in the air between them.

Lisa blinked at her, and a small smile tugged up one corner of her mouth. "I love you, too," she whispered.

"Well, good. I'm glad we got that settled." Ashley tried to keep the grin from spreading too wide, tried to keep from stealing the focus of what Lisa was about to do, but she couldn't help but feel like she could fly right about now. Lisa loved her. Yeah, she was pretty sure she could fly. She allowed herself a beat to just absorb that for a minute, to soak in that delicious warmth. Then she squeezed Lisa's hand and said, "You ready?"

With a clear of her throat and a determined nod, Lisa pulled the door handle and got out. Ashley followed and went around the car to stand next to her. She held out her hand and Lisa took it.

"Let's do this," she said as her Aunt Joyce opened the front door, a big, happy smile on her face, and threw out her arms to welcome her niece.

"Come in, come in," she said, hugging Lisa tightly, then ushering her inside. "And you must be Ashley," she said as she turned to face her.

"I am. We met at the beach party."

"We did. Ashley the Ambush Kisser."

Ashley's eyes flew open wide at the moniker and she looked to Lisa, who still held Ashley's hand but was looking toward the living room, then back to Aunt Joyce, who had a mischievous expression on her face and a twinkle in her eye. "Um..." Ashley felt her face heat up and couldn't think of a single thing to say.

Instead of continuing the teasing, though, Aunt Joyce did something else entirely. She laid her hand across Ashley's cheek in a gentle, tender display of kindness, and Ashley had no problem reading the expression on her face: gratitude. They shared a moment, Ashley and Aunt Joyce, a moment in which they both understood the depth of their love for Lisa. Ashley smiled back at the older woman and gave her a small nod of understanding. When she turned her gaze to Lisa, she, too, was smiling, albeit nervously.

"You ready?" Ashley asked her softly.

"I'm ready." Lisa turned and led them into the living room where her mother waited.

THE END

By Georgia Beers

Novels
Finding Home
Mine
Fresh Tracks
Too Close to Touch
Thy Neighbor's Wife
Turning the Page
Starting From Scratch
96 Hours
Slices of Life
Snow Globe
Olive Oil and White Bread
Zero Visibility
A Little Bit of Spice
Rescued Heart

Anthologies
Outsiders

www.georgiabeers.com